M000268215

BETWEEN TWO SHORES

To Howard Goldblatt

in admiration.

J. Tsin

This work of fiction is dedicated to my family.
It is inspired by my father who loved to
read detective stories and my mother who enjoyed
romance and drama.

It is a paean to the excellent teachers who taught me
English literature and Chinese politics.

BETWEEN TWO SHORES

T. L. TSIM

Between Two Shores
By T. L. Tsim

© **Dominic Tak Lung Tsim** 2020

All rights reserved. No part of this publication may be reproduced or transmitted in any form or by any means, electronic or mechanical, including photocopying, recording, or any information storage and retrieval system, without permission in writing from the publisher

ISBN: 978-988-78856-9-6

Published by Angelina Lai Fun Wong

Distributed by
The Chinese University of Hong Kong Press
The Chinese University of Hong Kong
Sha Tin, N.T., Hong Kong
Fax: +852 2603 7355
Email: cup@cuhk.edu.hk
Website: cup.cuhk.edu.hk

Printed in Hong Kong, China

List of Characters

(In order of appearance)

Historical Figures

Place Names

Although there really is a place called the Thousand Island Lake south of the city of Hangzhou, the name Jin-an County is entirely fictional.

For readers who wish to know the Chinese words and quotations which appear in the novel, we give hereunder the actual characters in the Chinese language:

P. 1   *"Wo men yao zhao lin tai tai."*「我們要找林太太」

P. 7   *chow mien*「炒麵」

P. 18   *xiao shun*「孝順」

P. 19   *yi*「義」

P. 53   'flowers in the mirror and moon in the water'
「鏡花水月」

P. 54   Chinese churros「油條」

P. 57   Legislative Yuan「立法院」

P. 77   "Taiwanese always fall asleep in the car.
They need a toilet without going far.
They buy love potions in the morning,
To help them with the night's whoring."
「上車睡覺；下車尿尿；
早上買藥；晚上打炮。」

P. 79   putonghua「普通話」

P.129   "history is our mirror"「以史為鑑」

P. 131 socialism「社會主義」

P. 134 *renzhi*「人治」

Life is the sum of all choices

On April 1st, 2003, Anne Gavin's phone rang in the middle of the night. She picked it up, half expecting to be hearing from her husband, Victor, who had forgotten about the time difference between Asia and America. A stranger's voice, loud and authoritative, spoke at the other end of the line, first in Mandarin Chinese and then in heavily accented English.

"*Wo men yao zhao lin tai tai.* We wish to find Mrs. Lin."

"Who is this?"

"We wish to find Mrs. Lin," the man repeated in stilted English.

"Who is this?" Anne asked again.

"We are the Public Security Bureau of Jin-an County in Hangzhou… in China. We have important news to tell him… er… her."

"I am Mrs. Lin."

"You are Mrs. Lin? You are the wife of Victor Lin Chung-li?"

"Yes, he is my husband. Why are you asking me this? What is happening?"

"Mrs. Lin, we are sorry to have to bring you the bad news, but your husband is dead. Lin Chung-li is dead."

Only ten days ago, Victor Lin was the living embodiment of hope and expectation as he packed his bags for a business trip to Taipei. By the time he arrived at Tom Bradley International Airport in the cool March evening air, it was already dark. He had called Anne from the office and said goodbye on the phone. He didn't want her to take him to the airport and then drive all the way back to Del Mar in the night, even though the weather report said the sky was going to be clear and the stars would be out that evening. Victor was travelling Dynasty Class, an exotic, expensive-sounding fare category created by a Taiwanese airline, one of the cheapest flying the Pacific. The airline was popular with Taiwanese travelers when they went home, because it offered a non-stop flight from Los Angeles to Taipei.

For Victor, however, LA was home now, although he was an ethnic Chinese, born in Taiwan to parents who were natives of Zhejiang Province south of the city of Shanghai. In Taiwan, where Victor grew up and went to school, those Chinese émigrés who had fled their native China in 1949 when the People's

Liberation Army swept to victory were all called Mainlanders. Victor was a Mainlander. He had made his way to the United States from Taiwan. His father was a member of Generalissimo Chiang Kai Shek's party, the defeated Kuomintang, KMT for short. But Victor saw no irony when he chose his English name. The émigré population in Taiwan always dreamt of eventual victory over the Communists even after long years of exile. It was for them an article of faith that some day they would be victorious and they would return.

Barely an hour before, as Victor speeded up the coastal highway with the ocean to his left, the bright orange clouds of a glorious Californian sunset had greeted him and lifted his spirit. The soft folds of white cumulus in the sky, Joni Mitchell's "ice-cream castles in the air", were particularly radiant that evening against the backlit twilight coming from across the Pacific. Spring Equinox was two days ago. It would soon be warm, Victor thought to himself, and the days would become longer. He liked that, and he knew Anne liked it too. They could loiter on the sandy beaches then, just talking about mundane, everyday things and greeting people who happened to be there as they themselves, doing nothing more demanding than walking their dogs or playing with their frisbees.

Victor had told Anne on the phone the cistern in their guest toilet was not flushing; he said he would fix the problem when he came back. He was an engineer by training and knew how to deal with such mechanical chores. They were his responsibility at home, whereas Anne would take charge of the kitchen and the interior decoration of the house. She had a particularly keen eye for the pattern of the curtains and carpets and the color of the fabric for the sofas. Anne was a naturally neat and tidy person, a homemaker, and Victor loved her dearly for that. He liked order in his universe.

Victor also wanted to change the boiler which they had inherited from the previous owner. It was now over six years old and he believed in forward planning. He would hate to have a boiler give them trouble in the middle of a wintry night. That would be a great nuisance and he knew Anne would not like it. But he had to find time for that and work out properly what needed to be done. Lately, though, his mind had been pre-occupied with, for him, more important things.

It was forward planning that had brought Victor to America. In his final year at National Taiwan University, he knew if he came within the first three in the Bachelor of Science graduation exam, he would have a realistic chance of landing a postgraduate scholarship to study at UCLA. And that was what he managed to do and why he was now working and living in California. Only no amount of forward planning by a professional engineer would have enabled him to foresee what was going to happen shortly after he landed in America. He could not have foreseen that the People's Republic of China, what his father called Communist China, would swing its doors open, embrace some aspects of a market economy and go full throttle for modernization. Following those changes and in just some twenty years, the country, which was once dubbed "the sick man of East Asia," had become an economic power-house in the new millennium, one of the world's top three economies, no less. And that was really why Victor Lin was making this trip now.

As he stood in the line waiting for his turn to check in, Victor noticed three of the big digital screens at the airport were not working. He wasn't surprised; that was LA for him and he had got used to the sloppiness around him. What did surprise Victor, however, was that the Taiwanese carrier he was travelling with had a check-in counter that was very close to China Southern, an airline of the People's Republic of China. It wasn't that long ago when many Americans, especially Californians, would call the PRC by the name "Red China." Beijing did not seem to mind the adjective. Indeed Chairman Mao Zedong was positively proud of it. His Red Guards had been taught the slogan "better red than expert". And for a long, long time, the most popular song in the PRC was "The East Is Red."

It was really quite confusing, particularly because the two Chinese airlines' large placards giving flight information in the Chinese language used different renditions, even different placements, of characters. It was traditional Chinese characters for the Taiwanese airline written from right to left, and simplified Chinese characters for the PRC airline written from left to right, in the exactly opposite direction. Not that it would matter to Americans, Victor thought to himself with some bemusement. How were they to know? And if they did, why would they care?

Victor had to take his bags to Station 8 for scanning. The PRC couple in front of him were talking to each other in the Hunanese accent of Chairman Mao, in voices so loud they could be heard from ten paces away. After the turn of the new millennium, even Victor had noticed they were coming to the United States in ever increasing numbers now, the *nouveaux riches* of China, well-heeled, well-dressed – designer clothes, handbags, shoes and all – but without being well-mannered. They often talked at the top of their voices and would not wait to be served or stay in line. To sophisticated Americans like Anne's mother, they looked like country bumpkins turned fashionable city upstarts. This was really quite unfair, Victor had told his mother-in-law when this topic came up in dinner conversation, because where these new visitors came from, nobody ever told them they should keep their voices down in public places, and nobody ever lined up for anything. The couple standing in front of him now was at least doing that, Victor noticed. But when the black airport attendant at Station 8 asked the two, in English, whether they were flying "Cathay Pacific", they did not understand the question and turned to Victor for help. He interpreted for them and waited patiently for his turn while their five pieces of luggage were being scanned. He then gave the attendant his own, much smaller, bag.

By the time the scanning was done, Victor was feeling a little peckish and wanted to check out the hot food counters on the mezzanine floor as he had been told his airline's lounge only offered snacks and drinks but not cooked food. The airport's closest up-escalator, however, was out of order – simply not working. Victor had to make his way to the end of the terminal's lobby to take the stairs and walk up. Long before he got to the mezzanine hall, the smell of food was all over the place. There was food of all kinds: pasta, *chow mien*, sushi, Korean barbecued meats, amongst other standard fares. He knew which to avoid – the Chinese food counter – because Chinese-style fast food in California was very greasy and the last thing he wanted in his stomach with such a long flight ahead, all of twelve hours if not more. As Victor drifted from one counter to the next, all the food there smelled very much alike, and the thought occurred to him that the eateries might actually have the same owner. It was a case of stale the food and stale the airport. What never ceased to amaze Victor was why, at the level of everyday living, the most powerful country on earth had such shabby standards. It just could not get the simple things right.

He finally settled for a McDonald's hamburger and an apple pie; at least they were tried and trusted, although Anne always warned him about their fat and sugar content and high cholesterol level. With those two in his stomach washed down with a cup of lukewarm coffee, Victor went downstairs again and walked, out of habit, into the Hudson News store. He saw many magazine covers with bikini-clad girls. One was particularly striking as it showed a very pregnant woman clad in a bulging bikini brief which barely covered the essentials, and this was just the second half of March, not even April. Victor was quite used to this by now. He knew Americans liked to be ahead of the game, especially in the world of fashion and showbiz. He also knew they liked sports and, in California, especially water sports. Victor played basketball himself and had become a fan of The Lakers since setting up home in Pasadena, although he now lived in Del Mar.

Inside the Hudson News store, Victor could see a great many sports magazines next to the girlie ones. He was also very used to that by now. He knew that sex and sports were the two great American preoccupations and that, while Walter Cronkite might think reading *The New York Times* was like eavesdropping on America talking to itself, it was the popular magazines on the news-stands that gave the truer flavor of what were uppermost on American minds. They provided the best introduction to the American way of life in this country which the older generation of Chinese immigrants still liked to call Gold Mountain.

Victor's searching eyes finally caught what he was looking for. He picked up a copy of the March edition of *PC World*. Computing was Victor's profession now. He had worked with semiconductors and computers throughout his career, ever since he left UCLA, and he was the number four guy in Advanced Computer Systems Inc. based in Newport. He could never be number one, though, and he knew it. Although Anne came from an Irish American family which hailed from Minnesota, although Victor played a good game of basketball and the two of them were members of the Del Mar Country Club and all that, Victor felt he would never be American enough to be made head of the company. He only came to America for graduate studies at the age of twenty four, when he was no longer young. Although he graduated Phi Beta Kappa from UCLA, an honor for outstanding all-rounders, Victor was not native, or not native enough to be fully at home in the country of his choice. He would always be an Asian-hyphenated-American. He knew that was as far as he would go in American eyes.

Victor had hoped that his children would be more accepted than he was, or at least would feel more accepted than he did, but he and Anne had no children. This was not for want of trying though. It was just that Victor's sperm count was unusually low. He and Anne tried in-vitro fertilization for two years, but it was to no avail. Then after he turned forty, which was three and a half years ago, he could not see the point any more. He had come to accept that some things might be pre-ordained. No one could argue with God or nature. And Victor was not keen on adopting. Like most ethnic Chinese men, he did not see the need to be a father to someone else's child.

Anne too was not the motherly type. Her Catholic parents divorced when she was twelve, much to everyone's surprise. It was a bitter experience for her mom and it was even more of a bitter experience for her, just when she was becoming aware of herself as a woman. Her only sister Meg, who was twelve years older, had married the year before and moved out. When the shouting around the house between her parents got unbearable, Anne could only find solace in her sister's home where she would go to lose herself in Jane Austen's novels and daydreams.

After she graduated from UCLA, being an editor of children's books was always Anne's first career choice. The world of fiction was more manageable, and infinitely more pleasant, than real people who were, all of them, born with flaws that could not be mended. Even her parents were no exception, and perhaps, she had always feared, she herself as well. And so, Anne decided, even though Victor would like to have a child, if she was not going to bear children, so be it. She was not sure she could be a better parent than her own mom. She always suspected that even with the best intention in the world, parenthood was not something anybody should take on lightly. It would take two, not just one, good parents to bring up happy, well-adjusted children – and Anne knew that only too well. So many things could go so wrong in the first twelve years, and then you would be blamed, as she had heard said in a Hollywood movie, for "having cheated your children of their childhood." Anne would not want that to happen to her. If it were God's will, then she would accept it with good grace. She would not want to go against nature in her youth only to regret what she had done in her old age.

The people Victor now saw most of all were his own parents, whom he had brought over from Taipei to LA after he had married Anne and secured for himself his first management position. Old Mr. and Mrs. Lin were already quite old when they came to live in America and they really liked it in California. It was the spacious bathrooms and modern kitchen in their semi detached apartment that they felt very comfortable in and attached to, as well as the manicured lawns and well spaced flower-beds outside their block. Like many East Asians who had settled on the West Coast of America, they loved the clean, spacious flushing toilets of American homes, also the big, well-stocked refrigerators, and the freshly watered lawns with radiant flowers that looked like they had been lavished with tender loving care. Victor's parents had saved up to send Victor to National Taiwan University. When he won a scholarship to study at UCLA, they were overjoyed. Victor had made them proud and they, in turn, actively encouraged him to go to Gold Mountain to seek his fortune. To be able to live in America was as much their dream as it was his.

Victor really did not need a lot of encouragement. Hollywood movies and American pop music had already done the persuading a long time ago, in his high school days. He really wanted to experience for himself the exhilaration of driving down America's highways in an open-top roadster, surfing the waves coming in from the ocean, playing volleyball on the beach, and slow-dancing with college girls of his age at social gatherings. The New World seemed such a fun place to be. All those things which were not readily available to teenagers in Taiwan could be had in the United States, or so he thought, because he had seen these in the movies. America in the late 1970's and early 1980's was paradise on earth to a great number of young Taiwanese, and being able to study there was an aspiration shared by many of Victor's background, especially his school and college friends. Their generation was almost completely sold on the American dream.

It was at UCLA that Victor met Anne Gavin, an easy-going undergraduate with slightly curly, ash blond hair and eyes that stared straight at you when she spoke, which she usually did with a bemused, engaging look and a half smile. It was Anne's gleaming white teeth that first caught Victor's attention; they were so well-formed she could have been a model for Colgate. And then her lipstick too, which was a most unusual shade between peach and orange that lit up her beautiful oval face. For Victor, whose own front teeth had been knocked out in a basketball match and had to be replaced, the American girl's teeth, her lips and her smile were singularly captivating. And he followed her gladly into Professor Arthur Freedman's modern history and politics class, even though he was a graduate student in computer science at UCLA.

After a few weeks, Anne began to notice Victor, and they first got to know each other socially at a Neil Diamond concert which they attended with other classmates. Strumming his guitar and looking soulful with his hypnotic eyes, the legend of the 1970's belted out the familiar words of his number one hit to his Californian fans –

LA's fine, the sun shines most of the time,
And the feeling is laid back.
Palm trees grow and rents are low but, you know,
I keep thinking about making my way back.
Well, I'm New York City born and raised,
But nowadays I'm lost between two shores.
LA's fine, but it ain't home.
New York's home, but it ain't mine no more.
"I am," I said, to no one there.
And no one heard at all, not even the chair...

Afterwards, still high from the evocative ballad music and literally walking on air with the familiar melodies ringing in his ears, Victor hummed out the Neil Diamond numbers and started to sing as the group walked back to their lodgings. Anne was attracted to his deep singing voice and thought of him as the reliable, dependable type. She also saw in him a sensitive soul with gentle Oriental eyes. Not at all like her own father who had ideas galore and boundless energy, but was volatile and given to sudden mood swings and inexplicable tantrums. She decided there and then that she would like to see Victor again and suggested meeting for a Saturday stroll on Santa Monica State beach.

On their first date, Anne said to Victor, "I would like to call you by your Chinese name. Can you tell me your Chinese name?"

"*Chung-li.* My Chinese name is *Chung-li.*"

"What does that mean, *Chung-li?*"

"Well, *chung* means in the middle, as in *chung-kuo,* the Middle Kingdom, which is the name for China; and *li* means standing up. However, the two characters, when put next to each other, can also mean being neutral, as in taking the middle ground between left and right and not siding with either. That's my given name, *Chung-li.* And my family name is *Lin,* which means forest. The three characters, taken together, mean standing in the middle of a forest, not knowing where to go." As Victor said this, he started to chuckle out loud.

"No!" said Anne, "You're having me on. Why would your parents give you such a name?"

"I don't know, but they did. *Lin Chung-li* is really my Chinese name," said Victor, "And it is a good description of me right now, lost in the middle of a big forest that is America. The vastness of your country simply overwhelms me."

Anne liked Victor's self-deprecating humor. "But China is vast too, isn't it?" she asked.

"It is, but I have never been there, so I don't really know what China is like and what living in China is like. I don't have any *feel* for it, you know." Victor replied.

"Have you never been to China at all?"

"No, never! I was born in Taiwan, the Republic of China. We are sworn enemies of the Communist state called the People's Republic of China just across the Taiwan Strait."

"Do you consider yourself a Taiwanese then?" asked Anne.

"No, no, I am Chinese, not Taiwanese. But I am not fiercely proud of being Chinese. I would not be so presumptuous as to say we are God's chosen people, for instance," and he chuckled again, "although I know some of my compatriots would dearly love to make that claim."

Anne smiled at this reference to the Jewish people of whom UCLA has a lot, and Victor, sensing that she was warming towards him, decided to tell her more. "I think many Chinese people are essentially irreligious. They don't need God to choose them and tell the rest of the world how great they are. They would choose themselves. The Chinese have a super high regard for themselves, haven't you noticed?" He smiled as he said this and picked up a pebble from the beach, which he then threw forcefully against the incoming waves. He was hoping it would trip a few times on the water, but it did not. The wind and the waves were both against him.

Anne was still laughing at the audacity of Victor's remarks but thought she must ask him an even more penetrating question if she was to know him better. "Tell me, *Chung-li,*" she looked at him straight in the face but with a glint in her eyes, "What does it mean to be Chinese? I'd like to know."

Slightly taken aback, Victor first paused for thought and then asked Anne a question in return, "We are speaking in general terms, are we? I cannot speak for all the Chinese in this world. They number more than a billion, much more…"

"Oh, yes, we are speaking in general terms – based on the people you know, the people you went to school with, the people you've met socially… Yeah, I am just curious. I really want to be enlightened."

Victor felt reassured and he began, "Well then, I'd say to be Chinese is to be self-conscious. We are very conscious of the fact that we are different from other peoples. We are very conscious of being looked down upon, bullied, pushed around, made fun of and passed over – when we know all the time that we are superior to the people who are doing all these things to us. And we want to show them. And so we work very hard to achieve material success in life. We are very down to earth, materialistic, and we take the external trappings of success very seriously, things like money, a big house, an expensive car and an important job title."

"I would say those are the aspirations of the average American too. We're no different," Anne rejoined.

"Maybe, but in two other respects, we are quite different from you. The first is the great importance we attach to the family. My father taught me the Japanese would put their country first, and the Americans would put themselves first," he made a face at Anne as he said this, "but the Chinese would put their family first. A lot of Chinese parents who really cannot stand each other would nonetheless stay together for the sake of their children. Not many Americans would do that, from what I've seen. Chinese people would also make great sacrifices to give their children a good education. And the children, in turn, are expected to repay their parents by being filial and obedient. The Chinese term for this is *xiao shun* – not just filial, but also obedient – there are two words here. There is no equivalent for such a term in American English, because this is not an American trait. You may be filial to your parents, but you are not obedient and beholden to them, I've noticed."

The primacy of the family and the essence of Chinese family traits, as Victor expressed them, touched a chord with Anne, who never forgave her wayward father for leaving her and her mother after a big row one Christmas Eve and never coming back.

"And the second? What is the second difference?" Anne quickly followed up.

"It is the strong bond we have with our friends. Chinese friendships are stable and long-lasting. We are expected to be loyal to our friends, to help them and to defend them. The Chinese bond of friendship is very strong and the relationship is reciprocal. This is the idea of *yi,* which again has no real English equivalent. In this country, I'm told, some people would sleep with their best friend's wife or their wife's best friend. That is a huge no-no in any Chinese community anywhere. Anyone who does that will be ostracized, out in the cold, considered totally untrustworthy – *unworthy* in every respect, period."

Anne's heart missed a beat when she heard that. It was too close to her own father's behavior for comfort. She did not want the conversation to go in that direction. And so she switched her questioning to Victor himself.

"You said Chinese people work very hard to achieve material success in life. Is that what motivates you too – material success?" she asked.

"Yes, absolutely. I am very Chinese in that regard." Victor turned and looked sideways at Anne and smiled broadly as he said this. He was being honest.

Encouraged by the directness of his response, Anne decided to ask again, "And are you filial, obedient and family-oriented too?"

"Well, I respect my father. I hold him in very high regard. He taught me most of the really important things in life, and I owe him a lot. I wouldn't be here if it were not for him. He worked really hard and saved a lot for my education. He made it all possible. I am the only son, so I am expected to take care of him in his old age, and my mom too, that goes without saying. You see, the family is our people's bedrock and safety net. In a society where there is no social security, it is the family that provides our people with an insurance policy, our mutual-aid fall-back of the first and last resort. Chinese family bonds are exceedingly strong."

"And how do you see us Americans now that you are living among us? Don't just tell me we are different, I know we are." Anne was laughing as she said this, her white teeth gleaming and her head slightly tilted. It was that bemused look again.

"Well, you are outwardly friendly, easy-going and inclusive," replied Victor as he looked at her open, beautiful face which embodied all those lovely qualities he so admired. Anne's laughter had put him at ease, and he went on, "And I like that – very much. But you have this move-on mentality. Nothing lasts very long with you. You change jobs, change professions, change cities, change friends, change marriage partners ever so often. There does not appear to be much permanence in your lives. But I am being judgmental and I am sorry." Victor realized he had become strident and sweeping and quickly apologized. "You handed me a trick question and I walked right into it. You probably think I'm being didactic. If I am, I can't help it. You see, I'm Chinese. But I'm sorry if I have offended you."

"No, it's not a trick question. I'd like to know how other people see us. And it is true, Americans like to take stock of their lives once every few years, and if they don't like what they see, they will change things. Yes, we do move on. You may see this as a weakness, but I think it is a strength too. It is a strength because we can cut our losses and not be bogged down by them. I suppose, from the tone of your voice, the Chinese don't do that?"

"No, not to the same extent, not *nearly* the same extent. We're good at making do, putting up, living with adversity and muddling through."

"What then, would you say, are your character weaknesses? Not your own, the Chinese people's, I mean."

"Well, we are, paradoxically, the opposite of you. We are not inclusive. We are quite selfish and self-centered. We do not make friends easily with people from other ethnic backgrounds. We are naturally reserved. In fact, I would go so far as to say we are exclusive. We do not treat other people all the same way, and we do not treat everybody as equals. We are not very trusting to begin with, and we are particularly distrustful of foreigners, er, I mean non-Chinese people. "

"Does that distrust apply in a boy-girl dating relationship too?" Anne asked, not quite innocently. And they both looked at each other and laughed out loud.

"What do you think?" said Victor, with a twinkle and mischief in his eyes.

On their second date, Anne decided to put forward an observation that had troubled her for some time. And so she began, "Don't misunderstand me, *Chung-li*, for what I am about to say to you." And then she stopped. Victor did not know how to react. His face was expressionless but his eyes were not. He was looking askance at Anne. She caught this and, with a quick smile on her face to put him at ease, Anne continued, "I think the Chinese people are very clever, very numerate, and especially hard-working. With these wonderful qualities, you can do better and should do better, but haven't really, not in this country and not on your own native soil either, it would seem. So what is holding the Chinese people back? Please tell me. I've had this question in my head a long time. You are my first Chinese friend and so you are the only one I can ask."

"You have listed the good traits, Anne. But there are many things wrong with this culture of ours. For one thing, it is really ancient, pre-Christian even, and held together by the teachings of Confucius who lived some two thousand six hundred years ago. And Confucius' view of the world is hierarchical, like a pyramid, with the emperor at the top, then the court, then the scholar gentry, and then the peasants, artisan-workers and finally the merchant-traders, in that order. The merchant-traders were considered the lowest of the low because they were not producers themselves and lived on other people's labor, and they were motivated by greed and always after a profit, which Confucius loathed and despised. The Sage gave very precise instructions on human behavior, within the family, within the emperor's court and between friends. In his scheme of things, it would be a well-ordered society if everybody knew his place and behaved accordingly; and absolute obedience was the *key* construct – absolute respect for authority and seniority. He really wanted a perfectly ordered world, one which is very rigid and structured. Confucius should have been an engineer, like me." Victor laughed out loud as he said that. "But then," he continued, "no Chinese engineer has been able to leave a legacy this big, this long, and this pervasive. Confucius pre-dated even The Great Wall!"

"And is there no concept of equality in this Chinese, er, Confucian world?" asked Anne.

"No, not really…" replied Victor.

"Not even after so many years of communism?"

"I doubt it," said Victor.

Anne was still pondering the point when Victor picked up the thread of his train of thought again. "And the problem of this very rigid social structure is this, you see. There is very little creativity to speak of. Most people lead very conventional lives. They have very narrow comfort zones, and there are many self-imposed no-go areas. This Confucian culture, this Chinese way of doing things, is so ingrained and so resilient that the Chinese people, even when they are living outside of China, cannot really learn from other cultures and other peoples. In this country, for instance, after so many generations, most Chinese restaurants still do not have decent, clean toilets."

"Perhaps this has to do with the people who use them?" Anne always thought that and the words just came out of her mouth.

"That may be," Victor who had never thought of that before was taken aback and slightly deflated. He was about to blame the restaurants but had to concede Anne might be right. "You have a point," he continued after a pause, "although I have to say some of the toilets were not clean and tidy to begin with. They are always awkwardly small and some double up as store-rooms. The washroom is often the most unsightly part of a Chinese restaurant. That's putting it mildly actually. Some are downright disgusting. But as long as the food is good and the price is cheap, these restaurants in Chinatown have no lack of customers. Maybe people who go there only care about what they take in and not what comes out."

"In Chinatown," Anne interceded, "restaurants compete with each other at the lowest level – in price. In such competitions, cleanliness and aesthetics are easy casualties."

"I only go to Chinatown for provisions, nothing else." Victor quickly said. "I don't eat there. I like places that are clean and where things are tidy – they don't have to be expensive. But what really gets me is the way some Chinese people choose to live in squalor even when they have the money to decorate their apartments and improve their wretched surroundings. I think they are inherently insecure and just love to see their money pile up under their beds. And they never pay any attention to the way they look; simple cleanliness, you know, eludes them, never mind elegance. The Chinese people can be beautiful; they just don't..."

It was Anne's turn to laugh out loud at this sudden, unexpected assertion and she felt obliged to ask, "What do you mean?"

"Well, they don't seem to know how to bring out the best in themselves. They don't spend much money on outward appearances. Somehow it's as if they can't be bothered. And their manners... well, need I say more? Why can't they learn? I ask myself. I have, even in the short time that I have been living here."

"That will change with the second and third generations," Anne said to Victor, for she wanted the conversation to end on a positive note. "A lot of new immigrants have that problem when they first arrive in this country. I have seen this happen to people I know, people I went to school with. America is a melting pot and education is a great leveler. It is possible to get out of one's cultural ghetto – with time, willingness and conscious effort."

"I happen to agree with you," the starry-eyed new arrival from Taiwan said to Anne. "We have to adapt and we have to change. That is the only way forward. Now that they are living in America, I do wish the people in Chinatown would leave their self-imposed distrustful, authoritarian and hierarchical baggage behind. These cultural shackles are what's holding them back, and their children too. If they do, if they break free, they can become the next Yo Yo Ma or the next I. M. Pei, instead of being stuck in menial jobs scraping a miserable living." As he said this, Victor was sure he would not become one of these people in Chinatown, because he would fit in; he wanted to fit in, and he would work on it. He would work hard; he was willing; and he was not stupid. He would break free from what Professor Freedman called "the Chinatown syndrome."

After she had returned home and was lying in bed, it occurred to Anne she might have asked Victor whether this Chinatown syndrome was class specific or typical of the Chinese people from a particular region of China. Maybe Victor was from a different socio-economic group or a different province. With a population of over one billion, there were bound to be regional, professional and other, perhaps more subtle, differences. She told herself she must remember to ask Victor that on their next date.

On her third night out with Victor, Anne had completely forgotten to ask Victor about the typical Chinaman in Chinatown. Hostilities had flared up between Taiwan and China again and the United States' Taiwan policy was being called into question in an article which appeared in *The New York Times*. The writer alleged that there was not much difference between the People's Republic of China, the PRC, and the Republic of China in Taiwan under President Chiang Ching-kuo, son of the Generalissimo. Both were one party states; both parties ruled with an iron hand; neither party would entertain freedom of the press or free elections; and then he went on to argue that the United States should make Taiwan open up its political process and allow its people more freedom as a condition for selling the island more military hardware.

Over dinner, Anne made the mistake of suggesting to Victor that geographically Taiwan was not really an integral part of China. On hearing this, her companion became very emotional.

"No, no, Taiwan *is* part of China." Victor insisted. "One day, these two parts will be reunited as one country. But the Beijing government would have to change its barbaric ways before this could happen. Taiwan is on its way to becoming a modern country now, but China is still mired in her feudalist, socialist ways. Of course, we have our problems in Taiwan too. I suspect, for instance, that some Taiwanese people really want independence from China. We are being squeezed from both ends – the Chinese Communists on one side and the indigenous Taiwanese Nationalists on the other."

As Victor sat and explained to Anne his distaste for the nascent Taiwan independence movement and the new face-off across the Taiwan Strait between the governments of China and Taiwan, and the origin of their separation, she began to understand why that Neil Diamond song resonated so strongly with him. The young man seated in front of her had been lost and wandering for a very long time.

As Victor recounted it, the Chinese saga was the history of a proud people who, having been humbled and humiliated by foreign powers many times over, still endeavored, and still managed, to stand up, again and again, never giving up the hard struggle, because they wanted their country to be strong and to take its place among the world's superpowers. If their country were strong, not only would the Chinese people all over the world be able to bathe in its reflected glory, this would also be proof positive that they themselves were the scions of a superior race, and that they need never feel inferior towards anybody in any country any longer. This was especially important for the Chinese abroad who felt they were always being discriminated against or even kicked around. It was not difficult to work up patriotic feelings among ethnic Chinese living on foreign shores.

Victor's simple history lesson ended with Chairman Mao Zedong's victory on the Mainland and Generalissimo Chiang Kai-shek's retreat to Taiwan in 1949. He told Anne how his own parents had come to settle in Taipei, having had to leave behind their land, their relatives, their friends and their careers in China, and how he grew up hating the Communists, because his parents had drummed many horror stories into his young mind. Although Victor was born in Taipei and had no first-hand experience of the atrocities of the civil war, the land reforms, the Great Leap Forward and the Cultural Revolution, the horrendous tales his parents told him had left their marks.

Victor told Anne about his dream for a new life in America, which was for him the land of hope, the land of opportunities and the land of fun. It was everything the two Chinas were not. He told her he wanted his green card and once he had that would find a way to bring his parents over. She listened to him intently and was particularly touched by his filial devotion and his Chinese idea of family and permanence. Among her college friends, never before had any young man of his age poured out his innermost feelings and fondest aspirations to her and laid himself bare in the manner that he had done, this earnest and vulnerable man with dark, deep-set eyes and the voice of Neil Diamond with a Chinese accent.

When she went home that evening, Anne kept hearing the refrain of the song *I Am, I Said*. And the words "nowadays I'm lost between two shores" took on a totally new, non-American meaning. Instead of referring to the East and West Coasts of the United States, the two shores first became China's Fujian Province and the island of Taiwan, and then morphed into the vast distance between the China Coast and the Californian beaches of the United States of America, with the wide Pacific Ocean in between.

Two years later, after they had both graduated and found their first jobs, Anne and Victor were married in a Catholic Church in Pasadena after Victor applied for and received his dispensation from Anne's parish. He needed that because he was not a Catholic. Anne's mother and sister were at the wedding, but not her father, who was not invited. Victor had wanted to bring his parents over from Taipei but his mother broke her leg while coming down the stairs of the old apartment building and had to be hospitalized for weeks and so had to miss the wedding. Victor's father, the dutiful husband that he was, also decided to stay behind to care for her and attend to her needs.

After the service at Anne's parish, the Irish priest who presided over the holy matrimony made a joke about Victor's huge fingers because his wedding ring was one size too small. Victor and Anne were the opposite of the stereotypical Asian-American couple. Whereas many tall, big Caucasian Americans had married petite Chinese girls, Victor was tall and muscular, whereas Anne was slim and willowy, although well-proportioned.

His wedding ring and the *Phi Beta Kappa* ring from UCLA were Victor's two most prized possessions. The ten-carat gold band with the BK insignia engraved on the top, and his own initials and year of election on the inside, had to be custom made by Hand & Hammer Silversmiths, because of his finger size. Victor was a basketball player and had very big fingers. "Useful for playing basketball, but awkward for rings," Father Hillary had said, with a wink at the groom.

Victor's first job was with a subsidiary of Intel, Anne's was with McMaster Publishing, in children's books. His company took full advantage of his technical competence in hardware and sent him all over the country to do trouble-shooting. He worked hard and was suitably remunerated for his contribution. With their combined income, they were soon able to buy themselves an apartment and started saving up to bring his parents over.

They were able to do that five years later. Victor flew to Taipei to accompany his parents on the flight back and help them deal with U.S. immigration when they came into Los Angeles, because old Mr. and Mrs. Lin did not understand or speak English. Anne had never seen Victor so happy as on that day when she greeted him and his parents at Tom Bradley International Airport. He was the proud son who had fulfilled his parents' dream. He was on a high even after the long flight and was very talkative, very cheerful on the drive home, busily pointing out the LA landmarks to his parents along the way. That evening, the English major that she was, Anne wrote down in her diary a line from T. S. Eliot to describe her Victor, "He had 'the look of flowers that are looked at', so happy was he."

Anne thoroughly endorsed Victor's filial piety, especially the way he looked up to his father, partly because she never felt that towards her own who, despite being a Catholic, had left her and her mother when she was a little girl turning into a teenager, at the most sensitive, vulnerable and needful period of her life.

Anne had been looking forward to getting to know Victor's parents and sharing many family meals and happy hours with them. In this, she would be disappointed, as she found they only knew a smatter of English words and considered themselves too old to learn a new language to the level of conversational proficiency. What she did not know was that they too were disappointed. Not in Victor for marrying a Caucasian American girl, but in Anne for not being able to produce for them any grandchildren even after several years of marriage. She did not know that, in Chinese society, of the three most un-filial things a son and daughter-in-law could do to his parents, the most reprehensible was to not give them grandchildren, especially grandsons.

Over time, Anne's relationship with her parents-in-law had fallen into the conventional mode of being polite and proper, but not close and caring. Victor, who had noticed that, started to go to his parents' home for lunches and dinners on his own, although he would always accompany Anne when she visited her own mother at Thanksgiving, Christmas and Easter. Victor tried hard to please his mother-in-law who was always welcoming and not at all formal; and he was liked for being attentive to her needs. Anne's mother could see that her son-in-law wanted very much to fit in and tried to help him along by including him in her dinner parties from time to time and encouraging him to go out more with his American friends and colleagues.

But Victor had become frustrated at work. Not that he could not cope, and not that he was not appreciated. Rather it was because he sensed that the company was merely making use of his strengths and was not developing his potential. Sure, he was good with hardware, had good technical skills and was good at trouble-shooting. But he could see that the colleagues who were making more money and getting promoted ahead of the engineers in the firm were the guys in marketing or the ones doing accounting and finance. And he wanted to be one of those.

Victor did not have a professional accounting qualification but he thought he could try marketing. After seven years in the same job, he asked for a transfer and actually applied for a marketing position, not once but twice. He was interviewed twice and was rejected twice. Each time, somebody else got the job. Not that he was no good but someone else was better, or so the interview board told him, someone who could speak without a foreign accent, someone who could "mix well" with clients, whatever that meant in the eyes of senior management. Victor was a friendly, sociable guy; he could do an excellent barbecue; he played basketball with his colleagues and loved to sing. But he could not hold down his drinks. Like most ethnic Chinese, he had a low tolerance for alcohol. And, again like most Chinese, he hated losing control of his faculties; he hated making a fool of himself in public. He could relate to people if they would open up to him, without having to first loosen up by drinking a lot of hard liquor. But, of course, as he would find out, that was not the American way.

Finally, after nine years with the same company, he got so fed up that he went to work for a small start-up. And that was his job now, number four in the company hierarchy, Senior Vice President of Advanced Computer Systems Inc. His job paid slightly above the market rate for positions at this level and was not excessively demanding. But Victor was not satisfied. He had seen Jews, Hispanics and Blacks become CEOs of medium-sized and even big American companies, but very few Asian Americans, except for those from the Indian sub-continent, who could somehow talk their way up the corporate ladder even when their business performance was on the way down. Victor could never talk like that. His father had taught him to be truthful and honest and to "tell it like it is." What Victor did not appreciate was that whereas the Jews and Indians knew how to buttress their own positions by building up their ethnic networks in the organizations they were working for, the Chinese liked to be the only Chinese in a white man's world and never bothered to help their own kind. As minorities went, they tended to behave like those women senior executives who would not do anything to advance the careers of other women.

Anne could sense Victor's frustration, although he had pushed it deep down and tried not to show it. She could almost see it in his eyes when he knitted his brows in the evening as he sat and read his Taiwanese magazines. This was a family trait which he had inherited from his father, who also had the habit of knitting his brows when he read his newspapers. For both father and son, reading was serious business that required undivided attention and instant reaction. Of late, Anne guessed, something must have been bothering Victor, something he had read in the Taiwanese magazines he subscribed to, which were all in Chinese, a language which Anne did not understand.

If she did, she would have known these magazines often carried stories of successful Taiwanese businessmen who had made it big in Taiwan and China. Some of them were not only known to Victor, a few were actually his classmates at secondary school and at his *alma mater,* National Taiwan University. They were not even scholarship boys, and he was. The only clever thing they had done was to have stayed behind in Taiwan or, having studied in the United States, to have chosen to return to the land of their birth. Victor's father always told him life was ironic; and young Lin could fully appreciate it now. Victor, who was head of his class, was making $220,000 a year, a very good salary for California to be sure. But his contemporaries in Taiwan were now millionaires many times over, some with a net worth of $100 million or more. Chief among them was Jason Fang, who had seen his fortune grow by leaps and bounds since he started his semi-conductor business in China after making it big in Taiwan. Fang was now reported to be worth some thirty billion New Taiwanese dollars, or about one billion in the American currency. Victor simply could not live that down.

"What? The man who is known as Taiwan's billion dollar man is Jason Fang? Tiny Fang who used to copy my assignments because he could not do calculus? How could that be? How did that happen?" Victor muttered to himself as he finished reading the lead article in his subscription-only Taiwanese magazine. He was very quiet that evening. He had kept up with Jason over the years because they had been buddies in high school and this was a trusting relationship that had lasted into middle age. For a number of years, Victor was ahead of Jason in the earnings stakes when America and Americans were riding high. In fact it was Victor who started Jason off on making semi-conductors in Taiwan. And now, according to Taiwan's *Commonwealth Magazine*, Jason Fang was finding Taiwan too small for his burgeoning ambitions and was planning to expand his operations in China and expand them manifold.

Shortly after that magazine story, Victor received an email from Jason. It was a business proposition between friends. "Come and work for me in China and I will make you a rich man. You're getting into your mid forties now. It's time to make some serious money before we both retire and go fishing on Sun Moon Lake. Come to Taipei next month and we'll discuss the details."

After work that day, Victor drove to his parents' house and told them about Jason Fang's offer. He thought it was his duty to do this before he broke the news to Anne. His father said he should not take the job; his father said he should not work in China because the Communists could not be trusted. They might be opening, welcoming and reforming now, but no one knew how long that would last; they could just as easily reverse themselves without any warning. You don't want to be there when they do that, Son, was what old Mr. Lin said to Victor. And then he started recounting the history of the Communist Party's many betrayals over the years, from the civil war to the War of Resistance against the Japanese and back to the civil war again.

"You've told me all that before, Pa, many times, and I am not challenging your version of events. But this time is different." Victor ended with a phrase he had heard used a lot by his American colleagues when they were talking about internet stocks at the turn of the millennium.

"No, Son, a culture that has lasted five thousand years just does not change in one generation," the old man retorted, as Victor's mother poured her son more jasmine tea and laid out his favorite Taiwanese pineapple shortcakes on the table.

But Victor insisted and explained why he wanted to give it a try as he ate his shortcake and drank his tea. In the end, his father, having said all he had to say, gave up talking. He knew his son's mind had been made up. Victor's mother just warned her son to be extra careful, as all Chinese mothers do when their children leave home for a long journey. She thought her son knew best and she should not stand in his way.

Before Victor rose to go, he said to his mother, "Ma, if I have time, I would like to visit Hangzhou, the place where you met Pa when you were attending the same university."

"No, Son," old Mrs. Lin stopped him immediately, her voice firm and abrupt; the look of fear had crept into her eyes. "Don't go back. Don't reveal yourself to anyone. Don't tell people who you are and who we are. Your father's family and mine were considered black elements because we were landlords and scholar gentry from the west of the city. During Land Reform in the early 1950's, my elder brother, your uncle, was shot and his body turned into fertilizer. I told you he died in the hands of the Communists. But I did not tell you how barbaric they were. They didn't just kill him. They tortured and humiliated him for days on end before shooting him in the head and leaving his body to rot in the fields." She stopped because she could not go on. There was a lump in her throat and tears were welling up in her eyes. After what seemed like a long pause, she finally said to her son, "Now you know."

Victor was silent on hearing this. A new dose of reality had crept in. It was not strong enough to make him change his mind but he now wanted to know what Anne thought.

Victor was late coming home that evening. He quickly showered and sat down to dinner with his wife. During dinner he did not say much when Anne asked him about his day at the office. After he had finished washing the dishes, Victor joined Anne in the sitting room where she was flipping through a copy of *Cosmopolitan*. It was then that he told her about Jason Fang's offer. He also told her he was inclined to accept. To Victor's great surprise, Anne was flabbergasted and flew into an uncharacteristic rage.

"Why?… To Taiwan? What for?" she howled at him.

"Not Taiwan, Anne, China! And you don't have to go if you don't want to. I'll go and set things up for Jason and then, when the thing can run itself and I get the serious money he promised, I'll come back if by then you still don't want me to work there," he pleaded.

"But that means I won't see you for weeks and months, maybe years! Look, I'm perfectly happy here. If you're not happy with your present job, you can always try to get another one. We should both stay in one place, in the same city, in the same country, at least in the same continent!"

"I'm not happy with being number four in my company, Anne. I know I can do better than this. I know you would like that holiday house in Hawaii, and I want to get that for you before we both grow old. We should retire somewhere in the middle of the Pacific between Asia and America where people are different shades of white, yellow and brown. That's where we would both fit in."

"I've told you this many times. My mom and I are simple folks from Ireland, and we want a simple, uncomplicated life, even though my grandfather was a Congressman and all that. I'm not like my sister Meg. I don't have her kind of ambition. I'm perfectly happy working as an editor of children's stories and perfectly happy that you're holding your present position in your company. We don't need a lot to live on, you know. We have some savings and we have no children to leave the money to."

"And it's my fault, of course, and don't I know it!" Victor raised his voice at the mention of children, getting ready for an argument that had been repeated many times before.

"I'm not saying that." She steered away from that diversion. They looked at each other closely and both decided against picking up the old quarrel again. The treatment for infertility which lasted more than two years was for them a very unpleasant experience.

Victor slumped on to the sofa, cleared his throat, stretched his neck to his left and right, and then finally came out with the words, "Anne, please try to understand. I want to do this. A chance like this comes around once in a lifetime. Even my parents understand that, even my Pa who was a member of the KMT that had fought the Communists for years has put aside his objections, so why can't you?"

"Because I have been brought up differently, that's why! Even you have. They may be Chinese, but you don't know them anymore! Can't you see, Victor? Communism is not compatible with the American way of life! We are opposites!" Anne raised her voice again.

"But it's different now. They're not following Communist policies any more. China was closed to the outside world for more than one generation and now its doors are open again and everything is happening – the fastest growth rate in the world, some of the tallest buildings in Asia, modern airports, designer clothes, hand phones, even Mercedes limos and so on. You name it and they're going for it – all these status symbols, capitalist things Americans like – well, the Chinese like them too. They want a piece of the goodies, just like everybody else. It's really happening now, Anne. Maybe before long, communism will simply disappear from the face of China and, when that happens, the Chinese people can be re-united again and we won't be lost between two shores any more. Can't you see, Anne? What I want and what I need is a career *worthy* of my life."

Hearing Victor say this with such anguish and pleading in his voice and knowing in her heart how much this material success meant to him, Anne stopped and looked intently at her husband of fifteen years. She took in a deep breath, bit her lip, and finally came out with the words, "Do you want me to come with you on this trip?"

"No,' replied Victor, the word finally slipping out in the middle of a very long sigh, "I can manage." The tone of his voice told Anne he had thought everything through. "There will be many business meetings with Jason and other people that may last well into the night. I don't want you to be bored just lying around waiting for me in a hotel room, not knowing when I'd be back. I'll do this alone and I'll come back within a week to ten days max."

Anne couldn't sleep that night. She was in two minds whether she should insist on going with Victor to see Jason or head back East with her mother for her sister Meg's fiftieth birthday, as she had promised to do. She also toyed with the idea of re-opening the conversation again and forcing him to abandon his plan with the threat of divorce. It would have to be the threat of divorce, she thought, because when he was in such a mood, nothing else would change, move or deter him. But Anne loved her husband and could feel his deep-seated frustrations, his disappointments with the way his career was going. Being Catholic, she had learned from her mother never to even mention the word divorce in any argument with her husband, as Mrs. Gavin found out to her everlasting regret.

Tossing about in her bed, Anne knew she was really in a quandary. She could see that it was *Madam Butterfly* in reverse.

Her Chinese husband had just announced he wanted to go back to Asia. He didn't say it was going to be a permanent move, but she felt it would eventually lead to that – one fine day and it would happen. Maybe it just had to. She knew she had been dreading this moment for the last five years. When his native country summoned with promises of riches and bounty, she always suspected, Victor would rise and answer the clarion call. It was easier for the husband in such matters. Not so easy for the wife. Anne was not alone in her predicament and dilemma. Many couples across many cultures have had to make that choice some time in their lives. She thought she could keep Victor in America, but now China was beckoning like the sirens in Ancient Greece, and he just could not resist its lure.

It was one of those unexpected ironies in life again, as Victor's father always said. Victor was not Chinatown bound. He had worked hard, consciously, to break free of its shackles. But he was also not as successful as he would have liked and secretly craved. Like many of his compatriots before him, and no doubt also many who would come after, Victor was toiling away in middle management, and a long way from taking his place in the glittering pantheon of Chinese American celebrities, which was where he wanted to be. And so he was seizing what he thought was his big chance.

In their love-hate relationship with their host country, Chinese Americans had gone through three quite distinct stages. In the first stage, making good money in America through dint of hard work, and then returning home to their native village in China to live like landed gentry, was the Chinese migrant workers' dream. This was the pattern for close to half a century from the 1900's onward, when travel was by ocean-going steamers and when the Golden Gate Bridge was the iconic symbol of the famous Gold Mountain. For many years thereafter and during the second stage, after China became a Communist country and closed its doors to Americans, making it big in America itself and getting a mention in the society pages of US media publications was the fond aspiration of the next generation of Chinese Americans. With the horror stories of the Great Leap Forward and the Cultural Revolution doing the rounds in family circles and media reports, assimilation in their adopted country seemed the only way forward and many took that route. Then came the third stage – after China's doors flung open again in 1979 and the growth rate of the Chinese economy started to outpace that of the United States. In this *new* third phase, some Chinese Americans' goal in life was to go back and make big money out of their native country, by taking advantage of their Chinese connections and American know-how, and then *return* to the United States to buy big houses with their China-acquired wealth. Californians of ethnic Chinese origin were in the forefront of that traffic.

On the plane that night, all Victor could think of was the compensation package he would be asking for. He definitely wanted the title of CEO and at least double what he was getting now, plus a bonus at year-end, and a sizeable allotment of incentive shares and stock options when the company was ready to be listed on Nasdaq. And three trips a year back to the United States of course. He would insist on that; well, at least two. The dream got sweeter when he heard the song *I am, I said* in his mind's ears rising above the humming engine noises of the aircraft as it made its way across the dark expanse of the Pacific.

> *Did you ever read about a frog who dreamed of being a king*
> *And then became one?*
> *Well, except for the names and a few other changes,*
> *If you talk about me, the story's the same one...*

"From six to nine inches!" said an ebullient Jason Fang from the soft leather sofa in his ultra modern office on the top floor of one of Taipei's tallest buildings. "We're going to do nine-inch semiconductors in China."

"But I heard you're not allowed to do that by the Taiwan government. That's against the law, Jason!" Victor Lin was surprised.

"Never mind the law, Vic, we're running a business here. It's the ideal combination, don't you see? We're in Taiwan and upstream, where the technology and licenses are. Across the Strait and just an hour and a half away, and downstream of course, there's the Mainland where the cheap labor is. Not just cheap, but also high-quality. And the two together mean world-beating products at developing-country prices. The only problem is: the Taiwan Government would not allow my company to run both operations as one entity. That's right! Our own government wants me to have two separate companies, two separate boards and two separate managements. We are to keep everything completely independent of each other and at arm's length, especially the accounting. As we're a company listed on the Taiwan stock market, our government could give us no end of trouble if we did not comply, in appearance at least. This is where you come in. With you as CEO for our PRC operation, we'll tell them we're doing six inches in China, not nine, and that you are running this Mainland company as a separate entity. The rest we don't have to tell."

"But it's still illegal," insisted Victor.

"Only in Taiwan. Not on the Mainland. On the Mainland, they want the state-of-the-art technology. They really don't want to wait, and they don't care!" said Jason, but he could see that Victor was not convinced.

"Look at it this way, old pal. The Taiwan Government will relax its own restrictions within a few years. It will have to. It must. It will all be legal then, even in Taiwan. It's just a matter of time. But I need to be ahead of the game. That's why I need to start the China operation now – to keep ourselves competitive against the South Koreans. They are already breathing heavily down our necks."

Jason paused at this point. He could see that Victor was trying to work out in his mind whether he should accept a proposition which lay in the grey area of dubious legality. "There's a quarter of a million dollars here for you, US dollars, of course. And that's just the sign-on fee." Jason then continued, "I'll give you 2% of the company's equity after you have set it up properly in the next twenty-four months, rising by half a percent a year for the following six years if we turn a decent and progressive profit, up to a ceiling of 5%. And you don't have to put up any capital. You will have Profit and Loss responsibility and you report directly to me." When Victor just looked at him but still did not say anything, Jason pressed him further, "Look, Victor, I am telling you – you can make what you want out of this. The sky's the limit, as they say in America. One day, this operation which you will be running in China may be bigger than what I now own in Taiwan. Just think of the size and scale of the Chinese market – we're talking about well over one billion consumers, my friend!"

The sums were simple enough for Victor. Five percent of a company as big as Jason's existing operation, if successful, would give him close to $50 million in equity. He would have to set it up properly first; there were legal risks in Taiwan of course, that was always the catch but, thankfully, not in China where he would be based. Jason could take care of those risks, Victor thought. Jason knew so many high-ranking government officials in Taiwan; they could not possibly move against him. And even if they did, he was sure to hold his old friend harmless.

"It's a start-up, right, Jason? So where is it going to be based?"

"In Suzhou, where the Singaporeans have lost a bundle but have solved the teething problems for the Mainland guys. And for us too. Sometimes there's no first-mover advantage where investing in China is concerned, as you might know. The early bird does not necessarily catch the worm. He needs to know where to look."

"I would have to check out the layout of the site, the facilities, the infrastructure, the logistics, the skill level of the labor force, the quality of the water and so on. When can we go?" Victor had not come all this way to say no and Jason knew it now.

Rising from his sofa, a delighted Jason said, "You can leave the day after tomorrow. You'll need to be there for a few days if you're going to check so many things on this trip. But you can leave the legal issues to me. I'm not going with you as I have some of my biggest American clients visiting Taipei this week. I'll have Michael Wu go with you. He is one of my executive assistants. He will have your program worked out and he will take care of your flights and hotels and other details. He will show you the things you want to look at and take you to see the people you should see."

"So why can't I go tomorrow?"

"Because tomorrow night I have arranged a reunion dinner for you, dear friend. You do want to meet the old gang, don't you?"

"You mean James, Paul and Bernie?"

"But of course! Who else? Bernie is travelling up from Tainan just to see you. It's been almost twenty years, he said, since he saw you last."

"That's true. So what is Bernie the Brain doing these days?" Victor asked.

"Didn't you know? Haven't you heard? He's become a monk. He is now Bernie the Monk. No, actually, he calls himself Abbot Mirror Moon now, from the old saying 'flowers in the mirror and moon in the water'. To him everything in this life is ephemeral, even illusory."

"Bernie a monk?"

"Yes, he said he's committed too many sins, made too many mistakes and wanted to atone for them," said Jason with a very broad smile which quickly turned into a sneer. He could barely hide his own disbelieving cynicism, even in jest.

"And James? And Paul? Are they still in the same jobs? I expect Paul is since he's an academic, and academics rarely change jobs in Taiwan."

Jason's personal secretary appeared at the entrance to the room after a quick knock on the door. This was the signal for Jason's next appointment. And so he said to Victor, "You'll find out when you see them."

"Alright then, I'll go to Suzhou the day after. But I have to be back by the middle of next week. I promised Anne that."

The next morning, the overcast Taipei weather typical of the spring season greeted Victor as in the days of old. California it was not. He decided not to take the sumptuous hotel breakfast but went instead to a roadside store selling soya milk and

Chinese churros, the kind he had eaten almost every day when he was a student. Victor really could not wait to re-acquaint himself with a long-lost but still familiar sensation – the taste of warm soya milk swirling in his mouth as the poor man's breakfast of fried churros went down his hungry throat. This Taiwanese specialty was always to Victor a precious, heavenly combination, now made even more precious by the long abstinence, and he soon decided to line up in the queue for a second helping.

His breakfast done and feeling nostalgic for more reminders of his past, Victor went for a stroll down memory lane at National Taiwan University. He entered from the university's main entrance with the glorious palm-lined boulevard, as he had done countless times when he was a student. The university had an early twentieth-century Japanese feel to it. The low-rise buildings were functional and bare. The colors were plain and subdued, quietly unostentatious. But the boulevard was an unusually impressive and particularly memorable sight for the students who had passed through the university's gates. So much would have happened in their formative college years.

As Victor looked at the palm trees again, he noticed they now seemed shorter than he remembered them to be. Memories are not reliable witnesses. It did not occur to him that his perspective had changed and that he had grown used to bigger and taller palms in California. Coming to the end of the line of palm trees, Victor made a 180 degree turn and faced the main entrance of the university again, now at a distance of about one hundred meters. Just at this moment, a group of undergraduates had rushed through the gate on their bicycles, laughing and shouting as they raced along the wide boulevard. Victor saw shadows of himself twenty four years ago and the past hit him like a dagger in the guts. It was at that moment, totally unexpectedly, that tears rolled out of his eyes. Memories of his youth came flooding back with the force of rushing tides. Victor found a bench at a quiet corner, sat down, steadied himself and cried. This was where he had spent four happy years of his life. This was his long lost Taiwan University.

It was a bitter-sweet moment and Victor was glad he was here by himself, because he wanted to reminisce alone, loiter at his own pace and savor everything he saw in silence. The bicycle yard where he used to park his bike was still there, as was the banyan tree where he and his buddies used to gather and wait before going to a movie. Victor took a peep at an empty lecture room and surveyed the inside in an arc as his head turned. He found they were still using wooden desks and wooden chairs after all these years. It was a surprise to him, but also strangely comforting.

At National Taiwan University, a lot might have changed in the intervening years between Victor's graduation and return, but some of the old rooms, labs and big lecture halls were still there; and Victor noticed they smelled the same. For a man looking for some remnants of his past, the familiar smell of those rooms was very reassuring. As were the smells of the busy streets, the car fumes, the badly lit shops, even the smell of the people rushing past – these had changed little for Victor. In some respects, Taipei was like Berlin and Vienna after the Second World War – the lack of permanence in people's lives had affected their behavior in a fundamental way. Much was makeshift and few believed they would be staying very long. Homes were rented, not bought. People did not want to commit, because to own was to belong, and the émigré population in Taiwan, of which the Lins were part, had no idea how long they would be there for. And they did not feel they belonged.

His tour of familiar places finished, Victor left from a side entrance of the university and headed towards Wenzhou Street where he and his buddies had spent countless evenings strolling from one end of the lane to the other and then back again, young men in their plastic flip-flops and shirt sleeves, loitering after dinner without any specific purpose, just happily chatting away or debating anything under the sun, from the latest Hollywood movies to Taiwanese politics, but in particular a subject which came up multiple times – who was the prettiest girl on campus.

Victor wondered what might have become of his life now if he had stayed in Taiwan all these past nineteen, almost twenty, years. He might have made more money, but would he have had a better lifestyle, he wondered? He might have seen the growing business opportunities ahead of Jason, but would he have dared take the risks and act on his hunches? And could he have marketed himself, his ideas and his company as well as Jason had done? And arranged the bank financing as skillfully? Perhaps yes, but then, perhaps not. Victor was enough of a realist to know that it was idle to speculate. His life had gone in a very different direction.

Victor's nostalgia had finally run its course. Leaving his university and Wenzhou Street behind now and with his eyes dry, he knew the past, his own past, was irredeemable.

At the reunion dinner, in his first remarks to his old friends, Victor could not resist teasing Bernie about his surprised conversion to Buddhism. He said he always thought Bernie was the most worldly and the most materialistic in their group of five. Jason quickly joined in and said he had expected Bernie to be a billionaire rather than a Buddhist. He said it was for Bernie's sake that he had arranged, reluctantly, a mostly vegetarian meal, except for the duck and pork dishes which, he remembered, were Victor's favorites. Everybody laughed. Victor nodded his head in acknowledgement and raised his glass to thank Jason for arranging the dinner, but his first questions were directed at James Jen, when he found out that James had become a career politician.

Victor asked James what he thought of the future of Taiwan next to a resurgent and increasingly assertive China, now that it had started to throw its economic, political and military weights about.

"It is not good," said the politically savvy James Jen who was now a KMT legislator in the Legislative Yuan. The air around him almost froze as he continued, his voice coarse from speaking at a mass rally that afternoon. "We Mainlanders are caught between a rock and a hard place, Beijing on the one hand and Taiwan's DPP on the other."

"But the Democratic Progressive Party was not a force in politics when I left!" said Victor. "I remember it was illegal to even form an opposition political party then. I know they have put their own guy in the Presidential Palace recently but how did that happen?"

"Well, they are certainly a force now. They are highly motivated and quite well organized. Solidarity with 'nativism' is their drawing card – Taiwan for the Taiwanese, you know. They won the last election because the KMT was hopelessly split and fielded two candidates instead of one."

At this point, Paul Chiang the learned Professor of the group weighed in as he straightened the metal-framed eye-glasses on the bridge of his flat nose. "Time is on the side of the DPP. When the Generalissimo came over to Taiwan in 1949, about a million and a half of us Mainlanders crossed the Taiwan Strait with him. The native Taiwanese outnumbered us in the ratio of roughly six to one. But we had control of the government, the armed forces and the mass media and they couldn't touch us then. They can now, well, certainly since 1987, when political parties other than the KMT became legal and the mass media were freed up. I can't see us winning many more elections going forward. That blasted six-to-one ratio is now closer to seven to one. As you know, many Mainlanders have emigrated to the United States, well, you yourself for one." Paul was pointing his hand at Victor as he said this. The eminent academic had always thought leaving Taiwan to fend for itself was something of a betrayal and he was not mincing words.

"But is there much to fear from a DPP ascendancy?" Victor ignored the reference to himself and asked the next question quickly to deflect it, and he went on to say, "Power sharing may not be such a bad thing, my friends. Changes of government do occur from time to time in Western countries, and it's all very peaceful, through the ballot box. Power can change hands without incident. I've seen this in action in the United States. Parties just take turns to govern with no alarming, long-lasting ill effects as far as I can see."

"Ah, but this is Taiwan," said James with a sigh indicating resignation and disappointment, "Here, when the DPP is in a position to dictate, they will want to settle the accounts with us, and after that they will want independence – from Beijing. They insist on calling themselves Taiwanese; they will not call themselves Chinese, you know. They are asserting their own separate identity. They want to call this island Formosa, using its Portuguese name, not Taiwan, which is, of course, its proper Chinese name. There isn't much room for compromise, I'm afraid. The situation is quite dire."

"Settle the accounts with us? What accounts?" asked Victor.

"The February 28th massacre of 1947 for one," said Bernie the Monk, he with the round face and shaved head who had been relatively quiet until now. Bernie had the look of a benign abbot who wanted to save the world through preaching enlightenment and forgiveness. "That's the fateful day. As you know, on that day the Nationalist Government killed a few thousand Taiwanese for organized rebellion against KMT rule. This took place before we were born, before our families moved here, but it did happen. Many DPP supporters see this as Taiwan's own version of the June 4th massacre at Tiananmen Square and have been clamouring for justice and retribution for years. Several KMT ministers since 1987 have conceded the crackdown was a mistake, but the DPP are still agitating for more than just an acknowledgment. I don't know where this is going to lead. I just hope people will see the futility of it all. All things temporal, all our cherished attachments, are illusory, my friends. Nothing is permanent. Buddhism is the only answer. Do you have time to come and see the grand temple in Tainan, Victor?"

"No, not Buddhism," Jason Fang, the host of the evening and the billion-dollar man, felt obliged to counter such negativism and he weighed in. "Please, Bernie! Buddhism is the abnegation of life and everything that is wonderful about living. And talking about living, if we want the good life to continue, we simply have to trust the good sense of the leaders in Beijing and put some of our eggs in China." Then, turning to his long-absent friend from the United States, Jason continued, "This may sound strange to you, Victor, but I have had fewer arguments with Communist Party officials in China than I do with the DPP here."

"Do you think the DPP will really take Taiwan down the road of independence?" Victor asked what was for him the truly important question.

"You bet," his friends Paul and Jason both replied, almost in unison.

At this point James the Politician came in with an observation which Victor had not heard before. Looking really serious now, James, a hangdog expression on his face, said, "I think when push comes to shove, the end game is this: Most people in Taiwan would accept a confederation, something like the European Union, with China and Taiwan as equal partners and each keeping its own army and autonomy. But I don't think Taiwanese people would accept a federation like the former USSR, especially one that would be dominated and dictated by the Chinese Communist Party. That would be my considered judgment. But the DPP's leaders do not want either. They want complete independence for Taiwan, and if that's not possible, they want the continuation of *de facto* separation, which is what we have now. But I doubt Beijing would allow this to continue for long."

"What can Beijing do about it?" asked Victor in all innocence; he had been away too long. "Do you think the Communists will go to war to recover Taiwan?"

"Not until Beijing is strong enough to take Taiwan by force," said James. "They're not there yet provided the Americans stand by us. Beijing's more intelligent leaders know this even if some hotheads do not. They need to reckon with the U.S. and with Japan. The Japanese will come in on Taiwan's side I think and, by so doing, drag the United States into war. Washington doesn't have much wriggle room under the terms of the US-Japan Security Treaty."

"I am not so sure," Paul the learned but skeptical professor of politics disagreed, "Why should the aged eagle spread its wings?"

Victor ignored the comment and continued to press James. "But you think this is a war Beijing cannot yet win?" he asked.

"That's right," the ever pragmatic Jason butted in again at this point, "I am optimistic that something could be worked out, but the DPP must have the wisdom not to provoke Beijing into taking premature and precipitous military action against its better judgment. That's not going to do anybody any good, least of all us businessmen."

"No, Beijing would not leave us alone for long," Paul the Professor warned, shaking his head as he said, "The generation that left with the Generalissimo, our parents' generation, is dying out fast. They account for less than seven percent of the population now, and many of them are no longer economically or politically active. They are the ones with a strong attachment to the Mainland, because they were born there, went to school there, got their first jobs there and probably got married there – my parents did. When they die out, and they will soon, Taiwanese identity will assert itself ever more forcefully, and the peaceful return of the island to the bosom of the motherland can only be a pipe dream."

"That's probably right," said James Jen in agreement. "The Communists really have no realistic hope of getting Taiwan back *peacefully* now after the way they messed up Hong Kong. I mean it's there for all to see, right? Beijing promised Hong Kong 'one country, two systems' with a high degree of autonomy for fifty years and all that, but look at Hong Kong now! Anybody can see that the Communist Party is running the city, not the Hong Kong Government. It's as if the cadres thought the rest of the world wasn't watching. But we are – we *all* are in Taiwan."

"I can agree with you for once James," said Bernie the Monk, "I had thought they would have the wisdom to deal with Hong Kong more advisedly, with more circumspection, but they didn't. It's all very strange to me how they've messed up. I put it down to fate when something, against many people's rational expectations, moves inexorably along an unfortunate trajectory that can only lead to a tragic ending. If the Communists were more Buddhist, this would not have happened. We do not believe in owning or controlling things, but they do. If anything, we Buddhists believe in giving away all our worldly possessions."

"It should have been a simple matter of living up to the promises they themselves made when they signed the Joint Declaration with the British in 1984," Paul Chiang, who had authored two seminal works on international treaties, was slightly indignant as he said this. His whole career was built on the sanctity of the written word. "The British had already handed over sovereignty in 1997. All that the Beijing government needed to do was wait fifty years and then it would all be theirs anyway – everything! Every instrument of government, lock, stock and barrel. They could do what they like after that; it would all be legal and in keeping with the Sino British Joint Declaration. Why couldn't they just wait? If they had done that, it would have shown the whole world they're as good as their word. It doesn't make good legal or strategic sense to me."

"Ah, but it does make political sense if you look at it from their point of view – they have a mortal and morbid fear of losing political control. That is why they are so eager to introduce legislation in Hong Kong to ban treason, secession, sedition and subversion!" said Bernie, who was always interested in the metaphysical plane in any discussion. "It is not just a Communist trait, I'm afraid; it is also a Chinese trait, my friends. We want to manage and run things the way we like to when we're in a position of power, and we will broach no disagreement. Chinese leaders are obsessed with power and control. What's more, they often confuse the two. What they're really after is absolute control, but when they cannot get this, they think it's because they don't have enough power, and so they go out and grab even more. But we Buddhists know that absolute power does not equate with absolute control. We know that absolute control is an illusion. It is simply not attainable in this life. The United States may be the most powerful country in the world, but it still cannot control all that is happening around the globe."

"Can we just bring the discussion back to substance and not metaphysics please?" said Jason who was slightly annoyed with Bernie because he really didn't understand what the holy monk was saying. Taking the cue from his host, Paul the Professor began, "I have to say I am with James. What Beijing is doing to Hong Kong – this Article 23 business – is setting a really bad example for Taiwan. I doubt many Taiwanese would want re-unification with China on the terms the British settled for. In fact, I doubt whether anybody in Taiwan would believe the Beijing Government after seeing what has happened in Hong Kong since 1997. Which actually makes me think that perhaps

Beijing is not pursuing the same strategy vis-à-vis Taiwan as it did in the case of Hong Kong. No, not at all. China's leaders are not really using Hong Kong as a showcase for Taiwan. If they were, they wouldn't have interfered as much as they have done. Which leads me to believe Beijing only has in mind the military option for re-unification with Taiwan. Not the *ultimate* option, mind you, but the *only* option. They're not really considering anything else. It's now just a question of timing."

"If that is the case," said James, "then, believe me, my friends, Beijing will act as soon as it is able to. It is not going to wait. Re-unification is the number one priority of every hubristic Chinese leader in Beijing."

"That may be, but how will the Taiwanese armed forces react to an outright invasion?" asked Victor.

"Our own government has said our military could only hold out for two weeks," said James who, as a legislator, was privy to some classified information, but was discreet and never named his sources. "The United States armed forces must come to our assistance before then or we cave in. This is why the diehards in the DPP would not recognize the principle of One China which Beijing has been pushing so forcefully since the first Singapore dialogue between us in 1992. They're afraid that if they agreed to One Country, an invasion of Taiwan by China would just be a civil war between two warring political parties within the same nation-state, and it wouldn't be any business of the Americans or the Japanese. They would have no legitimate reason to come in and help even if we asked them to."

The drift of the discussion had billionaire Jason Fang worried. The normally high-spirited and smooth-talking businessman was lost in thought and could not think of anything else to say to his friends. His business was going well, but politics was pulling in the opposite direction, and the shrewd businessman in him knew that sometime, somehow, something had to give.

Just then, the *pièce de résistance* of the evening arrived. Peking Duck, as it was still called in Taipei, was being served. The old pals clinked their glasses, readied their chopsticks and the conversation soon drifted to the good old days when they were young and carefree bachelor boys and did not yet know much about the real world in which they lived. Life consisted of writing essays, doing projects, taking exams and running after the pretty girls at the handful of fraternal universities in and around Taipei. They would all be middle-aged by now, these teenage dreamboats of their generation, many of them stuck in humdrum office or teaching jobs and some with teenage children. You would not want to look at them after this many years, not even for old time's sake, according to Jason Fang when some girls' names came up. "Never look back," Jason said. Jason should know; he had been the president of their alumni association for several years and attended many class reunions as its major donor and patron.

Bernie kept very quiet when the conversation turned to reminiscences about boys and girls in their undergraduate days, Victor noticed. He thought of asking Bernie about Kathy but quickly decided against it. This was hardly the time or occasion.

He remembered Bernie and Kathy had a long courtship which somehow did not end in marriage. He suspected that Bernie started seeing the transience of life and the futility of human relationships after his girl friend of many years ditched him for an American exchange student from Iowa. But Victor never expected his once worldly friend would become a monk.

After dinner, when Bernie was trying to engage Jason and sell him the idea of endowing a new wing of a Buddhist hospital in Tainan, Victor drew Paul and James to one side and said to them, "Jason is fabulously rich; he can do anything he wants and he can settle anywhere he wants. Bernie has resigned himself from the world; he is no longer interested in temporal, worldly things. But what about you two? What are your plans, my friends?"

James, ever the man of destiny even in his high school days, looked Victor in the eye and said, "My immediate plan is to win the next election in just over a year's time. There is high-level dialogue going on between our party and Beijing. I want to be there to influence events and serve the best interests of our people. We are fast approaching a turning point in history and I want to be there. I entered politics for that vital, critical moment, and we're getting close to that now, or will be soon."

Paul was never quite so straightforward and idealistic as James even in his younger days. He tucked his pair of eyeglasses upwards, gently pulled out a cigarette from his breast pocket, his first of the evening, then slowly came the words he wanted to say, "I am writing a book, probably the most important of my career, to rebut some of the things American academics have been saying about the impending collapse of China, because I don't think it's going to happen. If anything, China is in the ascendant. The Communist regime has loosened up a bit. These guys can now entertain private ownership. Chinese people's lives have improved quite substantially. This is not the kind of worrisome chaos situation that had preceded past collapses..."

At this juncture, James butted in, before Paul could finish what he wanted to say. James disagreed with Paul on principle and had argued with him on this point before. James said, with a touch of false modesty, "It is not for me to challenge our distinguished Professor of Politics, but I remember when you and I were students and attending the same class on political philosophy, old Professor Bai made us study Alexis de Tocqueville's *The Ancient Regime and the French Revolution* and quoted to us what appeared to be paradoxical advice but which turned out to be the embodiment of profound political wisdom. And this is de Tocqueville's observation that a bad government is most at risk when it is trying to reform itself. What do you say to that now, Paul?"

"Of course I remember the quote and I don't disagree with it. But it is still idle to speculate on the timing of the Communist Party's so-called 'impending collapse'. I honestly don't think anybody has a clue. That said, however, I should also say it is not idle to speculate on *how* China might break up, because there are plenty of precedents in our 5,000 year history. But James, seriously, I really would not wish the sudden collapse of the Chinese Communist Party Government on anybody. Because the Chinese model of disintegration is quite unlike what we've seen in the former USSR and the former Yugoslavia. In the Soviet model, the implosion was largely peaceful; the former Union of Soviet Socialist Republics broke up into fourteen sovereign states after 1991, without an outbreak of civil war. In the case of Yugoslavia, the break-up was not peaceful; a bloody civil war broke out in 1992; but it did not last long and was effectively over by 1999. In the Chinese scheme of things, when dynasties fell, this was inevitably followed by long periods of extremely brutal, barbarous civil wars, some of them lasting well over a hundred years, with a horrendous number of deaths and wave upon wave of desperate refugees fleeing for their lives. Human tragedy of the Chinese kind is epic in scale. It really does not bear thinking about, James."

The gathering of old friends ended with many sobering thoughts but not a single solution. The general feeling was that time's winged chariot was about to take China and Taiwan into uncharted territory.

Late that evening, Victor tried to call Anne from his hotel, to tell her he would have to go into China – to the city of Suzhou – for a few days before flying back. But because of the sixteen-hour time difference between the two shores of the Pacific Ocean, Anne was already on a plane to New York with her mother; they were going to her sister Meg's fiftieth birthday celebration and family reunion.

Victor put down the phone, feeling slightly disappointed. He wanted to tell Anne about what he had seen in Taipei, what he had felt at returning to his *alma mater,* and his conversation at dinner with his former mates. And he particularly wanted to tell her about the quarter-of-a-million sign-on fee.

Suzhou had the potential to be, Jason Fang had told him, the Silicon Valley of China. Only much cheaper, Victor found. The Singaporean investors might have had their fingers burned when they set up the Science Park in this city, but the Chinese were getting a great deal of warmth from the fire these pioneers started.

He did not expect this, but Victor Lin actually had very mixed feelings on first setting foot on Chinese soil. In Suzhou, he was going through culture shock. The New China that was spread out before him was like nothing he had pictured in his mind, and nothing like what his parents had told him over the years. He now began to understand why Jason was so excited about the prospects that were opening up for Taiwanese businessmen in the Mainland. The train station was modern, the highways were streamlined, the skyscrapers were many, and although some of the new buildings had outlandish designs borne of the runaway imagination of second-rate architects, they looked solid, well-constructed and expensive. The only jarring aspect to an otherwise impressive display of 'China in modernity' was the inadequate and sub-standard office lighting which he noticed once he ventured inside the grandiose buildings – not just one but many. The haphazard color schemes and curious interior designs also seemed like unfortunate consequences of someone's careless afterthoughts.

But Victor was not bothered by this incongruity. When he was growing up in Taipei, the behavior of the people there was not dissimilar. The well-to-do in Taiwan would put up a luminous front on the outside of buildings but skimp on what they considered the non-essentials. And lighting was certainly one of those, with the result that many offices and houses in old Taipei were always dimly lit. Appearances are important in Chinese societies, and so the facades often tell a different story from what lies within. In its modern side, Suzhou, the Chinese city Victor was actually driving through now with Michael Wu as his guide, would leave any city in Taiwan trailing. But even the best parts of the city were quite uneven in appearance, and Victor noticed there were large areas of poverty and squalor still.

As a computer scientist and engineer, Victor Lin was naturally drawn to new technological breakthroughs and emerging opportunities. And he could sense that Suzhou had plenty of these to offer going forward. Like most Americans, he was impressed by size and modernity, and he was interested in being part of a new beginning. Although he was critical of the Chinatown syndrome in Los Angeles and San Francisco, Victor was really quite proud of his ethnic roots. He had never denied them, and it felt good to see his native country emerge from the backwaters of under-development. Like many ethnic Chinese people around the world, he really wanted to see the end to almost two hundred years of humiliation.

But, on the other hand, when Victor saw the crowds in the streets of Suzhou, the way they were dressed, the way they talked, and the way they ate their food in restaurants and street corners, he knew he was no longer one of them. He was not trying to stay aloof, not consciously. There was the bond of blood between them, but Victor really felt he was a man apart in the Suzhou crowd, like a cousin that was distant, several times removed. What had created that distance was the many years of separation, the many years of living in another culture, among a different people, and being married to an American. He just felt he was not one of them anymore. Not superior or above, just on a different plane, not the same – beyond.

The truth of the matter was that Victor really didn't know what to make of China and where he might fit in, in this new scheme of things. He needed a great deal of soul-searching and the passage of time for first impressions to sink in and turn into considered opinions. Victor was not there yet. He was confused because he was not sure of his own identity, nor where he stood. To begin with, he was Taiwanese Chinese, and then Chinese American, and now he was back in his native China, and actually travelling down the streets of Suzhou for the first time in his life. This was not yet a full circle, but the rapid turnings along the way were enough to make his head spin.

While Victor was a student at UCLA, the writings of Maxine Hong Kingston were all the rage, especially her most successful book *China Men*. The title was so eye-catching and seemed so relevant to his predicament that Victor went and bought a copy immediately after the book came out and quickly finished reading it in two days. But he could not relate to what the author was on about. Years later, in a discussion of the book Victor had with a visiting literature scholar from Taipei, he found out why. Professor Liu explained to him that Hong, although an ethnic Chinese, was not in his opinion a Chinese writer. In his opinion, she was really an American writer, because her sensibilities and even her imagination were American, not just her choice of language. Liu's words were coming back to Victor Lin now. Perhaps his sensibilities and those of the native Suzhounese around him were no longer in tune? But had his own sensibilities changed so much in the last twenty years that he was no longer Chinese? Victor was beginning to ask questions about his own identity, now that he had seen his native China at first hand. Living amongst Americans had somehow moderated his Chinese-ness. He belonged to a breed called Chinese-Americans and they were a people in between, a people apart, neither Chinese nor American.

As Jason Fang had told him, Michael Wu was a great help and seemed to know the ins and outs of everything in Suzhou. But in the course of their many conversations on the plane and in the car, Victor also noticed that Michael did not have a sense of the big picture and the future direction of American tech companies in the United States. He was more of a fixer, perhaps even a general manager, but was much too narrowly focused to be entrusted with strategic expansion for which making the right critical choices was absolutely vital. No, Victor concluded in his head, Jason was right not to entrust his expansion plan to Michael Wu. Efficient and knowledgeable as he was, the man would not make a suitable chief executive for the entire China operation. He did not have a strategic and coherent vision.

After two days of inspection tours followed by numerous meetings, Victor had finished the preliminary due diligence he wanted to do to help him make up his mind. He called Jason and told him he would take the job and accept the terms offered. He proposed to start in two months. That would give him time to serve his notice to his current employer and also spend more time with Anne, he thought. He was not taking the re-location lightly.

Victor was booked to fly out from Shanghai on Monday, thinking he would need at least four days to size things up in Suzhou. But all the work he needed to do was already done by Thursday afternoon and he could not change to an earlier flight. Michael Wu advised him not to bother visiting the famous Suzhou gardens on this trip as he would have all the time in the world to do this after he took up residence in the city. And so Victor decided to take a side trip to Hangzhou on Friday and see the legendary West Lake his mother had told him so much about over the years. Although his parents were not actually born in Hangzhou itself, they considered the city home and often spoke of it in glowing terms. Because of that, Hangzhou had always held a special fascination for the young Lin.

Victor's maternal grandfather was an art teacher and had taught Victor's mother to write and paint in the classical style. He had impressed upon her that just as the shimmering light of the Côte d'Azur had been the inspiration of many French Impressionists, so Hangzhou's morning mists on verdant hills had stirred the imagination of many generations of Chinese painters, and they had tried to capture the poetry of those moments on their paper scrolls. Victor's mother in turn had tried to convey the magic of those images to her son when he was a small child growing up in Taiwan. Victor remembered the little tales his mother told him particularly well. If there was one place near Suzhou he would love to see more than any other, it was Hangzhou where his parents went to university and where they first met. So he told Michael Wu that was where he wanted to go, and Michael got him the train ticket, booked him the hotel and arranged a car to greet him at the Hangzhou train terminal as he arrived.

Everything worked out as planned. Except that Victor had not expected to be greeted by the famous Hangzhou drizzle at this time of the year. His driver who met him at the station held out an umbrella and opened the car door for him. He had just buckled himself up in the car, and was looking at the large crowd through his car window, when the young chauffeur introduced himself as Ah Sheng and handed him a bottle of mineral water, before starting the car engine and driving off. Victor acknowledged the thoughtful gesture with a smile and thanked his driver politely but left the water untouched. Shortly after the car got into the city traffic, everything ground to a crawl as people and vehicles got in each other's way. Victor had plenty of opportunities to gaze at the somewhat chaotic street scenes and the many passers-by. Trying to make conversation, Ah Sheng looked into his rear mirror and said to Victor, "You don't look Taiwanese."

"Oh?" a surprised Victor raised his voice. "Why do you say this? I didn't know we looked any different!" said he, feeling slightly offended by the driver's over-familiar comment.

"No, but I mean you don't behave like a Taiwanese on the Mainland," the driver explained himself.

"And how *does* a Taiwanese behave in the Mainland?" Victor became curious.

"Well, they're not very well-mannered for a start, they wouldn't have thanked me for the water for instance, and they are very blatant about their, shall we say, evening activities. They would ask me to set them up within minutes of getting into my car once they see the pretty girls on the streets. We have a rhyming doggerel in Hangzhou which describes how a Taiwanese behaves. You want to hear it? Mind you, it's a bit rude."

"Yeah, why not? We're in a traffic jam anyway, aren't we? So tell me."

"OK, here it goes," Ah Sheng winked at him in the mirror and blurted out the rhyming couplets:

"Taiwanese always fall asleep in the car.
They need a toilet without going far.
They buy love potions in the morning,
To help them with the night's whoring."

Victor burst out laughing – loud. He had to admit that even though the doggerel was indeed raw, it was really quite clever and probably summed up the locals' disdain for their Taiwanese visitors of which, thankfully, according to this driver, he was not one. Almost twenty years of living in the United States had Americanized Victor. Even his physical features had changed somewhat. His skin had become quite coarse from too much sun, his nose more prominent, and his gait had developed the casual nonchalance of the laid-back Californian. In any case, Victor was not a native Taiwanese. His parents were born and raised in Zhejiang Province in the Mainland just south of Hangzhou. They only went over to Taiwan in 1949 with Generalissimo Chiang Kai-shek during the great retreat. Victor was born in Taipei and went to school there. His family knew other émigré families and he played with their boys. They could tell the native Taiwanese from their own kind – they were different in their looks, their accent and their manners. Native Taiwanese, the scions of farmers and fishermen of Fujian Province, were darker, shorter, and spoke a southern dialect called Min-nan, not Mandarin Chinese.

"That's pretty good," Victor said to the driver, "Now I'm glad you don't think I look Taiwanese." They both burst out laughing as they acknowledged a naughty joke unashamedly shared.

The ice having been broken, Victor felt he could engage the driver in a more serious conversation, and so he asked, "Do you not resent them, the Taiwanese, I mean, coming here to sow their wild oats with your women?"

"Resent?" his driver asked, "Oh, come on, we're all Chinese, aren't we? And they are my customers, just as you are. I make good money out of them."

"You mean you take them to the girls and they give you big tips. Is that it?" Victor taunted his driver.

"Oh no. No, no. Hong Kong clients give big tips. Taiwanese clients don't tip much. It's that damned Japanese influence, you know – fifty years of Japanese rule after the Manchu government gave away Taiwan to Japan and they've picked up a lot of bad Japanese habits. Japanese don't tip, and the Taiwanese, well, they learned from the damned Japanese. In Hong Kong, they learned from the British. And the British do tip. Not a lot, mind you, but they do tip. Hong Kong people give the biggest tips. They should, they've had it so good for so long. Not like us. We are only beginning to turn the corner."

"I'll give you a big tip if you'll take me to my hotel in the next ten minutes, then wait for me in the lobby and take me around the city for a tour of your most famous sights. But I need to use the toilet first."

The driver gave a loud chuckle at the mention of toilet, since Victor was behaving exactly like a typical Taiwanese visitor in the Hangzhou doggerel. Through the rear mirror, he could see that Victor was blushing as he realized what he had just said. To save him further embarrassment, the cheeky driver ventured a question. "If you're not Taiwanese,' he said, "You must be American. Am I right? You can't be from Hong Kong or Singapore; your *putonghua* is too good."

"I've lived in America for some twenty years. My wife is American."

That was Victor's truthful answer, but he could not tell whether the driver understood the fine distinction he was trying to make and the complex emotion behind those few words.

After a quick check-in and a quick toilet routine, Victor came downstairs and consulted the concierge about the following day's program. He then rejoined his driver and was soon quite captivated by everything he saw on the road. As his car made its arduous way through the congested Hangzhou city traffic, Victor remembered what his mother had told him – that the house she grew up in had been torn down and the whole area had been turned into factory buildings. She told him not to even bother going there and that, instead, he should go and visit the West Lake if he had the chance. She told Victor the scenery at and around the West Lake was the most beautiful, and rightly celebrated in the city's folklore, such as the tragic story of Lady White Snake.

Like most old women, Victor's mother would repeat the same words and whole sentences over and over again, and these had found their way into Victor's consciousness and conjured up in his mind an impression of a city that was small and old, quaint and picturesque. But the city he was now confronted with, in the brand new and very shiny limousine he was traveling in, was anything but that. It was big, sprawling and had a central business district lined with modern buildings that might best be described as neo Western. In the early spring drizzle, the mists that would obscure the hills beyond the city had already disappeared and, as so often happens to itinerant tourists, Victor did not get to see what he had come to see – Chinese landscape paintings in their real, three-dimensional setting.

But, notwithstanding the disappointment of a wish unfulfilled, Victor thought the less populated West Lake area of the city really did justify the oft-repeated phrase which described Hangzhou as "heaven on earth." It was a pity, he thought, that he did not have more time and had to resort to a car tour of such a magnificent place. It would have taken him hours to walk around the Lake and visit all ten designated scenic spots and the twenty-four bridges of different styles and construction. Victor knew he could not possibly do that in one afternoon. He also knew he should not tire himself out on his first day in the city, because on the following day he was hoping to do a full-day tour of The Thousand Island Lake which was a good two hour ride to the south of Hangzhou. This was what the hotel concierge had told him.

But, seeing that the drizzly weather had subsided, Victor could not resist walking the last mile when he saw the logo of his hotel appear in the distance. So he told Ah Sheng to stop the car and let him off at Broken Bridge where Lady White Snake, a demon that had taken human form for the love of her beau, fought her last losing battle against the Holy Monk who had been sent to banish her from her hapless husband.

Victor thanked Ah Sheng as he got out of the car, reminded him to be on time the next morning for the trip to the Thousand Island Lake, and gave him a big tip. Ah Sheng looked at the two large bills and realized he had a satisfied American customer. He drove off with a smile on his face after making his customary half bow.

That evening, Victor was going to have dinner at the hotel restaurant alone. While walking through the hotel lobby, he had caught a glimpse of a rather tall, curvaceous and heavily made-up girl at the bar, with long, dark and shiny hair. He was not particularly drawn to her curves. He had noticed, when he walked back to the hotel that afternoon, a plastic surgeon's clinic at the street corner opposite. The clinic displayed a big banner spread across the breadth of the building to advertise its special service – breast enlargement – and the characters on the banner read, "No breast is too small for us". Victor had a long, uninhibited laugh when he set eyes on the protruding advertisement. The audacity of Chinese business adverts could be very disarming.

After Victor finished his meal, he rose to go back to his room. He noticed the girl was still there, apparently still drinking by herself, although he only saw a glass of water on the counter in front of her. And when Victor went past her and headed for the elevator lobby, the girl stood up and followed him. She entered the elevator after he did but did not look at or push any of the buttons on the panel. When the lift stopped on Victor's floor, she did not make any move and just let him walk past.

Victor went into his room, but had scarcely taken his jacket off when the door-bell rang. He opened the door and the girl with the long shiny hair was standing right in front of him.

"Room service?" the over-long eyelashes in a smoothly made-up face batted out an invitation.

"No, I didn't ask for room service," he replied.

"Yes, but did you want it?" she leaned forward and moved her body a little closer until the front of her dress was almost touching his shirt.

Feeling embarrassed, he backed off a little and said, "I'm married, I'm afraid." As he did this, the smell of strongly scented perfume followed him and took full possession of his personal airspace.

"You don't have to be afraid," the girl pulled out a packet of condoms.

"That's not what I meant…" Victor quickly stepped back, closed the door shut and put on the latch.

The next morning, Victor donned his casual slacks and jacket and went down to breakfast at the hotel restaurant. The lady of the night was no longer there, nor did he expect her to be in broad daylight. He was now all excited about going to the Thousand Island Lake which in his mind conjured up vivid images of nature in its florid glory. Having lived in California almost twenty years, Victor really felt uncomfortable in the dampness of the Hangzhou air and was easily persuaded to take a day trip to the south where, the concierge had told him yesterday, he could expect sunnier weather.

Leaving behind the crawling traffic in the city, the car sped down the almost deserted super highway and headed south, in the direction of the Thousand Island Lake. Ah Sheng was in a confident, talkative mood and launched into an account of the stupendous achievements of the New China since Deng Xiaoping, the paramount leader, started the country on the road to Economic Reform, the Open Door and the Four Modernizations. That was in 1978, he said, and in less than one generation, China had been transformed. Every major city now boasted of skyscrapers, a new airport, luxury hotels and traffic jams. "Yes," said Ah Sheng, "Traffic jam is a sign of our prosperity. Last year, Ferrari started selling their cars in China. I mean, could you believe that? Ferraris in China! I notice these things when I read the newspapers and magazines, you know. I am a professional driver after all."

"But you don't drive a Ferrari, do you?" said Victor, needling him and trying to bring him down to earth.

"No, but still life is much better now than it was in my parents' generation. They could only ride bicycles when they were my age," replied Ah Sheng. "Do you drive a Ferrari?" he asked as he shot him a cheeky glance in his rear mirror. Ah Sheng was no pushover in verbal combat and was giving as good as he got.

"No, but I could if I really wanted to. I decided to spend my money on my house instead."

"Ah, a house! In China, that's something we all want but cannot have. You know, I am thirty-six now and still not married, all because I don't own my apartment. Without one, it's not easy to get a good marriage partner."

"I read a newspaper report that there is this park in Shanghai where marriages could be arranged by the parents. You might want to try that," said Victor, humoring him again.

"Ah, Shanghainese girls! Who in Hangzhou would want to marry a Shanghainese girl! They're not for us. They've got eyes that look skywards. No, they won't bother with us, and quite frankly, I wouldn't consider them either – too much trouble! Do you know what Shanghainese husbands are expected to do? Their wives expect them to leave work at noon, go home and prepare lunch – for the wife! And do I want to do that? No way! No, never!"

"Does that mean you intend to stay single all your life?" Victor was beginning to find Ah Sheng interesting.

"No, I am saving up. But it's not easy, you know. We have to pay for so many things now – apartment, pension, medical bills, and for those who have children, schooling. Half my earnings go into savings."

"Half? That's quite a lot!"

"How much do you save?" It was Ah Sheng's turn to ask.

"Well, certainly not half, not nearly that. In America, the savings rate is generally low. Quite a lot of American families are up to their ears in debt. But, Americans are eternal optimists. They live for today. They invented hire purchase, you know. Their philosophy is: enjoy now, pay later."

"In China, we live for tomorrow. And we make ourselves ready for disappointments and major reversals. Our history has prepared us for that."

"Chinese history books are not to be trusted, you know. Chinese history gets rewritten ever so often – dictated by the political considerations of the people in power and the needs of the moment. They don't tell you what really happened."

"I thought it was the Japanese who do that."

"Well, the Chinese do it too."

"Do you have any proof this is so?"

"OK, let me try this on you." Victor knew he was on solid ground when he said this; he had done research and written a paper on this very subject for Professor Freedman's class at UCLA. "When you think of China," Victor began, "the Chinese people and the territorial reach of the country, what comes to your mind?"

"Well, that it is a country that is made up of five major races, the Hans, the Manchus, the Mongols, the Muslims and the Tibetans, and that the country traverses Manchuria in the north-east, Inner Mongolia in the north, the Muslim province of Xinjiang in the west, Tibet in the south-west – and with the Han Chinese right in the middle. It is 9.6 million square kilometers of land and that makes us the third biggest country on earth after Russia and Canada. I learned all that in primary school and have never forgotten it, you know." Ah Sheng belted out all this information with a self-satisfied grin. Rote-learning was an indispensable part of Chinese schooling.

"But Manchuria and Mongolia were never part of the Middle Kingdom. The Islamic Xinjiang Province was conquered by the second Manchu Emperor, as was Tibet. Taiwan too only became part of the Manchu Empire in 1683. And so, if you look at the territorial reach of the Middle Kingdom in the Ming Dynasty, before the Manchurians established the last dynasty, it was not even a third of China's current size. And that was really the extent of Han China which the Manchus conquered in 1644. But I bet you have never come across that in the history books that you've read."

"But we overthrew the Manchus in 1911 and it's only right that we should inherit their empire."

"*Might* is no longer automatically *right* in the modern age. That was the law of the jungle which belonged to The Dark Ages. The rest of the civilized world has moved on since the end of the Second World War. Today, some countries are willing to give up part of their sovereignty in exchange for a lasting peace. That's what Europe is doing. In the civilized world, we are all talking and seeking peaceful co-existence now. Such an ideal may be elusive, but it's still the only sensible way forward. The alternative is war, terrorism and endless strife. There is no peace and no respite if you go down that road."

Victor was surprised to hear himself push this American line of thinking to a Chinese person, when in all the twenty years that he had been living in the United States, he had become more and more conscious of his own ethnic and cultural identity, his unique Chinese-ness, especially when he was in the company of his American friends. And especially when he found them talkative and quarrelsome after a few drinks, which was quite often. Victor had become more and more aware of his own ambivalence, internal conflicts and divided loyalties; they would surface and unsettle him from time to time, particularly when China or Taiwan featured in the evening news. It would have been a lot easier if he were more one-sided in his thinking and his feelings, but he could not help himself. His mind and his heart were often at two different places; his soul was always drifting between two shores.

Ah Sheng the driver could hardly be expected to argue with Victor on this subject. But Victor himself knew that the situation was complex and not amenable to simple, straightforward solutions. He had asked himself this question multiple times – could any Chinese leader, any Chinese government, ever give up control of Tibet where the Yellow River and the Yangtze River have their sources and where every major river in Asia originates? The Middle Kingdom had been at war with the many nomadic tribes to its west, its north and its north-east for hundreds of years. It had only been successfully conquered twice in its five thousand year history. Both times the invaders, the Mongols in 1271 and the Manchus in 1644, stormed into China from the north and easily overran the Han Chinese on the central plains. There just weren't many defensible strongholds once the barbarians breached The Great Wall. Could China give up what is now Inner Mongolia, Manchuria, Xinjiang and Tibet and still feel safe with what was left? Those, Victor knew only too well, were big questions and there were no easy answers.

"If our country is powerful enough, we're not afraid of anything or anybody. Nobody can push us around anymore." Ah Sheng finally shut up after making this, to him, definitive statement, gleaned from what he had heard in Party broadcasts that had been repeated many times over many years. Victor knew that for Ah Sheng, as for many Chinese people, this was the equivalent of the gospel truth. Had he not lived in the United States for twenty years, had he not been influenced by the liberal American media which Anne subscribed to, had he not attended political science lectures at UCLA and written his A-graded papers for his professor, Victor Lin would probably have thought so too.

Feeling slightly deflated, Ah Sheng no longer wanted to talk and Victor soon dozed off.

The car finally came to a stop with a thud. Ah Sheng turned to Victor, who had just woken up, and said, "This is it, Mr. Lin. This is the Thousand Island Lake."

Victor opened the car door, stepped out and told Ah Sheng to pick him up at five o'clock at the exact same spot and to wait for him if he was late. He said he would give Ah Sheng a big tip for the day's journey once he was safely back in Hangzhou.

"Alright then, Mr. Lin. Ahead of you is a no car area. So please just walk straight on, follow the road, go down the slope and you will find the pier. I'll be waiting for you here at five o'clock."

Half way down the slope and even before he got to the pier of the Thousand Island Lake, the moment Victor started looking at what was around him, he realized he had made a mistake to have come here. He should never have listened to the recommendation of the hotel concierge who had told him he might find better weather if he travelled south. This had not happened. The area was overcast, just as it was in Hangzhou, the air was dense and pregnant with foreboding.

He should have known better. It did not take him long to realize that this "famous" tourist spot was actually an artificial lake, not a natural one. The tourist brochure he was now holding in his hand confirmed it. The Chinese can fake anything, so why not a lake? And why not call the many mounds jutting out of the water thousand islands? Who's counting anyway? If you are not a Christian, it's not a sin to tell a lie. The young men selling fake Hermes and Prada bags at the approach to the pier area assured him those were Grade A fakes and that was why they were asking RMB 150 *yuan* for them; but only twenty dollars if he could pay them in the US currency.

After he got to the water's edge, Victor focused his eyes on the remote distance out on the lake, on the faraway landscape, as far away as his eyes could see. But there was nothing much out there for his sadly expectant eyes. He was now very disappointed and decided that he really preferred the lakes and islands in Minnesota – by far. He remembered the Minnesota scene very well. He remembered the glaze of the sun in his eyes through the aircraft's window when the plane took off from Minneapolis for Los Angeles one mid-autumn afternoon. And when he looked down, he saw these little pools of water on the Minnesota plains. These were lakes of different sizes, dotted with small islands here and there, all basking in and reflecting the sun's receding rays. The leaves were a sea of yellow and orange flames, radiant and welcoming, the way they must always have been, even before the dawn of human existence. It was nature in its primeval glory – exuberant but serene, confident but unassuming, and utterly content in its own quiet beauty.

The Thousand Island Lake spread out before him now could not have been more different. Victor had been looking for a rural, scenic spot with birds, wildlife and greenery, punctuated perhaps by a lone pagoda or a quaint temple here and there, and hopefully the solitary figure of a fisherman in his boat waiting for his day's catch. But instead he found himself stranded on a commercial hub of a place with far too many hawkers and tourists. If he had wanted crowds, he could have stayed in Hangzhou. He had asked the hotel concierge for a recommendation because the guy told him the weather in Hangzhou was going to be bad. And, of all places, he recommended this artificial, touristy place because he thought it would be sunny.

Victor knew he had to get away from the din, but he had told Ah Sheng to pick him up at five in the afternoon and the man had driven off. There was nothing he wanted to see on shore, so he drifted in the direction of the ticket office on the landing pier and lined up to buy his voucher for a tour of the lake, just like the other tourists now standing in front of him. They were Thai, Indonesian or Malaysian Chinese, he was sure. He could tell from the occasional English words and phrases they used that they were from Southeast Asia; they all spoke with a lilt half the time. This was a very flashy group, he thought, as he noticed the expensive jewelry the women were wearing – a lot of jade and even a few green emeralds and sparkling diamonds. But there was a demure woman with a sad face who stood apart from the rest. She wore a dark grey dress and was not talking to anybody, just staring blankly into space. She stood out because she was the opposite of loud. She looked composed and moved without disturbing the air around her. She also looked sad. And she wore no jewelry.

Victor got his ticket but had to wait for the boat to come in. He turned around and saw some young vendors pushing their fake merchandise in the path of the tourists at the pier. He simply ignored them and started walking towards a small hotel some two hundred meters down the road where he was hoping to get a cup of coffee. But within minutes, a light drizzle began descending and soon became a downpour. Victor had to rush for cover under a leafy plane tree. Two street vendors were there before him, still trying to cover up their haul of fake watches to protect them from the sheets of rain that were sliding down.

As Victor stood there waiting for the rain to pass, one of the young men plying the fake watches started shouting discounts at him. "Rolex and Patek Philippe for two hundred *yuan*! Reduced from two hundred and fifty. Best buy of the day! You won't get this price anywhere else," said the shabby, short guy as he pushed two watches under Victor's nose. "Only 25 dollars! Dirt cheap!" Victor pushed his hand away to show he was not interested. "These are Grade A fakes, did you know? They are much better than the Grade B ones you get in town. We don't normally sell them at this price, but the rain… well, the rain is not good for business," said he with a sigh and a shrug, looking for sympathy now.

Victor started to look away. As he did so, the taller, paler of the two young men was staring intently at Victor's Phi Beta Kappa ring which had been presented to him by the Dean on graduation. The young man broke into a grin and said with a gleam in his eyes, "I'll exchange five of these watches for what you're wearing around your finger." Victor just smiled back and shook his head. "Can I take a look?" the young man asked. "No," Victor replied curtly and thought this would be the end of it. But the Short One cut in and said, with a flattening of his thin lips to show disdain, "How do you know yours is not a fake?"

Victor ignored him but didn't want to be pestered any further. So he stepped aside and kept his distance. When the rain had died down, Victor decided to walk back to the pier. A line of people had already lined up there and were waiting to board. Amongst them, some rough looking men with unkempt hair and unwashed faces were smoking and cursing as they talked. Meanwhile, mists had started to gather on the lake in the weak and fading light.

The phone rang in the middle of the night. "Mrs. Lin, we are sorry to have to bring you the bad news, but your husband is dead. Lin Chung-li is dead."

Anne ghosted through Tom Bradley International Airport, a widow at thirty eight. She could not yet take it in. What happened in China? What really happened? She had to find out, because the man on the phone who said he was calling from the Public Security Bureau of Jin-an County did not tell her very much. He only said her husband was travelling on a river boat that was doing a tour of the Thousand Island Lake; it capsized and he drowned. That was all he was able to tell her in very stilted English with a thick Chinese accent – no other details. Only that and the address of the Bureau's headquarters in Hangzhou, the name of the official in charge of the case, a certain Assistant Commissioner Rong Hua, and a telephone number to call if she wanted to gather her husband's belongings. When she pressed the caller and said she wanted to speak to the Assistant Commissioner himself, she was told the senior cadre would only be available to meet the families of the deceased on Saturday at ten in the morning – in the city of Hangzhou itself.

After she put her phone down, Anne immediately thought of Victor's parents. She wanted to tell them what she had just heard, but knew she must do this in person and with the help of Victor's second cousin who was also their family doctor. While waiting for Dr. Tsai to drive over, Anne told herself she must go to the Thousand Island Lake, to the scene of the accident, and find out more. She wanted to know the full circumstances of Victor's death, because she could not believe he drowned; he had always been a strong swimmer. She simply had to find out, even though she feared the truth might be more than she could bear. She thought she owed that to Victor's parents and also to herself.

When Anne broke the news to Old Mr. and Mrs. Lin with Dr. Tsai by her side, they could not believe what they had heard. They did not want to. At first they both shook their heads, then Victor's mother gave out a sharp cry and collapsed. Anne could not have dealt with the situation had it not been for Dr. Tsai, who quickly rushed over and put the old lady flat on a sofa and took her pulse. He then told Old Mr. Lin and Anne that it was going to be alright. Anne asked whether she should call an ambulance, but Dr. Tsai said this would not be necessary and told Anne to just wait. Old Mrs. Lin did come to shortly after that, but started crying so loud that the good doctor decided to take her into her bedroom to calm her down. While all this was happening, Victor's father just sat in a corner and wept, without speaking to or facing anybody, because he was grieving deeply inside. The old man was all but shattered. Victor was their only son, on whom they had depended for everything. Their loss was both material and total. They had expected him to lead a long and healthy life and to take charge at their funerals – to look after all those tedious arrangements and intricate rituals a filial son would have to deal with on such occasions. But instead, in a cruel twist of fate, the reverse was now happening. Their son's life had ended before their own.

Unable to speak Chinese, Anne could not even comfort her father-in-law in the language he would understand. She could only move over, hold him tight and cry into his broad shoulder, until they were both exhausted and slumped onto the sofa. The silence which followed lasted a very long time. The sun's rays were coming into the apartment at a much lower angle now, and Dr. Tsai emerged from Old Mrs. Lin's room to tell the two of them that she had gone to sleep. He also advised Anne to go home and get some rest while he dealt with looking after the two old people whom he called Uncle and Auntie.

"Here, take one of these Stilnox tablets if you need to. It'll give you several hours' sleep," he said.

Anne really wanted to stay but realized she would only give Dr. Tsai more work to do. So she wiped the traces of her own tears from her face, thanked Dr. Tsai and quietly went out of the door.

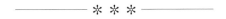

On the plane crossing the vast expanse of the Pacific in the dark of the night, Anne Gavin's normally well-organized mind was in shambles. "What really happened? And why? I would need his death certificate to show the insurance company. I would need to tell Victor's employer and I haven't even done that. Why is this happening to me? And where is Victor's body? I've got to bring his body back and give Victor a Christian burial, among the whispering cypresses he so loved. I want him in his favorite suit. He would like that, I know. But where is his favorite suit? Did he take that with him? And his favorite tie? Which is his favorite tie? Oh, yes, and after that a memorial service at the church where we were married – to commemorate Victor's life. I would need his baptism certificate for that, when he converted, but where did I put it…" Questions and impending actions, past, present and future got all tangled up in the fast-flowing stream of Anne's consciousness, causing her mind to race out of control and giving her a splitting headache. She desperately wanted to sleep but could not. The ever cautious Dr. Tsai had only given her four sleeping tablets and she had already used them all.

At the thought of the memorial service, Anne saw visions of the church in Pasadena and the kindly Irish priest who joked about Victor's big fingers. Just at that moment, an announcement from the pilot was coming through the public address system. The plane had already flown past Japan and would be landing in Shanghai in an hour.

When Anne came into the public arrivals lounge in Shanghai, a man holding a placard with her name written across it was waiting for her. Next to this man stood another in a black business suit with matching black tie. When Anne acknowledged the man with the placard, it was this other person who stepped forward and introduced himself as Michael Wu and gave her his name card. He explained that Victor's father had called Jason Fang and given him her flight details and that Jason had sent him to greet her and attend to her needs.

After they had all got into the car and the chauffeur had started to drive off, Michael Wu handed Anne an envelope and said this was from his boss, Mr. Fang. Anne tore open the envelope and realized immediately it was a letter of condolence from Jason. The letter was short and the English was formal. Jason used the standard words that Chinese people tend to use on such occasions, because he did not know Anne well and because he did not know what he could say in the circumstance. Next to the letter was a thick pile of hundred dollar bills. Anne knew cash gifts were standard practice at Chinese funerals, to help defray the costs and console the family of the deceased. She took the letter and pushed back the cash Michael Wu's way. She said simply, "You can return this to Mr. Fang."

Michael Wu understood. Anne did not want to take Jason Fang's money. It was the lure of money that had brought tragedy onto her family. If only Victor had been able to resist it, if only she herself had insisted, this would not have happened, and he would still be with her in Del Mar now, lounging across the sofa in front of their television set and watching the LA Lakers trounce another visiting team.

Michael Wu quietly took back the envelope and put it in his breast pocket. But, feeling embarrassed, he started to apologize for Jason and explained that he could not be with Anne because he was at a Young Presidents Conference where he was due to give a speech on the new business opportunities that were opening up in China. It was arranged three months ago and Jason could not get out of it now, Michael took great pains to emphasize. He also told Anne the Public Security Bureau in Hangzhou had impounded the personal effects of Victor in the hotel he was staying in, including his suitcase and briefcase, but these would be returned to her when she showed up and if there were no suspicious circumstances or untoward complications like espionage, unpaid debts, rival claims and family disputes over probate.

Michael Wu told Anne he helped run Jason Fang's business operation in Taiwan and had to hurry back that very evening and so would not be able to accompany her all the way to the Public Security Bureau in Hangzhou. He said he would come with her as far as the train terminus in Shanghai. After they got there, he would put her on a train to Hangzhou and arrange a car and chauffeur to meet her on arrival and take her to the hotel she would be staying in. This personal chauffeur would be at her disposal throughout her stay in Hangzhou.

Anne called the Public Security Bureau number after she had checked into her hotel in Hangzhou. She was told by Assistant

Commissioner Rong's underling to come into the bureau office the next day at ten o'clock.

The following morning, after a long and sleepless night ended with just a short nap, Anne left her hotel and walked into the Public Security Bureau in a daze. She was late. Shock, grief, jet-lag and the feeling of being a stranger in a strange land had combined to make a zombie of her. She asked for Assistant Commissioner Rong Hua and was led by a minder into a room that was very nearly full – of unhappy strangers with weary, pallid faces and eyes swollen from crying. Someone was already speaking to the assembled. "That's Commissioner Ma," Anne's minder pointed to the speaker, "And Assistant Commissioner Rong is on his left." And he motioned her to sit down on one of the few empty seats at the back.

"The boat was struck by lightning, capsized and the passengers drowned – that's all there was to it. It was dark. There were no survivors. It's all in the newspapers." The rough and authoritative voice of Commissioner Ma barked out at the anguished faces of the closest and dearest of the deceased. The Commissioner's words were translated into English by a listless interpreter who said this was for the benefit of the foreigners among the assembled.

Anne found it strange that the public security head should have cited newspaper reports to lend credibility to his version of what happened. Surely the police should be the ones doing the investigation, not the reporters, she thought to herself.

"Exactly how many people drowned?" A Chinese person who had his hand raised asked in English, with a distinctly British accent. He was seated to Anne's right, one row in front and just a few chairs away. Anne turned her head, leaned forward slightly and took a look at the gentleman. He was well dressed and well groomed, in a dark grey business suit with a black tie, not at all the kind of person she would expect to find in a Chinese public security bureau. He looked fifty-ish but might be younger, or older. Anne knew from her contacts with Chinese people in California that they didn't seem to age between forty and sixty-five.

Before answering, Commissioner Ma quickly went through his brief again and talked to his two underlings, first to the one on his left, then to the one on his right. The older one of the two, the one on his left, who was big and fat, with a pale complexion, spiky hair and shifty eyes, pointed to the brief again and again. That would be Assistant Commissioner Rong, Anne thought to herself. The one on the Commissioner's right was younger looking, had angular features and a high forehead, and was wearing horn-rimmed glasses. He was the one who was now conferring earnestly with the Commissioner. "We don't know yet," this person finally said in English, "All we know is that there were no survivors."

"How many people were on the boat?" The Chinese gentleman with the British accent asked again in English.

"We don't know that either. We are waiting for more relatives to come forward."

"Did all the crew drown too?"

"Dr. Han, I had already told you! There were no survivors. Everybody drowned." The Commissioner suddenly butted in and answered the question in English, without waiting for the translation from his subordinate. He was obviously getting impatient, even annoyed, as he had raised his voice in addressing his Chinese interlocutor whom he somehow knew by name.

"But my husband was a good swimmer. I find it hard to believe he simply drowned, Inspector, er, I mean Commissioner!" Anne raised her hand and cut in, "I want to see the autopsy report and death certificate. I assume you will be taking us to the mortuary, maybe after this meeting?"

At this point, Assistant Commissioner Rong took over and said through the interpreter, "No, there is no need for that, we do not have large mortuaries in our county and bodies don't keep in this kind of weather." His eyes then shifted from left to right, and he continued, "We had to cremate the deceased after a forensic examination the day following the accident. I'm afraid you have arrived too late to look at the bodies. We do not have individual autopsy reports. We have a non-specific, general report if you want to look at that."

"What?" "How could you do that?" "Why didn't you contact us sooner?" "Why didn't you tell us on the phone?" The interpreter's words caused an uproar in the room as the assembled crowd shouted numerous questions at him.

Ignoring the uproar, the interpreter read out from a sheet of paper in a loud voice, "You can collect the ashes from 4:00 o'clock in the afternoon starting from Monday next week. These are matched to photographs and personal effects of the deceased." As he was making the announcement, Commissioner Ma and his two assistants were already rising from their chairs. All three started to move quickly down the aisle at the centre of the room as the interpreter continued with reading out his brief, "The Municipal Government is paying 40,000 *yuan* to each family by way of compensation. Assistant Commissioner Rong Hua will deal with any further questions on details in his own office at the end of the corridor outside the hall. He is from Jin-an County where the accident occurred."

The assembled, an assorted crowd of people, some speaking English with Southeast Asian accents, quickly rose to their feet and went after Assistant Commissioner Rong through the open door.

Anne was on her feet too, and muttering to herself, "Oh, this is outrageous!"

"But not unexpected," Dr. Han was also muttering to himself as he picked up his black brief case and started to leave. "They're a law unto themselves."

Anne's ears pricked up at the use of the word "unto". This Chinese gentleman clearly had a good education, and probably in the humanities. She looked at him and said, "I don't know about you, but I'm going to my embassy to ask for help. My husband's insurance company will want more documentary details than what I've just heard!"

They started to walk out of the room together. "I went to mine yesterday – I went to the British Consulate. But because my sister was from Hong Kong and the city is no longer a British colony after 1997, and because I didn't have her birth certificate with me, the consular officials here said they're unable to offer much assistance. I think I will have to go higher up the hierarchy to get help of any kind really."

"Well, my husband was American, as American as I am, although he was ethnically Chinese. The U.S. Consulate here cannot *not* give me help."

"You'd still have to wait until Monday, as would I. The offices are closed until then. I'm going to the Thousand Island Lake tomorrow, to burn some incense for my sister. Ancient Chinese custom, you know. We have to burn the incense *in situ*, on the site where the deceased died. You can come along with me if you wish and do the same for your husband, if you believe in these things, following Chinese customs, I mean. You may not, since you consider your husband American. Well, it's entirely up to you."

"He's a Chinese American, originally from Taiwan, originally from China of course. The family, that is. I think his parents would like me to burn some incense for him, yes I believe so. Would you show me how this is done if I come with you? I have the use of a car. My husband's business associate has made the arrangement."

"Alright then, we can go together. I'm David, David Han."

"And I'm Anne, Anne Lin."

The two strangers, united in their bereavement and having no one else to turn to, decided to swap hotel details and discovered they were staying at the same hotel by the West Lake. That made matters easy and they arranged to meet at the lobby the next day after breakfast. As Anne Gavin and David Han left the public security bureau, one of Commissioner Ma's two assistants, the cadre with the high forehead and horn-rimmed glasses, and who spoke English, was watching them cross the courtyard from an upstairs window.

"Assistant Commissioner Li, Sir, the big boss is looking for you," a man's voice echoed down the poorly lit and harshly resounding corridor of power.

Li Neng was only the Acting Assistant Commissioner. But in China his subordinates would call him Assistant Commissioner anyway, out of respect and to make him feel the impending promotion was all but settled, just a matter of formality. Everyone working in Chinese bureaucracies knew that flattery, loyalty and blind obedience offered the fastest way up the greasy pole of career advancement. And they would do accordingly.

"The journey will take around two hours, if the traffic allows," David Han said to Anne tersely, after talking with the driver of the car in his native tongue. His eyes looked tired from lack of sleep. Without the matching tie now, his jacket and shirt appeared slumped and ruffled. "If it's alright with you, we'll hire a boat and go out on the lake after we get there. We can burn the incense on the boat in the middle of the lake. After we've done that, we'll go back to the town of Jin-an and have lunch there before we head back. Shall we do that?" David Han asked. "It'll be late afternoon by the time we arrive back at the hotel."

"Yes, I'll just follow your lead," said Anne as she tied a grayish-green scarf around her head of ash blond hair. In her pastel green dress and slightly darker sweater, she looked particularly frail and worn against the overcast sky. She took with her a light brown mackintosh which she did not wear as she got into the car.

Ah Sheng the driver watched without any expression on his face, but he was secretly trying to figure out in his mind who and what this Chinese gentleman was, he who was carrying a paper bag full of joss sticks and paper nuggets of gold, traditional Chinese offerings to the dead. Being experienced and street smart, Ah Sheng could tell, from the man's bearing, manners and the way he spoke, that this was an educated Chinese gentleman from overseas. He was also quite sure the pale and sad looking American lady was not his wife from the way he opened the car door for her at the hotel entrance – the man was very proper and careful, almost deliberate. But Ah Sheng could not tell what the relationship was between the two passengers who were now in his car. And he decided to keep quiet and just listen and observe.

After leaving the city, the highway the car was speeding down was first class in every way – modern, wide, without any bumps, and with soothing green fields on both sides of the road. But there was hardly any traffic. Not long after, David Han began to stir. He was arching his neck left and right to get a better look at the countryside after some big character billboards appeared. Something was catching his attention.

Anne, who had been watching him, finally spoke, "What do those characters say, if you don't mind my asking?"

"Oh, just that this stretch used to be the home base of Sun Quan who ruled over the Kingdom of Wu during the Three Kingdoms Period in Chinese history."

At the mention of the name Sun Quan, Ah Sheng's ears pricked up, because Sun was an historical character famous in Chinese literature and folklore; even children would know about his political exploits which featured in the historical novel *The Romance of The Three Kingdoms*. But Ah Sheng could not follow the conversation in English that was taking place between his two passengers and soon lost interest.

"The Three Kingdoms?" asked Anne, "I thought your dynasties were all unitary states and had names like Han and Tang. Am I wrong?"

"No, you are not wrong. Those were the more stable dynasties, but in between stable dynasties we had periods of civil war. And the Three Kingdoms was a civil-war period which followed the collapse of the Han Dynasty. It lasted quite a long time, with the generals battling it out among themselves. In the last century, China went through another civil war period, only then these generals were called warlords. Most people know that Chinese dynasties could last a few hundred years. What they may not know is that civil-war periods in between dynasties could last just as long. Sometimes even longer."

"Is China going through a dynastic period now or is the country still in the midst of a civil war period, since Taiwan remains out of reach and... unbowed, shall we say? What do you think?" Anne asked.

"I think this is really a dynasty. The KMT lost the war a long time ago. We are now in the reign of the Communist Dynasty. But, notwithstanding that, long-lasting peace is still elusive. When I was a young student, I had this misconception that Chinese dynasties were super stable structures and lasted a long time. The truth is that some dynasties were really quite weak and precarious, not stable at all, and some did not last very long. The Southern Song and Ming Dynasties were plagued by internal strife, foreign invasions and peasants' revolts, for instance."

"Troubled they might have been, but from what I have seen in museums in LA, San Francisco, DC and New York, these two dynasties produced some of the most exquisite paintings, ceramics and furniture in Chinese history. And some of the best poetry and theatre too, my late husband told me. How do you explain that?" Anne asked again.

"I can't, except to say that Chinese civilization followed its own trajectory quite independently of state power. But my mentor Professor Yu who taught Chinese history at Yale thought that Chinese civilization was most vibrant and alive when the central government was weak and ineffectual, and *not* when the central government was strong and domineering. Paradoxical, isn't it?"

"This is new to me. I have not heard this before. Do you agree with that? Do you agree with this view?" Anne was getting really interested, because she had assumed that a powerful state laid at the heart of cultural ascendancy.

"I have a slightly different take, not inconsistent with Professor Yu's thesis, but maybe complements it. I believe the end of some once glorious Chinese dynasties was preceded by a flowering of the arts, be they poetry, drama, music or artistic expression of other kinds. When the emperor and his court spent more time on leisure and trivial pursuits, and neglected the defense of the realm and the basic needs of the people, well, that was when the rot set in, followed by decline and fall. Pleasure-loving and hedonistic Athens would always lose to muscular and hardy Sparta, not at the first invasion perhaps, but eventually, because the hungry and deprived are much more strongly motivated and much more determined than the well-fed and sated."

"If you are right, then Britain and the United States are the most at risk, are they not, since the arts scenes in both countries are at their most creative and most vibrant at this point in time? Well, I think they are anyway, from a Western perspective."

"I agree. Britain has been for some time, and the United States is moving in that direction. Don't get me wrong. I love the theatre, opera and ballet myself. But I also believe in striking a proper balance and in moderation. If an overwhelming number of people want to be rock stars and no one wants to be a rocket scientist, then I would be worried about that country's future."

"I wouldn't," Anne was quick to express disagreement. "I am a pacifist. I think the problem with my country is the animalistic instinct of the right wing of the Republican Party for world domination, and it will get my country as well as the world into serious trouble one day." Anne's maternal grandfather was a Democratic Congressman for the State of Minnesota and liberalism ran strong in her blood.

At this point, a road sign suddenly caught David Han's eyes and he followed it until the crossroads it was pointing to was past. He then turned his head away from the scenery and said to Anne, without much emotion, "That was the birth place of my sister's husband."

"Did he die too, er, with your sister…on the boat?" Anne asked.

"No, he died a few years ago… of acute leukemia. It was very sudden. He was quite young, not even forty," David replied, biting his lower lip. "My sister was a widow at thirty nine. And now she has joined him." And then he looked away, signaling that this would be the end of their conversation on this topic.

"I am sorry. I shouldn't have asked." Anne could sense that underneath the placid exterior of an upper crust Chinese gentleman who was very much in control of himself, David Han might be hurting deeply inside from two deaths in the family in close succession.

"It's fortunate that they did not have any children," all of a sudden David reversed himself. He somehow felt the urge to talk and decided to volunteer the information. "Having young children without both parents would have made matters even worse, much worse."

"I suppose you're right, although… speaking for myself, I would have loved to have a son or daughter with me right now. The loss of Victor would not be quite so… total."

"These things are not up to us," David said matter-of-factly.

"No, they're not." Anne could only concur, knowing her own circumstance. But, after a pause, she really wanted to continue the conversation; she was seeing in David a kindred spirit who not only shared her sense of loss, but also her sense of helplessness.

"Victor was an only son," she said to him. She was going to tell him more. "My parents-in-law must have had expectations. In fact, I was sure they did. It would have really endeared me to them if I had had a son and a daughter. Well, at least a son to carry on the Lin family name. But..." She suddenly stopped in mid sentence, not knowing if she should go on in this personal vein. She decided she should not, as a lump was gathering in her throat. Instead, after a pause, she asked him, "Are you your sister's only next of kin?"

"Yes, but we didn't see much of each other when we were growing up. There's a ten-year age gap between us. My parents had me when they were quite young but did not have another child until they were in their late thirties. So I was doing my postgraduate studies in London when Carol, my sister, was just starting secondary school in Hong Kong."

"Oh, so you're a Hong Kong family?"

"Yes, but originally we're from Jiangxi Province."

"And where's that? My knowledge of Chinese geography is really limited."

"That's the province to the southwest of Hangzhou, and we're now travelling due south, away from Hangzhou."

"So roughly speaking, you are from these parts?"

"Yes, but only very roughly. That's why I understand and speak *putonghua*. But there is intense rivalry between the different provinces around here, and people can tell just by your accent where you hail from."

"But you didn't grow up here, or did you? You have a very British accent when you speak English. You said you went to university in London…" Anne stopped there and waited for David Han to fill in the missing information.

"No, I did not grow up in China; I was not even born here. My parents left China with my grandparents in 1949, but they didn't go to Taiwan with Generalissimo Chiang Kai-shek. They went to the British Crown Colony of Hong Kong. I was born and raised in Hong Kong, but I won a scholarship to study at the University of London. Maybe that explains the British accent."

"It is quite pronounced, your accent. Through Victor's friends, I got to know some Chinese people from Hong Kong who had also studied in Britain before they settled in America, but they don't have your diction and intonation. I read English Lit at UCLA and we English majors notice such things." Anne tried to explain. She was curious; she half wanted to compliment him on his command of the English language, but was not sure how he would take that, and she did not want to upset her travelling companion, so she came across as being slightly apologetic.

"I think it may have to do with the fact that I worked in London for a number of years after I left university. Until you work with a people, you don't really know them, that's what I always say. This is not generally appreciated, but I believe it. A great many Chinese students go to English-speaking countries to study, but come back without knowing much about the language or the culture of the place where they spent three or four years of their lives. And that's because they kept themselves to themselves, or they socialized only with their own set and never really mixed with the people in their host countries."

David Han's words encouraged Anne Gavin to share her own views on the somewhat controversial subject and she began, "My mother and I discussed this often between ourselves, because Victor was a Chinese American. We, my mother and I that is, both came to the view that Chinese students who come to our country are only interested in learning the skills and technology that would further their careers, they're not interested in the people and the culture of the United States. They believe the Chinese are a superior race and that the Chinese culture is a superior culture, far superior to any other, including the American of course. It's just that in the last two hundred years the Chinese people have lagged behind us in science and technology, but not in anything else, and not for long now. And they don't think they need to learn anything else from us. We think they are wrong, because the advances in science and technology our country has made are hatched, nurtured and sustained by the freedoms our people enjoy. The innovators and mavericks like Steve Jobs and Bill Gates are not just the products of American schools and universities, they are also the products of American culture and, in particular, our freedoms."

"I agree with you, but you will not find many Chinese people who do. The Chinese ruling elite want modernization. They've wanted that for almost two hundred years now. But they want modernization without Westernization. They want to take the Western technology without also taking the Western values. Especially not democracy, freedom, human rights and the separation of powers. Because democracy and freedom might be their undoing. Why would anybody who is wielding absolute power want to risk being voted out?"

"Not even if this democratic way of selection is for the good of their own country? Are they so selfish and power hungry?"

"Yes," David gave a sharp, terse, resolute reply. And then he went on, "They are also afraid. Given the country's bloody history, China's leaders are more concerned with maintaining their hold on power than anything else. As for the Chinese students in America, you need to understand where they are 'coming from', to use an American expression I've picked up. For almost two hundred years, the Chinese people were pushed around, humiliated and bullied by the Great Powers of the day. The British, the French, the Russians, the Germans, the Japanese and the Americans – yes, the Americans too – they were all there, at the table to share in the partition of China at the end of the nineteenth century, the way some of them carved out colonies in Africa. The Big Powers all had their territorial concessions at China's treaty ports and the Russians took the lion's share of land. It's all written up in our history books, lest this sorry and shameful chapter of our history be forgotten. But, these very same history books also taught Chinese children the Chinese civilization is a superior civilization which goes back many thousands of years, the world's *only* continuing civilization, because the modern day Romans, Greeks and Egyptians are but a pale reflection of their ancients, whereas the modern-day Chinese are essentially the same people who built The Great Wall and modeled the terracotta soldiers of Xi'an. The constant interplay of this inferiority-superiority complex – they're both sides of the same coin of course – is at the heart of Chinese behavior today, as a country and as a people." David Han began to speak ever faster as he got to the end of his last few sentences. His complete fluency suggested to Anne that he had made this point many times before.

"If I may be so bold…" said Anne, hesitating a little. She was going to say 'you're speaking like Victor' but decided against it. Nonetheless, her curiosity was aroused and so she put this question to David, "Could I ask whether you went through the same learning process as other Chinese students at school and whether you subscribe to this view yourself – what you just told me?"

"I did. I read those same history books. But going overseas and being exposed to another culture and reading history books written by other people who looked at the evidence from different angles, and who sometimes drew different conclusions, have opened up my mind. Chinese history books written in the Chinese language and the ones written in English, Japanese or Korean give very different perspectives and interpretations. Sometimes they can't even agree on the facts. Now I see through the half truths my parents fed me and some of the outright lies our own history books taught me."

"I hope you don't mind my asking, but what have you learned, specifically I mean, from reading other peoples' interpretation of Chinese history and their views on Chinese culture?" Anne tried her best to be polite and inquisitive at the same time.

"Oh, mainly that the Chinese version is not the only plausible version, that the Chinese way is not the *only* way, and that, sometimes, the Chinese way is not even the *best* way," David said with emphasis, and also with the tone of finality.

"What you've just said is really quite profound, and so elegant in its simplicity. Thank you. In English Lit, we call this an aphorism." Anne regretted it as soon as she said that, because it sounded patronizing. She immediately corrected herself, "I hope you don't mind what I just said. I am an editor of story books for children, and children learn quickly when concepts are put to them simply. And so I notice these things. I make mental notes when I come across language which is simple and elegant. I was actually trying to commit what you just said to memory – that the Chinese way is not the only way. And, for that matter, neither is the American way. Really, I mean that and I mean that as a compliment." Anne managed to spread her lips a little to squeeze out a half smile, to show that she really meant well.

"That's alright. I talk too much anyway. My ex-wife always thought that. She used to complain that I had these pet subjects and I took ages to come to the point. It's true. I could be very long-winded even when I was giving instructions to our maid. I'm afraid my ex-wife had no patience with me and I'm afraid she might have been right. But we academics are like that – we try to prepare the ground carefully so that even people who disagree with us cannot attack us with impunity." David Han's choice of words continued to fascinate Anne – his use of the word "impunity" and the word "instructions" instead of "orders" really betrayed his learned but slightly pedantic sophistication.

"So, what do you teach? I imagine you must be a professor in the humanities."

"Yes, that's right. Cultural studies, actually. China, more specifically. Academics who deal in cultural studies believe you cannot really understand a country and a people through its politics and economics alone. You can study those of course, but you can only really grasp the essence of a country through understanding its culture and its values. Because they determine people's behavior."

"I suppose that must give the indigenous scholars a certain advantage, compared to the likes of us, for instance, since we do not even know your language, let alone your culture."

"Your husband was a Chinese American, wasn't he? That must give you some insights, surely?"

"Not enough." Anne really did not know how to carry on the conversation at this point. On the one hand, she did not know David Han well enough to tell him what she had learned in all those years of marriage – how difficult it had been to cope and sustain a marital relationship across two cultures as different as the American and the Chinese. On the other hand, she was finding the conversation stimulating and wanted to continue the discussion, even as an intellectual exercise in itself. But Anne was not at her best either physically or emotionally now to carry on talking at this point. The travelling and jet-lag from the time difference were taking their toll, and the sense of loss and the hollowness within which had followed Anne these last few days would suddenly emerge and interrupt her train of thought. Scattered and unrelated memories would spring to mind all at once. They led nowhere really, but they confused and crowded out what she wanted to concentrate on. They made sustained logical thinking impossible.

And so Anne chose not to pick up the conversation from where she left off. She turned her head to look outside the car window and soon dozed off. David Han took that as a sign to stop talking and quietly leant back in his seat.

After a short while, and seeing that the American lady had fallen asleep, Ah Sheng the driver tried to engage the Chinese gentleman in conversation, but quietly, in a low voice. He began by telling David Han in *putonghua* there was an accident at the Thousand Island Lake a week ago and that many people died.

"I know," said David Han, "that's why I am going there, and so is this lady." He gestured with his head and touched the bag of protruding incense sticks and paper nuggets. "We are making offerings to the deceased."

"You are related then?" Ah Sheng asked.

"No," he said simply, because he did not want to tell the driver anything more.

"I took a client to the Lake a week ago, an American Chinese or Chinese American, whatever you call them, and he also died."

"Oh?" Alerted, David sat up and said, "Go on. Tell me more."

"Well, his company hired my car. It's the same company that has hired me to service this lady next to you. And he asked me to take him to the Thousand Island Lake and wait for him there, and to take him back to Hangzhou afterwards. Only he never made it back. I waited and waited. Then the fire brigade turned up, and the public security people also turned up; and I heard from the crowd that the boat had capsized and a lot of people drowned."

"You said the fire brigade was there?" David asked. "Was there a fire on board?"

"I believe there was. Some of the bodies they brought back were very badly charred. I saw them with my own eyes."

"So some died in a fire? They did not all drown?" David was speaking to himself now, "Then why did they tell us the boat capsized and everybody drowned?"

"Chinese superstition," David Han said with a shake of his head, not once but a few times, as he lighted a bundle of joss sticks with a huge one in the middle, thick as a carrot and about four times as long. With the lit incense in hand, he bowed three times in the direction of the water and poked the joss sticks into a traditional incense burner that was covered in dirt and ashes. He watched, motionless, as the incense burned and sent its consolatory message to the nether world. David knew, from what his mother told him, that if the smoke from the joss sticks bent and turned, this was a sign that the offering was being received and appreciated by its intended. But if it did not, if the smoke went straight up but did not twist and meander, the offering had been made in vain. He never believed it. He always thought his mother was a superstitious, gullible woman.

At the sacrificial altar that had been set up at the stern of the boat, the smoke was turning and curling as it moved skyward into oblivion. David said nothing and displayed not a trace of emotion. He had obviously done this before; it was just a ritual to him. He gave a packet of the same incense offering to Anne. She took the packet with studied care; he lighted the incense for her and stepped aside. And, following his lead, she also bowed three times in the direction of the water, muttering as she did, "Vic… Chung-li… may your soul rest in peace… in God's arms… We miss you so much, so very much, your father, your mother, me… especially me." As she said this, she could no longer hold back her tears and she burst out crying. David turned and looked away, embarrassed to see her outpouring of grief.

When she was able to stop the sobbing, Anne dried her eyes with a handkerchief and tried to make normal conversation. She said to David, "Americans have superstitions too, you know."

"But not as much as the Chinese – not by a long chalk. There's a difference in degree, a big difference." David Han also wanted to engage to ease over the embarrassment. He seemed to know that in such situations a serious conversation might help.

"Well, there may be, but does it really matter so much?" Anne rejoined.

"Yes, it does. Our superstition is a reason for our weakness – our inability to move forward – because it stands in the way of science and enlightenment," David said.

"How so? Please explain."

"Well, I'm sure you know about the four Chinese inventions. Because Chinese people are very fond of telling everybody they invented the compass, paper, printing and gun-powder."

"Yes, I do recall Victor telling me that, and my parents-in-law too, more than once."

"And did they tell you we used our gun powder for firecrackers and fireworks whereas when this stuff got into the hands of the Europeans, they used it for muskets and cannons? I mean as weapons of destruction and not any longer for a peaceful, recreational purpose."

'Yes, Victor mentioned that too. You both say the same thing. Was that what your Chinese history books told you?"

"Yes. But what our history books didn't tell us is that those are the only important inventions in a history of more than five thousand years, with a population that was almost one fifth of mankind. It really isn't very much, is it? Considering what the West has been able to come up with since the invention of the steam engine and electricity, all in just two hundred years."

"What would account for that, er, shall we say long hibernation of the mind?" She was treading carefully and trying not to offend.

"You have touched upon my favorite subject. And we've got time to kill – it would take us about fifty minutes to an hour to get back to the pier – so I will share with you my thesis written while I was at the University of London some twenty-five years ago. If you don't mind being bored, that is."

"No, I am fine with that."

"Let me first tell the coxswain of our boat to re-start the engine and head back." David Han walked to the front of the boat and talked to the man on the wheel. When he sat down with Anne again, the noise coming from the direction of the boat's engine forced David to raise his voice, making him sound authoritative.

"My thesis asserts that the triumph of the West had much to do with two things – the scientific method of enquiry and the freedom of thought borne of a multi-polar, non-conformist society – but China had neither. Western science is evidence-based. Once it was proven beyond doubt that the earth is round, not flat, the 'old knowledge' was discarded and the 'new knowledge' was taught in its place. In this way, the sum of human knowledge expands, is widely disseminated, and a new generation of scientists can build on the work of the previous one. Which is why Western science moves forward and is able to push further afield the frontiers of human knowledge. This is what leads to the ascent of man. This is what has taken the West to where it is today."

"You know, I'm really surprised that China has not followed the same path in its long history. It's only sensible…" said Anne.

"You're right. China has not. Science lost out to superstition and lying. Untruths, falsehoods and outright lies were not discarded and they have clogged up the Chinese mind. And, at the same time, new scientific knowledge has not been taken on board and built upon. Truth, honesty and an enquiring mind that challenges orthodoxy lay the foundation for scientific progress. Science and mathematics cannot thrive if scientists and mathematicians are prepared to accept, as a matter of habit, that truth is malleable and that two and two can make five if the authorities say so. I really do believe that respect for empirical findings and intellectual honesty are necessary conditions for the advancement of science. It is a critical failing when people act and behave not on the basis of scientific evidence, but on the basis of hangovers from the past, authoritative but erroneous judgement, and political expedience." David paused at this point to watch Anne's reaction.

Seeing that Anne seemed to have taken his words on board, David Han continued, "Another critical failing is when they do not record their mistakes faithfully for the edification of the next generation. This edification is important and necessary. It enables a people to learn from past mistakes and not repeat them. But, instead of the unvarnished truth, we tend to get whitewashed accounts of what really happened. This habitual cover-up and lying is not conducive to science and progress."

On this point that David was making, Anne finally found her voice and she said, "I might be wrong, but don't the Chinese people have this saying that 'history is our mirror'? Victor used to buy a magazine from Chinatown called *The Mirror* and he told me that's what that name implied. And I thought at the time how appropriate a name that was for a news magazine."

"Yes, there is such a Chinese proverb but the advice is rarely followed. Instead, we have had a lot of re-writing and re-editing of history over the years to hide the mistakes and failures of the past. If a people really learned from history, they would not be repeating the same mistakes over and over again. I'm afraid some of the history we teach at our schools might have been doctored. And, in China today, there are no alternative versions to challenge the authorized texts."

"I defer to your knowledge of Chinese history, but it is astonishing for a people to have made so little real progress over hundreds of years, until the modern era."

"Ah, but I haven't finished; there is a third critical failing. This is when the elite keep essential knowledge to themselves and not share it with other people, so that when they die, that knowledge dies with them. Add to that the burning of books considered subversive and the killing of scholars considered seditious and the sum of human knowledge available to the Chinese people could actually *shrink* instead of *grow*. Or at least *stagnate*. China suffered from that too – an unwillingness to share. Pure selfishness."

"Was that because you didn't have patent laws which would have offered protection to the originator of that new knowledge or those new inventions?" asked Anne.

"Yes, that is one explanation. China never had patent laws until the modern era. But, even if it did, patent laws could only protect in peace time, when there was law and order, trust in the law courts, the judges and the legal process. Patent laws by themselves would be quite useless if the country was in a state of war, or in a general state of lawlessness most of the time – because the people in power just wanted to do as they pleased."

"Your exposition is very eloquent and I do not mean to challenge your thesis, and I certainly do not have any counter arguments to suggest the contrary. But I still find it hard to believe these reasons alone would account for China's hundreds of years of under development." Anne said to David in response.

"Well, this brings me back to my opening statement, that a multi-polar, free-thinking, non-conformist society is a boon to the ascent of man. China had the opposite of that – the state-sponsored mind control apparatus works like a straitjacket strapped around the freedom of thought, of enquiry and of expression. Because of that, without these freedoms, this country never had the benefit of a Renaissance, a Reformation or The Enlightenment. There is not much chance for innovative, original thinking to come to the fore if orthodoxy reigns supreme and authority cannot be challenged. After Confucius, there were very few new ideas in social and political philosophy – for some two thousand years, in fact. Even the current official creed – Marxism Leninism – is a Western import. But it is a Chinese form of Marxism. They call it 'socialism with Chinese characteristics'. I call it Chinese feudalism with socialist features."

"But, wait a minute. This is the first time I have set foot in this country, and it is eye-opening. I can see that traditional infrastructure is being replaced by modern ones everywhere I look. So much is new now that the general impression I have is that China is fast becoming a modern country and leaving its past behind. Is this not so?" asked Anne.

"It is only the appearance of change, not the substance. On the face of it, the Chinese people are now donning Western suits, drinking red wines and driving around in their new European cars instead of riding bicycles. It is all part of a headlong rush towards modernity on the part of a people long denied. But, underneath it all, things have changed little, especially not in that which really matters most – the opening up of the Chinese mind. Old beliefs die hard; Chinese values are very resilient, even in British administered Hong Kong. The force of that feudal tradition is virtually insurmountable when the culture is several thousand years old and has become the behavioral norm of over one billion people. A few maverick Chinese leaders can think out of the box, sure, but there are not enough of them, and they are not in positions of power to make a difference." David Han was despairing as he got to the end of what he wanted to say.

"My husband Victor and I had this discussion before. He was in computers but had a degree in engineering. Like you, he believed the scientific method is what has propelled the important technological advances in the West. And we both agree that freedom and the democratic institutions of the United States are the cornerstones of our strength – our ability for renewal. We also believe our universities are great incubators and repositories of knowledge. But in the West we take all comers and we do share such knowledge, and it is easy for Chinese people to simply pick this up from our books, the Internet, and our universities. We are very open about it, you know. I don't just mean the books on science and technology, but also the books on politics, law and philosophy."

"Yes, I know. You may have an open society. But unfortunately we don't. Not in China. Information access is severely restricted in this country. Chinese rulers believe an ignorant population is easier to govern than an informed one. Thought control has been practiced in China for many hundreds, even thousands, of years – it goes all the way back to our dynastic days – deviation from the norm is punished with heavy penalties, and dissidence is a crime. It is essentially rule by force and rule by fear – good for the ruler, but not for the people, and not for the country! A society such as this instinctively inhibits and expunges new ideas. It does not really move forward and never quite sheds its hierarchical, feudal heritage."

"It won't if its elite are only interested in science subjects like chemistry, physics, aerodynamics, engineering and computer science; or even business studies, finance and MBAs," said Anne. "I have not come across many Chinese students in my country that are taking degrees in law and philosophy, politics, history and literature – the humanities."

"Well, there you are. Most Chinese students are only interested in Western science and technology. They are not interested in Western ideas of freedom, democracy, human rights, the rule of law…"

"But China's leaders claim they practice the rule of law." Anne was surprised David had mentioned the rule of law in the same breath as the other "dreaded" Western values.

"I'm sorry, but China's leaders really don't understand the philosophy and the many sophisticated constructs behind the term. They do not know how it is all supposed to work and why. They think writing laws on to the statute books and administering them is the rule of law. But they don't want an independent judiciary or trial by jury; they do not recognize the supremacy of law over and above the authority of the Communist Party; and they would not entertain such essential constructs as *habeas corpus*, due process, equality before the law and presumption of innocence. This last bit really highlights the fundamental difference between the practice of law in common law jurisdictions and the practice of law in China. There is no presumption of innocence in Chinese courts. The burden of proof is not on the prosecution but on the accused."

"So what do they do in their law courts?"

"In criminal trials, China's law courts are really there to convict and they take instruction from the Party. What they have is, at best, rule *by* law. Chinese mandarins in China's dynastic days and their modern day equivalents, the Party cadres, all believe in rolling the three functions of government into one – legislative, executive and judicial – because they think this is the most efficient way of administering justice and running the country. But actually, some of China's dissidents say their government does not even practice rule by law, because what had been written into the constitution is often not being honored. They say the country is essentially run by the top leader and his court. They call this *renzhi,* the rule of man."

"Well, playing the Devil's advocate, I could argue that if the ruler is an enlightened and benevolent leader, the country can still make very impressive progress, as China seems to have done, no?"

"Yes, but that means we are back to the Moses syndrome of political leadership again and again. That is to say, China needs a good leader, a prophet who can take the people to the Promised Land. Under a good leader who follows enlightened policies, China moves forward. But under a bad leader, China regresses and languishes in the backwaters of stagnation. And then one bad government leads to another that is even worse, until there is a popular uprising or military coup to end it, maybe even a civil war. It is cyclical and China has not been able to break out of this vicious spiral."

"You may be right about China, but as a liberal thinking person, it seems to me the United States' model of democracy with a bicameral Congress may not be right for other countries."

"Maybe not, I never said it was. But I can see two vital pillars of strength in your system of government. In countries like the United States and the United Kingdom where democracy and the rule of law are entrenched, there is no fear of political chaos accompanying a change of political leadership, because the transition from one leader to another is through the ballot box and it is the people who do the choosing on the basis of one man one vote. The other pillar of strength is the checks and balances inherent in countries which practice the separation of powers between the executive, legislative and judicial branches of government. This enables you to moderate the mistakes of a bad political leader, even one at the very top. There is no possibility of the Great Leap Forward or the Great Proletarian Cultural Revolution ever taking place in the United States of America, I don't think."

"Perhaps not, but our current President is bad enough as political leaders go."

"He has not hurt the real economy and your stock market is doing well in spite of him. Your mass media can criticize him and his policies at will, as can you. If people do that here in China, they will be put behind bars, often without trial."

"Will the authorities here do that to you if you're an American or hold a foreign passport? Or do they treat us somewhat differently?"

"We'll see. Because I am going to challenge them as soon as I get back to Hangzhou."

"You are? What's your, er, your grievance? Aside from the fact that they have not given us much information."

"That's it. That's exactly it. I am not sure my sister died from drowning. In fact, I suspect foul play. The boat which Commissioner Ma said had capsized was burnt apparently. Because some of the bodies they brought back on shore were charred. That's what our driver told me when you fell asleep in the car coming out. He's the same driver who drove your husband to this place a week ago. He said the fire brigade was there and he saw the burnt bodies. I want to get to the bottom of this."

Anne raised her eyes and looked at David in shock, her stare confused. The purr of the boat's engine got louder and louder in the silence between them.

Young Bo took a deep breath as he surveyed the half-deserted main street of Jin-an County in the night. It was dark. The moon was in hiding, deep behind the thick clouds. The air was chilly for the time of year. There were only a few fast-walking pedestrians on the road, eager to find solace in the comfort of hearth and home. Bo had no home to return to. Both his parents were dead and he was their only child. He had taken up a bed space in an old and damp tenement building on the edge of town. That was all he had in this world, aside from the cash in his long wallet and his haul of fake watches.

After carefully wrapping up his counterfeit wares – the Rolex and Patek Philippe fakes – Bo rushed over to join his buddy Jie at their usual meeting place. This was the street corner two blocks from the movie house. He knew his street partner Jie would be there before him, as Jie never bothered to put his watches back into their boxes. He would just wrap them in cellophane, dump them onto a thick piece of table-cloth, tie up the four corners to make a bundle, and away he would go. Jie couldn't be bothered with what's behind him. He had a rage to live the next experience.

Bo was different from Jie, although they were about the same age, both of them in their early twenties. For one thing, Bo would shave and brush his teeth every day, and wash his hair often. For another, he was trying to save and not spend all his money. He wanted to improve himself. Bo might have missed going to university because his grades were just below the cut, but he had an intellectual curiosity about the world outside of China, especially Europe and the United States, a curiosity which Jie did not share. Bo knew he was selling fake watches but he did not want to do that for the rest of his life. He saw no future in what he was doing and he wanted a way out. He had even talked to Jie about it. But Jie paid no attention and could not see what other future the two of them might have aside from being vagabonds.

Bo was beholden to Jie, even though he was taller and bigger, because Jie was more savvy, street smart, and he was the one who had the underworld connection that got them the fake merchandise. For Jie, there was never any moral dilemma in selling counterfeit goods. He loved to turn a fast buck and he was just happy doing what he did best – smooth-talking tourists into parting with their money and making a tidy profit in the process.

"Look what I've got this time," an excited Jie told Bo when the two had sat down at their usual dingy little haunt at the edge of the city the night before. "Some genuine watches for a change, some bracelets and a few rings. The bosses took the expensive jewelry for themselves, the emeralds and diamonds, but even these leftovers cost me a lot – 15,000 *yuan* in all. But we should be able to sell them at three times that amount. Easy!"

Bo glanced over the pile of new merchandise which Jie had brought with him and noticed that it was indeed somewhat different. He picked up a big ring, obviously a man's ring, and began to look it over closely.

"You like this ring?" Jie asked, "Ah Fei's gang wanted eight hundred *yuan* for this, but I managed to get it down to five."

"I want this for myself, Jie. I want to keep it. So let's do a separate deal on this one, shall we?" said Bo.

"As you wish, Buddy," replied Jie. "I am more interested in what we're going to be doing tonight."

Bo did not answer. He was looking at the inscription on the inside of the ring. He saw two letters of the alphabet – a V and an L – followed by four numerals. It could not be a Louis Vuitton ring then, Bo thought to himself, the initials for that would have been LV.

"Well, how about this?" asked Jie.

"How about what?" replied Bo, somewhat absent-mindedly, still distracted by what he was looking at, and imagining the lettering might be some kind of secret society code and the year of induction.

"Why, Assistant Commissioner Rong's house, of course. This is their movie night, Buddy, and they're bound to be showing naughty movies from Hong Kong again. Don't you want to see them? The one we saw last week was hot, real hot." Jie rubbed his own palms as he said this, in a lewd gesture suggesting a sexual act. "You can't see these show-all scenes in our movie houses. Not even in the DVD versions. They would have been cut," he continued.

"I know, I know," said Bo, "but what if we got caught? What then? We were lucky the last few times, but…"

"No buts and what ifs please, Bo! I want to enjoy myself tonight. There's nothing else to do in this damned weather. Even the factory girls are in hiding!" As he said this, Jie pulled Bo's shirt sleeve and dragged him along with determination. They took three turns after hitting the main street and disappeared into the greenery which lined the poshest residential district in Jin-an County.

Jie took Bo quickly through the wood until they came to a wire fence. They circled the fence from the outside and came to a stop when they found the tall plane tree whose thick branches overhung the enclosed compound within. Jie climbed the tree with his bare hands, found a strong, sturdy branch, tied a rope around it, one he had hidden there for the last four weeks, slid down onto the grass lawn behind the fence and he was in. Bo followed closely behind, and soon the two buddies were climbing the water-pipe attached to the exterior wall of the imposing mansion. This was a mansion worthy of an Assistant Commissioner of the Public Security Bureau. It was just one of three residences Rong Hua owned, the one he used for entertaining his special guests. His regular residence, where he lived with his wife and daughter, was a splendid villa closer to the centre of the city.

Having reached the top where the roof was, the two young men stole into the big house by inserting a small knife through the keyhole of a door in the attic. Once inside, Jie pulled out a finger-size flashlight and crawled his way to where the top beam rested on the brick structure. There was a hidden alcove just big enough for two people. From here, they poked their heads out and could see that, some twenty five feet down from where they were looking, servants were milling in and out, making preparation for some big event. Jie winked and smiled knowingly to Bo as he switched off his flash. The busy servants were a good sign. He was sure the two of them would get to see what they had come here for tonight. The youngsters then pulled out a couple of buns, some knick-knacks and started eating in silence. They knew they had to wait.

In the vast open space under the ceiling, several servants were patting the cushions on the large sofas and laying the tea-tables with snacks, tea cups with lid-covers, and also wet towels. The precious white liquor *moutai* was taken out of the cupboard and unwrapped. The master of the house certainly knew his *moutai* – there were several bottles of the most expensive kind, one which was favored by high-ranking military officers and public security top brass. Among the people in this closely knit circle, you could not be a brother until you had shared their *moutai*. The huge television screen with surround-sound loudspeakers mounted on the four corners of the walls was being tested with a DVD sampler. The colors were dazzling, although much too sharp and artificial, not really true to life.

The door to the lounge suddenly swung open and in walked the big, fat and very powerful body of Assistant Commissioner Rong Hua, with two bodyguards either side of him, followed by an entourage of giggly, tipsy young ladies in their shiny, tight-fitting dresses. Several men in dark business suits followed on from behind, led by a man in a light cashmere suit. He was slightly built and quite pale. The light color suit made him look even smaller than he was. Some of the men were red-faced from earlier drinking but clearly sober. They were talking to one another in the Cantonese dialect of Hong Kong movies, but they were not talking to any of the ladies. These men knew the rules and the routines. They had seen it all. Indeed they stage-managed such happenings all the time, from their base in Hong Kong to an expanding list of major Chinese cities where their rich clients were based. The chatty young things who were standing around in a semi-circle were starlets who aspired to be leading ladies in the increasingly lucrative, high-grossing Chinese film industry. To the men in black business suits, the girls' "stable minders" as they were called in the trade, this was just a standard brothel scene in a Hong Kong movie. In China, the real world and the world of make-believe have much in common; the resemblance is uncanny and it is intentional. Real life and fantasy are indistinguishable in some people's minds.

Assistant Commissioner Rong with the spiky crew-cut walked towards and slumped into the centre of the big sofa facing the screen. His big frame caused the sofa to sag under his weight. He motioned two girls to come forward and, when they did, he pulled them down to sit with him, one on each side. Rong then told his male guests to help themselves to the plentiful food and *moutai*, while he helped himself to the nubile bodies of his female companions. He enjoyed the open touching and patting of these luscious young women in front of other men. Being able to run his thick and rugged hands over their soft tantalizing bodies when these younger and better looking dudes around him could only watch gave him a sense of power and a shot of adrenaline through his aging body. And he needed that.

The girl in the pastel lilac dress on his left pushed Rong's roving hands away. He, smirching and laughing in quick succession, turned his lascivious attention to the girl in the pink dress on his right. He tried to pull down her already low-cut dress from the side. She gave a shout and moved away as much as she could, turning her head as she did.

Bo's heartbeat quickened in an instant. He recognized an image in his head which had laid dormant for a good many years, ever since he left his middle school 401 High. He instinctively moved his head forward and tried to look more closely. But the girl had turned her back away from his line of vision by now and he could no longer see her face.

"A gift for my lady friends," called out Assistant Commissioner Rong. As he did so, a middle-aged woman brought out a jewel box and put it on the tea-table in front of the Assistant Commissioner. He opened the box and several glittering pieces of jewelry were strewn all over the rich velvet lining. The Assistant Commissioner picked up a shiny necklace and gave it to the buxom girl in the lilac dress who gave a cry of grateful acknowledgment as she doffed it around her neck. He then took another glimmering necklace and dangled it in front of the girl in pink on his right. The girl smiled but said, "Assistant Commissioner, may I take a smaller piece from your treasure box instead? I rather like the green emerald brooch and have a dress that goes well with it. I will wear them both for you tomorrow night." At this point, Bo was almost sure who she was; he recognized the voice even though he could only see her back now. A familiar image was coming back to him from the lone recess of his mind.

To the Assistant Commissioner, the pretty girl's teasing, smiling eyes were perfectly matched by her luminous red lips and gleaming white teeth. Whereupon he shouted in approval, "You do know your jewelry, my young temptress. This one is worth much more. But, so be it, if you're going to wear this for me tomorrow."

As the Assistant Commissioner smiled his self-satisfied smile, the fair-skinned man in the light cashmere suit who sported a pair of expensive eye-glasses and a thick gold bracelet on his wrist leant forward from where he was standing and said to him, "Boss Rong, you should see Mimi in her birthday suit on the screen. I brought this especially for you all the way from Hong Kong." He winked mischievously at the girl in the pink dress as he took out a DVD from his breast pocket. "This will enhance your viewing pleasure. The last scene was shot but cut out for the theatrical release, because it was too hot even for the Hong Kong audience. So nobody aside from the production staff has seen it until now." He smiled knowingly at the Assistant Commissioner while handing over the DVD to his man servant, whereupon the Assistant Commissioner shouted, "Lights out, everyone. It's movie time!"

Jie had not noticed anything wrong until Bo's sweaty palm touched him by mistake. He had to wipe the sweat away on his pants and gestured Bo to do the same. Bo was not paying attention to Jie. His eyes were fixed on the screen. The movie that was being shown was a typical Hong Kong police story, full of improbable macho action, but short on plot and characterization. Fast car chases and other standard clichés abounded, but there was no real dialogue of any depth or sophistication; obviously a big budget production which the mass audience liked, although most of the money had been spent on the car smashes and other explosive details. In such movies, the female roles were often superfluous and dispensable. In this one, however, the girl who played a police inspector was very attractive. She had insinuating eyes and pouting, sensuous lips – not the kind you would associate with a police officer exactly. But with a face like hers, the producer obviously thought, the audience would soon suspend disbelief and let her carry the plot along in the darkness of the cinema.

The suspense quickened in the movie when the girl stumbled upon evidence which led her to the Mr. Big of a heroin-smuggling ring. But her cover was blown by a telephone call at a silly moment which could only have happened in a Hong Kong police story. Mr. Big who could not tolerate betrayal set his henchmen upon her like hungry hyenas upon a hapless gazelle. Having caught her by the hair, they tied and hanged her up with a rope and proceeded to tear off her layers of garment one by one, to maximize the effect this would have on the eagerly-waiting, eyes-ogling male audience. Until finally, there was only one stitch of clothing left on her young and curvaceous body. At the climax of this scene, as the evil-looking leader of the gang cut off her flimsy panty with a knife and revealed her full and pulsating body in all its nakedness, a sharp cry burst out from the attic of the Assistant Commissioner's house. Bo could not contain himself any longer. The girl on the screen was his long-lost dream girl, his teenage goddess, from his school 401 High.

"Who's there?" The head of Assistant Commissioner Rong's bodyguards shouted as he followed the direction of Bo's cry. "Quick, the attic! Someone's there. Go after him!"

The two young men rushed out of the attic, slid hurriedly down the water pipe on the external wall of the big mansion, and bolted across the courtyard like frightened wild horses. Bo got to the rope first and quickly pulled himself up the tree to safety. Jie followed just a few paces behind. They both jumped on to the road outside the fence and ran for dear life. But Assistant Commissioner Rong's guards had caught a glimpse of what they were wearing before they vanished out of sight.

After David and Anne got back on shore, they found two restaurants which looked, from the outside, cleaner than the others. The two eateries were just ten meters apart and Anne thought they should get Ah Sheng to help them decide which might be a better choice for lunch. So David went up the road to look for their driver at the place where he had dropped them off earlier in the day and where he said he would be waiting. Anne decided to stay close to the pier and not to walk up the slope again. She was just loitering at the lakeside when her eyes were drawn towards a line of vendors plying souvenirs and fake merchandise.

Anne stopped in front of one selling fake watches, attracted by a sign hand-written in English with the words "Genuine Fakes". She was amused by the intentional oxymoron and was intrigued enough to look at the young vendor in front of her. He was pale and tall and clean shaven, with rather earnest eyes and shiny, well-groomed hair.

"High-class Swiss ladies' watches. Only thirty US dollars for one," he said to Anne. "Two for fifty," he raised his voice and shouted in English.

As Bo shuffled his hands smoothly through the merchandise he was peddling, Anne noticed something incongruous on the middle finger of his right hand. She could see an insignia ring, the kind popular with American college students who would have worn it on their little finger, as Victor had done with his since graduation. She started to watch the young man's hand and fingers intently until, perhaps out of embarrassment because the ring was constantly slipping off, Bo held back his right hand and started to re-adjust the ring by squeezing it.

"May I see your ring?" Anne said to the young vendor standing in front of her.

"It's not for sale," replied Bo, sounding slightly defensive.

"But can I look at it?" Anne insisted.

"No, it's not for sale," said Bo again, this time with a wave of his left hand for emphasis.

"I'll give you *two* hundred US dollars," Anne said with emphasis.

"Are you joking? This is 21 carat gold and it's heavy."

"I can give you a better price if you would let me look at it first."

"Like how much? Give me an idea." Bo's curiosity was getting the better of him; he wanted to know how much the ring could sell for.

"Let's say a thousand US dollars," Anne knew she was bluffing; she did not have so much cash in her purse; but she simply must look at the ring. A frightening suspicion was whirling in her head.

"OK, but be quick about it, and I only take cash," as he uttered those words, Bo let the ring slip down from his right middle finger and handed it over to Anne.

The initials OBK were unmistakable even at a distance of three feet. When Anne raised the ring to her eye level and looked at the inside, her heart sank and tears started to well up. She could see the initials VL and the numerals giving Victor's year of graduation when he was inducted into the OBK fraternity. She started to look for her handkerchief in her handbag. Noticing something strange was happening, Bo tried to snatch the ring back from her but could not. Anne was clutching the ring so hard her nails were stuck into the palm of her hand.

Pointing a clutched fist at Bo, Anne said to him, slowly but in a loud, angry, and stone-cold voice, "I will give you two thousand dollars for this ring if you would tell me how it ended up in your hands. Tell me where you got it from and who gave it to you."

"Forget it, lady. It's not for sale. I got it from a friend."

"No way, young man. This ring belonged to my husband and he died on board a ferry boat at the Lake out there. If you won't tell me who gave it to you, I'm going to call the police."

By this time the brawl between a foreign woman and a young Chinese man had caught the attention of the passing crowd who were now pressing forward to see what was happening. Bo quickly sized up the situation and started packing his merchandise. He then turned suddenly and tried to pull away. Anne would have none of this and was holding on to his shirt sleeve with her one free hand. This was not enough to stop the Chinese youth. He wrestled free, swung around and forced open Anne's other hand. The ring fell on the ground with a reverberating cling and started to roll away. The Chinese youth dashed forward, picked it up in a flash and darted off with his bundle of fake watches. Anne ran after him but he was too fast for her and vanished into the crowd after turning the first street corner.

When David Han returned with Ah Sheng, a visibly shaken and clearly distraught Anne Gavin told him what had happened.

"Are you absolutely sure that was your husband's ring?" asked David.

"Yes, I am absolutely sure. He had it on his little finger all these years – since graduation! And his initials are there, engraved into the inside of the ring. VL – Victor Lin. Trust me, I did not dream this up."

"In that case, I suggest we go to the public security people here right away. They must know who these street vendors are and where they may be hiding. Ah Sheng, please get us to the local Public Security Bureau."

They rushed back to the car. Ah Sheng started the engine but did not know where to go. It was then that he told David he was not from these parts. Ah Sheng drove off anyway, hoping to find another driver at the top of the road from whom he could ask for direction. Just then, Anne Gavin remembered the name of Assistant Commissioner Rong Hua and took out his contact details from a notebook in her wallet and gave this to David who read it out to Ah Sheng. But Ah Sheng was still clueless. David suggested going back to Hangzhou first. But Anne was adamant she must speak to Rong as he was in charge of public security at the Thousand Island Lake and he was the officer on the case. David then took the notebook with the address on it, got out of the car and stopped a passer-by. When he came back and gave directions to Ah Sheng, his chauffeur now knew which roads to take. Within seven minutes, the car stopped in front of the Office of Public Security of Jin-an County. Anne and David rushed in and asked for Assistant Commissioner Rong Hua.

"You cannot come in here and ask to see the Assistant Commissioner just like that," the officious man at the reception desk said to them in the grand manner to which he had grown accustomed. David Han always feared something like this might happen, but had not the heart to tell Anne. And that was exactly how things turned out. The two of them were told the Assistant Commissioner had gone to Hangzhou for the day and in any case would not be able to see them without an appointment. When Anne insisted on staying and was making a big fuss at the reception hall, the Duty Officer came out and offered to take down the details of what she wanted to report.

Anne gave to the Duty Officer the background to her husband's death at the Thousand Island Lake, followed by a detailed account of what happened at the pier earlier on, her physical struggle with the young hawker and why. She also gave the officer a description of the appearance of the young man. She said she wanted the Public Security Bureau to get to the bottom of this and she wanted Assistant Commissioner Rong to take personal charge – because her husband, an American, had died and because she suspected foul play might have caused his death. To make sure that this case and she herself would be taken seriously, Anne let it be known that she had a cousin working on The Council on Foreign Relations in Washington, and that he knew the US Assistant Secretary of State for East Asia who knew China's Vice Foreign Minister.

David Han interpreted for her throughout the interview. He knew the reference to The Council on Foreign Relations in Washington would not mean anything to a local official but translated that anyway. He made sure the man had every detail written down. Having heard what happened, David too began to suspect foul play was involved, but knew they did not yet have the proof to nail the case down. Afterwards, in the car going back to Hangzhou, David and Anne both agreed they must seek the help of their respective consulates. David, in particular, feared that the Public Security Bureau of Jin-an County was not to be trusted because it would want to sweep things under the carpet once the two of them were out of the picture.

Early the next morning, Anne and David went to the Public Security Bureau in Hangzhou as planned. They asked to see Assistant Commissioner Rong Hua. After waiting half an hour, another officer came out to let them know that the Assistant Commissioner had already returned to Jin-an County in the night and that they would have to go there if they wanted to see him. Infuriated but unable to do anything about it, Anne and David were on their way out when the *other* Assistant Commissioner, Li Neng, the one with the high forehead, quietly slipped in through a side door and asked them to join him in his office.

After offering the two visitors the exquisite *dragon well* tea of the Hangzhou region, the mild-mannered and bespectacled Acting Assistant Commissioner Li began in very proper English, "If you are here to complain, and I expect you are, you must tell me everything... I want to know what you know – every detail." As he said this, he took out a Chinese notepad.

"Well, it's about the Thousand Island Lake. I think you were at Commissioner Ma's briefing when he said the boat capsized and all the people on board drowned and the bodies had been cremated." Anne paused, took a breath, looked at Li Neng straight in the eyes and continued, "Well, we went to the Lake yesterday, Dr. Han and I, and we heard an eyewitness account that some of the bodies were charred. And then, to my astonishment, I found my husband's ring, yes, his graduation ring – yesterday, at the Thousand Island Lake – on the finger of a roadside vendor selling fake merchandise! I immediately reported this to the Public Security Bureau there and I wanted Assistant Commissioner Rong to follow this up. The bureau's Duty Officer told us he would be here, in Hangzhou. But he obviously is not. The junior guy we saw just now said he had gone back to the Lake. We're obviously being given the run around!" said an exasperated and agitated Anne Gavin.

The Acting Assistant Commissioner did not respond right away. He was writing on his notepad. "Assistant Commissioner Li," David Han butted in at this point, "You should be receiving a report from Jin-an County, shouldn't you? We reported the case yesterday."

"I know. The report was here this morning and I have read it. I expect Assistant Commissioner Rong has too."

"You mean Assistant Commissioner Rong was here this morning?" a surprised Anne Gavin quickly asked.

"I didn't say that." Li quickly corrected her.

"If he wasn't, how else could he have read the report?" Anne was incredulous.

"His department drafted the report and I expect him to have read it. But that's not important. I want to hear it from *your* mouth, what *you* know, what *you* have found out, gone through, *your* version. I don't want to miss any details. They may be important."

As he said that, something in Assistant Commissioner Li's manner – his deliberately slow enunciation and the way he looked at the two of them as he wrote on his notepad – suggested to David Han that something might be happening behind the scene, so he nodded to Anne. After a quick glance to acknowledge his nod, Anne began. She told Li Neng everything that had transpired at the Thousand Island Lake the day before. After she finished, David took over.

"The boat did not just capsize, did it?" he asked Li Neng, "There was a fire on board, wasn't there? We have an eyewitness who said he had seen burnt and charred bodies being recovered from the lake."

Li stopped him from speaking with a motion of his hand, took a file out of his desk drawer and checked what was there. He then said to Anne and David, "Leave this with me. I will contact you at your hotel later this week. I need time to… find… er… work things out."

"You have to get the young man selling fake watches and follow his trail," said Anne, "that's what you must do. When you get him, I expect you will be able to find out very much more."

"Maybe, but this is really Assistant Commissioner Rong's case. Let me see what I can do."

Anne wanted to bring up The Council on Foreign Relations again. "I have a cousin who works for… " she began, but David interrupted her by rising to his feet and extending his hand to say good-bye to the Acting Assistant Commissioner.

Once outside the Bureau, Anne wanted to know why David Han stopped her just now from putting more pressure on the Chinese official they had just spoken with.

"Because it occurred to me he is really trying to help us, that's why! If he is already on side, on our side that is, you don't want to spoil things by overdoing it." David explained.

"How do you know that? How do you know this is not one of those good cop, bad cop tricks?" asked Anne.

"I don't know this for sure. But the fact that he is even looking into a colleague's case is highly irregular, especially in China. I have a feeling he is not altogether happy with Assistant Commissioner Rong and the way Rong has been conducting the investigation. I suspect there is something between these two, and Li probably needs time to build up his case. I think we should help him; we would be helping ourselves if he is going after the real culprits…"

"I am not sure I'd go along with your hunch. I am going to my consulate to enlist official help," said Anne.

"And I'll go to mine, although I do not hold out much hope. Shall we meet for dinner and compare notes, then plan our next move?"

Anne nodded her head absent-mindedly. Her thoughts were still revolving around Li Neng's words.

"I have checked with the hotel concierge about dinner," David said. "There are two recommendations. The first is a traditional Hangzhou eatery. I've eaten there before, two nights ago. It's crammed, not very clean, and very noisy, but the food is really good. You won't get it anywhere else. Very local. The second is just our hotel restaurant upstairs on the top floor called The Clouds. It is very spacious, the lighting is soft and the place is clean and very comfortable. I have eaten there too. The food is not bad, standard hotel fare, you know. Caters to international tastes, plays it safe – that sort of thing. So why don't you choose?'

"I wouldn't want to eat in a place that's crowded and noisy. We might want to go through a few things together – quietly."

"That's true. It's decided then and I'll meet you at The Clouds on the top floor of our hotel. I'll book the table for, shall we say, 6:30? Dinner tends to be early in China, I am sure you know."

"I don't actually, but 6:30's fine. See you then."

"This is quite pleasant," said Anne to David, as she stared at the view of the West Lake from the top floor of the hotel restaurant. The Clouds is quite an appropriate name for this place, she thought to herself.

"Yes it is," replied David. "Would you like some tea or do you prefer something stronger?" he asked.

"Tea is good," said Anne. "Why don't you order for us both? I am not keen on abalone, but I eat everything else. I have never quite understood the fuss about abalones among Chinese people."

"It's an acquired taste, like haggis."

"Scottish haggis? Well, I don't like that either."

"Nor I. I just brought that up to illustrate a point – that we are all creatures of habit, of our own upbringing. But have no fear. Abalone is a Cantonese delicacy. I don't think they do that here." David stopped looking at the menu, paused and then said, "If we are going to talk about our experiences at the two consulates, shall we just order the set menu? It would save time." David asked Anne.

"Yes, why don't we? I am quite famished."

After the order had been taken and before the food arrived, David began. "My meeting at the British Consulate, my second in four days, was quite useless, much as I had expected it to be. The junior consular official I saw there said he was aware of what he called 'the accident' and that he had noted down 'one Hong Kong British national drowned' – those were his very words – but he said they were not in a position to do much as my sister was traveling on a Mainland Travel Permit issued by the Chinese Government to Chinese nationals overseas. Apparently my sister did not use her British passport to get into China. So, there! I just knew they would hide behind some technicalities like that and do as little as possible. Didn't I tell you? Now I will have to go higher up in order to get these people to take notice and act. I have actually done that of course. I am just waiting for a positive reply. No more underlings for me. They are a waste of time."

"Well, my meeting at the US Consulate was more productive, I guess. It turned out the consular officer who received me also studied at UCLA and was several years my senior. He already knew about Victor and what happened at the Thousand Island Lake. When I told him about Victor's ring on this young street vendor's finger, and the charred bodies our driver said he had seen, and when I asked him whether foul play might have been involved, he said he wouldn't be surprised if it had, and he said he would look into it. So, I am hopeful…"

"I'm glad at least one of us is getting somewhere. If you are able to find out what really happened, that would help me too. I can then put pressure on the British Consulate to do more than just going through the motions and giving me their standard no-action, can't-do-anything reply."

By this time, the first dishes – four appetizers of varying colors and textures – were being laid on the table, and David proceeded to heap them on Anne's plate one after the other with a pair of very delicate silver-plated serving chopsticks.

Anne found the appetizers quite delicious, not at all like the food that was served in Chinese restaurants in LA, and not what

David had led her to expect. "Tell me, David," she began, calling him by his given name, "These dishes we are having here, they are not the same as the ones I'm used to in California. Is this a different cuisine?"

"I don't really know anything about the Chinese food in California, but this is the Hangzhou cuisine and it is very refined. Hangzhou is famous for its painters and scholars, its silk, its tea, and its food. Chinese scholars have good tastes, you know. The green tea at Assistant Commissioner Li's office today was exquisite. Didn't you notice?"

"I noticed a special fragrance and a somewhat peculiar taste, yes. But does that mean the Assistant Commissioner is from a scholar background?"

"He might be; he has good manners. Unlike our man Rong, who is at best a rough diamond, I'd say. And I am being charitable."

"I'm not really a tea drinker, so could not tell so much from the one cup of tea I had, but I do love this food." said Anne as she went for another helping herself. "Is this the best Chinese cuisine then, the Hangzhou cuisine?" she asked David.

"Not for the Cantonese in Hong Kong," replied David. "For them, the Cantonese cuisine is the best. It's certainly the freshest, I'll give them that. Guangdong Province is the land of plenty; it is one of the most prosperous regions in China, and Canton, now called Guangzhou, is the provincial capital of the whole Pearl River Delta. And *that* is the home of Cantonese cooking.

But, to answer your question, the Hangzhou cuisine is one of the four best cuisines in China, yes."

"Oh? So what are the others, if we count Cantonese and Hangzhou as the first two?"

"You know what? Your former President, Ronald Reagan, asked that of China's paramount leader Deng Xiaoping when they had dinner at the Great Hall of the People some years ago – at a state banquet – and Deng reportedly said to Reagan then that the richest, most prosperous regions produced the best cuisines. It stands to reason, doesn't it? And these are: Guangdong (Cantonese), Sichuan (Deng's own native province), the Shanghai-Nanjing-Hangzhou area where we are now, and finally Beijing, the capital." At this point, David paused and proffered his own opinion, "I do not agree with Deng Xiaoping actually. I do not think much of Sichuan food; it is too spicy and too oily for me. What's more, it's the same spicy hot flavor for nearly all the dishes."

"Ah, well," said Anne, "then that's the Chinese food they serve in most restaurants in California."

"No wonder..." as David said this, there was a big commotion at the entrance to the restaurant, and the waiting staff was almost falling over each other to greet the new arrivals. An entourage of glamorous-looking people, both men and women, had walked in, with six muscular bouncers positioned in front of, alongside and also at the back of, the pack. Except for the important-looking man in the middle who wore beige, all the other men were in pitch black suits, and the women wore long silk dresses with a sheen that glittered under the arc lights.

"Welcome, Boss Pang." the *maître d'hôtel* stepped forward and bowed to the rather pale, unhealthy looking but very well dressed man in the middle. He was in a light cashmere suit and was smoking a cigar as he swaggered his way in. "This way please, Boss Pang. Let me show you to your private room, Boss Pang." The *maître d'* was all smiles as he said this. He obviously knew who the client was. He was putting on his best obsequious behavior.

Pang and his entourage of at least twelve people moved towards and then past Anne and David's table. Anne saw the two young women either side of this "Boss Pang" and could not take her eyes off them. The girl in the halter-neck lavender dress was the first to swing by in her four-inch heels; she left a whiff of perfume behind her. The other girl, taller and fairer, and in the pastel green dress that was not so revealing, was less theatrical. But the green emerald brooch worn just below her left shoulder was dazzling; this was placed above her pulsating bosom for maximum attention-grabbing effect. Anne did not like this girl's perfume. It was not a cheap perfume; there was just too much of it. David also saw Boss Pang and the two girls but showed no particular interest and continued eating. After they had drifted past, Anne's eyes wandered back and asked David to give her more tea which he duly did.

Shortly after disappearing into their private room, the two girls came out again, and were talking into their mobile phones. They went to the two far corners of the restaurant, taking up one corner each. Anne could not understand what they were saying as they walked past, but David could, although he pretended not to have heard. He did frown ever so slightly and lowered his head.

The taller of the two girls, the less theatrical one in the pastel green dress, had smooth, ivory-color skin, which Anne noticed. Her well-made-up face was accentuated by a smear of red lipstick on her tiny contoured lips and a beauty mole on the right side of her cheek. Anne had never seen such a stunning Chinese girl before, certainly not in California, where dressing casually and acting naturally was the norm. The unusual mix of oriental mystique and exaggerated western styling quite overwhelmed her.

But Anne had noticed that David was not even looking at this exquisite beauty, or for that matter the other, more curvaceous but shorter girl. Curiosity finally got the better of her and she asked him, somewhat sheepishly, "That girl in the pastel green dress at the corner of the room there on our right – she is unbelievably attractive, don't you think?"

"Not particularly. Not to me."

"Why? Don't you find her… alluring? She is so special. When she walked into the room, I could not take my eyes off her."

"That's only because you didn't hear her speak. If you had understood what she was saying, you'd know why I wouldn't want to be anywhere near that girl. I mean, she was swearing into the phone at her driver! The girl is really common. The veneer of sophistication which you see is just a put-on job. I draw the line at women swearing in public. Besides, I know of this big boss she's with, this man called Boss Pang. You don't want to go anywhere near him or his girls. He owns a film studio in Hong

Kong, makes soft porn and *kung fu* movies. And he has triad connections. The triads are the Chinese mafias."

"Well, never mind him. I'm more interested in her. Could you tell, really, from the few sentences that she spoke just now as she walked past that she was not well brought up?"

"Yes," David said most emphatically.

"Well, I can't."

"I thought not. That's why so many Americans have been fooled by wily Chinese girls," he said with a heave of his shoulders, and then quickly qualified himself, "Although not all of them are like that, I should add."

Anne was surprised by the forthright observation. She really had no answer to that. And, as she was thinking to herself, David continued, "If it's any consolation to you, we Chinese men make that mistake too when we look at American or British women. Some of my friends' patrician parents in Hong Kong have found, to their eternal shame, that their sons and heirs to the family fortunes have married American tarts or British barmaids. It is not easy to detect social origin across cultures. Once you cross the cultural divide, you are just a novice in the dating game. You forget your own culture's taboos; and you don't yet know the taboos of the new culture. It is as if you have been stripped naked, and only physical attraction remains. Now Alexis de Tocqueville was the clever one…"

"Alexis de Tocqueville the French philosopher? Oh? What about him?"

"Well, he noticed that the British abroad behaved differently from the French abroad. At the breakfast table in a foreign hotel, he noticed the French tourists would talk to total strangers from their own country – on first acquaintance, that is – whereas the British would not. But then he noticed that after a few days, the French contingent would also start to sit at different tables from each other, just like the British did, only the Brits had done this right from the start. And de Tocqueville concluded from this observation that whereas the British could tell each other's class origin by just listening to the first few words their countrymen spoke, the French could not. They needed a few talking sessions to find out. And when they did find out one another's class origins and if these were quite different, they would go their separate ways too, as you might expect."

"I'm sorry, but America is not a class-ridden society, as the British and the French no doubt were over two hundred years ago. The only class distinction in America is green – green is the color of our money, our banknotes are called greenbacks, as I'm sure you know. We respect success, we admire people who have made their own way in this world and not relied on birthright or inheritance. What I'd like to know is – where do educated Chinese people stand in all this?"

"Oh, I think the Chinese are as bad as the British. This comes from having a self-professed superior culture and a large empire over several thousand years. I'm sure America will also come to that eventually – what's the expression again? – oh yes, in the fullness of time. The British poet W. H. Auden used to say he could sum up most things in life in four words. It's either a case of "not yet" or a case of "no longer". America is young. It is *not yet* a class-ridden society, as you said, but it will get there in the end. The Chinese and the British, on the other hand, are the world's worst snobs. It was said of the Duke of Wellington that he harbored social snobbery for his intellectual equals, and intellectual snobbery for his social equals. Upper class Chinese men understand that very well, I'd say. But not when they venture into another culture. When they venture into another culture, they behave like most men tend to do – they lose their sense of proportion and propriety."

"This may be so with men, but it doesn't work quite like that with women," Anne said quietly.

"How so? What do you mean?" asked David.

"Well, for women, it's not just physical attraction. Looks just aren't that important. It's many things. We tend to put more store on a man's innate qualities, his strengths, his personality, his character, the attributes we admire; these are much more important than physical appearance. The American women who marry Chinese men that I know..."

At this point, a tall, silver-haired and distinguished looking American was escorting a young and heavily made-up Chinese girl into the restaurant. They were taken to a far table with a view of the West Lake. Anne motioned to David and said, "Look at those two over there who have just come in. Is that girl a Chinese barmaid too?"

"I don't know. I need to hear her talk first. But, given the age difference, they are at least an incongruous pair," said David, as he took a quick look at the couple again. "He seems well-mannered. He didn't sit down until she had done so."

"He should be. He's a diplomat. This is the American consular official I saw this afternoon. His name is Robert Denning. Oops! He's just seen me and is now coming over. Here, let me introduce you."

"Hello, Anne, we meet again." So saying, a smiling Robert Denning held out his hand.

"Hello, Robert, this is David Han, whom I had told you about…"

"Speak, you scum! How did you get this ring?" the hoarse-voiced Senior Inspector Deng shouted at Jie and Bo at the top of his larynx, as he pointed at the ring that was now held between his two fat and rugged fingers. The two young men were on their knees and at an angle to each other.

"I… " began Jie, but before he could come out with what he was going to say, the Inspector smacked him across the face and said, "Speak up. I can't hear you. I may be an old man but don't think you can lie and fool me. I have many ways of finding out." The Senior Inspector leant forward and threatened with a roll of his round and protruding eyeballs.

"I got this from our source in the black market," Jie was really scared but managed to finish his sentence.

"Where? Which one? Who? Give me name and location or I'll beat the food out of you. I want precise details."

"Ah Fei at the corner of Peace Alley. He does wholesale. We are just his retail guys."

"And where does this Ah Fei get his merchandise from?" the Senior Inspector spat out the words, slowly this time, as he knew he was getting somewhere. His eyes rolled from Jie to Bo and back again. He began to move his big frame diagonally across the room as he waited for an answer. At the mention of the name Ah Fei, the other two public security officers who had been leaning on a wall at the back of the room exchanged a knowing glance with each other and started to lurch threateningly forward, towards Jie and Bo.

"I don't know…" said Jie, he saw the look of the two men who had just moved forward.

"What do you mean you don't know, Scum! Selling counterfeit goods is illegal. I can lock you up for ten years on that charge. Lead me to Ah Fei's gang and I can reduce that to five."

As Jie considered what to do in his mind, the Senior Inspector's hand phone rang. "Come into my office, Deng – this is urgent!" an authoritative voice called out on the phone. The Senior Inspector stopped the interrogation right away and hurried out, leaving the other two officers in the room to watch over the young detainees.

These two now stepped forward to confront the pair of hapless young men who were still on their knees. "Listen here! You must not lead the Senior Inspector to Ah Fei. If you do, you die. You understand, you bloody jerks? You die. We will make sure of that." The tall one with pimply skin belted out the dire warning to Jie and Bo.

"Do what we tell you and you will get off lightly," said the short one through his tobacco stained teeth as he lit a cigarette and took a puff.

Bo was incredulous. But he quickly grasped what was happening and responded with a nod of his head. As he did so, he could see that Jie was doing the same thing. But Bo remembered what Jie had just said earlier, and so, pointing his finger at his mate, he said to his two interlocutors, "But my pal here has just told the Senior Inspector Ah Fei touted his wares at Peace Alley!"

"No, he doesn't," came the reply from the tall thin man with the pimply face, "not any more, hell! And you are not going to tell Old Deng his other warrens if you know them. Is that clearly understood?"

"Yes, Sir!" replied Bo, just as Jie nodded his head in agreement.

When Senior Inspector Deng reappeared in the interrogation room, the taller of the two officers who had remained pointed his index finger at Jie and said, "This scumbag made up the story. Peace Alley is our area. There is no hoodlum called Ah Fei. He's plain lying. It's almost dinner time, Deng, and you need to eat before you can take your medicine. Leave the matter to us. We will get the truth out of him yet."

The Senior Inspector looked at his watch and said, "Alright, but we need a confession fast. Make sure you get that." And, as he headed for the door, he turned and said in his hoarse, menacing voice, "Use torture if necessary. My Assistant Commissioner wants a quick result. That's his order."

After Senior Inspector Deng had left the room, the short one with bad teeth and bad breath spat on the floor and cursed. "Li Neng is just an Acting Assistant Commissioner and already Deng is behaving as if he headed the whole bloody Bureau. Assistant Commissioner, my foot!" and he cursed again.

The tall one was now turning his attention to Jie. He moved closer and ordered the young man, "When the Senior Inspector comes back, this is the story you will tell him. Ah Fei does not exist; you made him up. Some other hoodlum sold you the haul of counterfeit goods and the ring was among them. You don't know where this came from. You just paid the usual price and tried to sell this merchandise in the open market, like you always did. Is that clear?"

"Yes, Sir!" responded Jie.

"Which other hoodlum, Sir? The Senior Inspector will want a name." Bo was thinking ahead.

"Tell him you don't know the guy, stupid! Tell him the guy's a white face in the black market and you haven't dealt with him before."

"But if the Senior Inspector does not believe us. What do we say then?" Bo asked again.

"We will back you up. You just stick to that story, and tell it over and over again," said the tall one. "I might have to beat you in front of the Senior Inspector. But that is better than a knife in your guts and then being dumped into the lake to feed the fishes. You understand?"

"Yes, Sir!" said Bo sheepishly. "But don't beat me up too hard," he pleaded with his interrogators. "I have a weak heart. Both my parents died of heart diseases in their forties. If I die in my cell because you beat me... well, that's going to be awkward for you."

"Shut up!" the short one took over at this point, "You will be charged for two criminal offences, for breaking into Assistant Commissioner Rong's house, and for selling counterfeit goods. You will confess to both and we will make sure you get off lightly. But not another word about Ah Fei if you want to live!" Jie and Bo nodded their heads in unison and in silence.

At this point, the door opened and in walked Senior Inspector Deng. He pushed a fat and balding middle-aged man to the ground and kicked his behind. Jie and Bo recognized the man instantly. The tall officer and his much shorter side-kick recognized him too. The fat man was Ah Fei.

"Do you know these two at the corner there?" shouted Senior Inspector Deng at Ah Fei who was fat rather than heavily built, and had an oily face with bushy eyebrows. He was almost completely bald and appeared clumsy and very middle-aged but might have been younger. He looked at Jie and Bo, his eyes blinking but he did not answer the Senior Inspector's question. He also noticed the two other men in the room.

"You're an old-timer. You know what we do to hoodlums who do not cooperate. So you had better tell us what you know now. We have painful ways of making you talk. You will eventually; everybody does. It will be easier on yourself if you do so quickly. You should know that I am not a patient man," the Senior Inspector threatened by pressing his knuckles against each other and flexing his bulging fingers. They made a crackling sound.

"Yes, I have dealt with them," Ah Fei nodded his head and acknowledged he knew Jie and Bo.

"You have? Good!" the Senior Inspector continued. Pointing at a ring held between his thumb and index finger, he said to Ah Fei, "Now tell me where and from whom you got this ring."

"Someone sold it to me at the Thousand Island Lake," Ah Fei replied in his flat monotone.

"Who did? I want his name and his whereabouts."

"I don't really know him. Many people sell counterfeit goods at the Thousand Island..."

"Oh no, you're lying! This is not counterfeit goods, you scum. This is genuine. It is an unusual ring. It may not be worth very much in price, but it is very precious to the person who owned it. It is a man's ring, and we know he died at the Thousand Island Lake. Now his wife is here kicking up a big fuss for us. We want truthful answers. No lies!"

Bo could put two and two together. He had a good inkling of what this was about. He knew that he and Jie were in serious trouble this time. It was not about selling counterfeit goods. Somebody died.

Ah Fei was silent. He was considering in his mind how best to respond and what to say.

"You know what happened to the people on Boat Number 9413 at the Thousand Island Lake, don't you?" the Senior Inspector raised his voice an octave. Ah Fei nodded his head but still did not say a word.

"There was a foreigner among them," continued the Senior Inspector.

"A foreigner?" Ah Fei looked surprised.

"Yes, an American."

"An American?" Ah Fei's brows knitted together and he seemed even more puzzled.

"Yes, a *Chinese* American. He died." Senior Inspector Deng walked up to Ah Fei and suddenly shouted at the top of his voice into the fat man's ear, "And you took this ring from his finger!"

Ah Fei was shaken, and his body instinctively started back, professing as he did, "I only bought things, Sir. I was not at the scene of the accident. I am a timid man by nature, I would not want to look at charred bodies, much less take the ring off a dead man's hand."

"So the bodies were charred, were they? Jin-an County's report said they all drowned!"

"Some of the bodies were charred, er, that's what I was told." Ah Fei's eyes caught just in time the facial expression of the two men in the shadow, at the back of Senior Inspector Deng, both ashen-faced and signaling with their deathly looks that he should stop the confessional. He tried to make amends, "Maybe the boat was hit by lightning and a fire broke out before it capsized?" Ah Fei made an attempt to make good the lie.

At this point, the short one with the bad teeth behind the Senior Inspector's back had moved towards the door and quietly slipped out. Bo saw that and wondered to himself what was going to happen next.

"Bloody liar!" The Senior Inspector shouted at Ah Fei and whacked him across the face. "There was no lightning on the lake that day and you know it. We had already checked with the Weather Bureau. Rain yes, but no lightning. You were there, weren't you, when the so-called accident took place, and you know exactly what happened, don't you? Just give me the facts now. I want the facts. Not what you think. Not your guesswork. One more lie and I turn you over to the torture department.

They are real professionals at making people talk. In any case, your two young accomplices here have already told us what they know. If you think you can pull wool over my eyes, you'd better think again. I am not called Iron Finger Deng for nothing. You know what I use my iron finger for, huh?"

Ah Fei was still wiping the blood coming out of his nose and mouth with the dirty shirt sleeve of his left hand. Senior Inspector Deng pulled back a little and crossed his arms. He was very menacing even as he waited, his heavy frame and bulging biceps suggested the use of brute force was always going to be the next option. The room was filled with foreboding for Jie and Bo. And even more so for the tall one with the pimply skin.

Ah Fei was just about to speak again when the door to the interrogation room opened and in walked Assistant Commissioner Rong with the short man behind him.

"Deng, I am taking over the interrogation. You can rest now or go to dinner. Let me deal with this rascal." The Assistant Commissioner said as if this was absolutely the normal thing to do, except that Senior Inspector Deng knew it was not.

"But, Sir, I was just about getting somewhere with this crook. He is my chief suspect and he was about to tell me what happened on the Lake. We're going to crack this case soon. Please, Sir, let me continue."

"It is not for you to decide. This is our department's case. You report to Li Neng. You do not report to me. My men should have stopped you a long time ago but you pulled rank on them. Now I am pulling rank on you. So leave."

"Your men and ours got the two young hoodlums together – at the corner of the movie house. But Ah Fei here was our catch. My guys got him. Sorry, Sir, our department – my boss Acting Assistant Commissioner Li's department – got Ah Fei. That is why we have the right to interrogate him first. Can we work together on this one? We won't take sole credit for it. Our department just wants to wrap things up quickly. The American woman and this Chinese man from Hong Kong, they have been to see my boss and they have got their two consulates involved. My boss said even Vice Mayor Sun is involved now and wanted a quick wrap up. The Vice Mayor had just called him. Please, Sir, let me finish what I started."

"No, Deng! Damn you, Deng! No, no, no! Do you not hear me? No!" Assistant Commissioner Rong was really furious now, and he was barking out his words at the Senior Inspector, "You have exceeded your authority. This is a Jin-an County case and I am the officer-in-charge. You can only interview this suspect after we are done with him, and only with our consent. When we get a confession from this piece of shit, we will report the case to Commissioner Ma ourselves and that will be the end of that. It is not your business. Now go. I will speak to Li Neng about this. I will speak to him myself."

"I am here, Rong." The Acting Assistant Commissioner had glided into the room without a sound and was now standing behind his peer who was turning to face him. "I have just spoken with Commissioner Ma and Vice Mayor Sun – both of them. Let's talk in my room."

Assistant Commissioner Rong was caught unaware. Anger was turning to fury when he realized who he would have to deal with. He stared at Acting Assistant Commissioner Li and gritted his teeth; he was breathing fire inside. The air was tense with an impending confrontation between the two heads of departments. Rong was more senior and experienced. But Li was the rising star with better academic credentials. After what seemed like a minute of silence, the eye-lids finally came down and Rong said to his men, "Lock these three up! I will deal with them yet."

"Sir," Senior Inspector Deng moved over to his boss and whispered to him through the side of his mouth, "The fat one is ours; we got him!" Li nodded his head slightly to indicate that he had understood but said in a voice everybody could hear, "Let them go to the same cell, our high security cell, since this is obviously what Assistant Commissioner Rong wants. I am sure he has no objection to putting them all into Cell 14?" Turning to Rong now, the Acting Assistant Commissioner said, "We'll let our underlings deal with this, shall we? In the meantime, I need to relate to you the new instructions from *our* bosses."

Cell Number 14 was a cell with hidden cameras and micro-phones. Every move and conversation was recorded. It was brighter than normal cells to facilitate the recording. The ceiling and open windows were set very high up, and there were no sharp or soft objects of any kind to forestall all attempts at suicide. Acting Assistant Commissioner Li Neng had good reason to choose this cell.

Now that the two heads of the two public security departments had gone into private discussion and the three suspects were taken to the more spacious Cell 14, the pressure on the three custodians was lifted somewhat, and suddenly Jie and Bo both felt very hungry. Ah Fei was still licking the cut inside his mouth, although the nose bleed had stopped. They looked at one another and Jie was the first to start talking.

"I don't think we can get off lightly," he whispered.

"No, I suppose not," said Bo, "I don't like the look on The Tall One's face."

"So what really happened, Uncle Fei? Why are we in such deep shit?" Jie asked Ah Fei.

When there was no reply, Jie pressed on with his second question, "Did you know that the merchandise you sold us a few days ago was from dead men's bodies?"

Ah Fei did not respond at all. He didn't even acknowledge the question or the person asking it.

"They have been bashing us, Uncle Fei, but we know nothing. Can you tell them we know nothing? We just bought from you. That's all we did. Please spare us. We don't want to be locked away for the next ten years of our lives." Jie was pleading with Ah Fei; he had grasped the seriousness of the situation.

Bo joined in and continued the pleading, "Uncle Fei. You know we have nothing to do with this. We are just the retail outlets for your goods. I have been saving up for another go at college. I haven't done any of the things young people of my age want to do. If I go to jail now, I will be middle-aged when I come out… if I come out."

Ah Fei was still silent. Leaning his back forward to hide his hands, he started writing on his right palm with his left index finger. The words were, "Admit nothing."

Reading the words which Ah Fei wrote out twice, Jie and Bo stopped talking. But after a while, Bo could not stand the silence and started again. "I am really very hungry," he said, "When I get out, I am going to get myself a bowl of beef noodles at our bolt-hole behind the corner of Peace Alley."

"Shut up!" Ah Fei suddenly shouted at him and then started writing on his palm again the words, 'Think before speak!'

"I can't think, Uncle Fei. I know nothing. So I really can't tell them anything." Jie was raising his voice and was almost shouting now out of desperation.

At this point, their jailer came in with a bowl of plain noodles, but no beef. He signaled Bo to come forward and then said to him, "You can eat this in the next room."

Bo went through the door and, as it was being shut behind him, Jie wanted to follow but was stopped by another guard. Bo heard Jie's voice call out, "Hey, what about me? What about me?"

In the next room, the tall man with the pimply face, whom Bo called The Tall One, was waiting. He just said "Eat" and watched in silence as Bo gobbled up the noodles and downed the last drop of soup. He then licked up the last few scraps of chopped spring onions which had stuck to the bottom of the bowl.

Squeezing a half smile out of his craggy, pimply face, The Tall One said, "Work with me and you will get more than just plain noodles. I will be able to get you out of here with just a fine. You can have your beef noodles then, you understand?" And then he continued, "We know you broke into Assistant Commissioner Rong's mansion. Now, don't argue. We already know. We saw you run away with your mate. What were you hoping to find at the Commissioner's place?"

"Nothing, Sir. We just do these things for fun." Bo thought that was a safe, non-incriminatory answer.

"Fun? What fun?"

"Movies. We love to watch movies." There was no harm in admitting to that, he thought, it was not stealing after all. He was not taking anything away.

"You can see these in movie houses. Tickets are cheap. Why did you have to see movies at Assistant Commissioner Rong's house?"

"Ah, well," Bo stopped a little before he answered, "Because they are Hong Kong movies... and because they are uncensored, you know, even the off-cuts were put back in."

"So you like uncensored movies. And how many times have you done this?"

"Not many. Three, four times at most. I don't remember exactly."

"One of you gave a sharp cry from the attic that evening. It was you, wasn't it? What made you do that?"

"I was, er, overcome."

"Overcome? By what?"

"By the rape scene, Sir."

"Haven't you seen a rape scene before? Movies are full of them now."

"Yes, but this one was special. I knew the actress."

"What? You knew Mimi Tian?" The Tall One was surprised.

"Yes, we went to the same school, 401 High, Sir... except she was called Liu Mei then."

"But she's several years older than you."

"I didn't say she was in the same class as me, Sir, no. She was my senior; she was five years ahead of me. But she was the belle of the school. All of us young boys knew and adored her."

"Was that so?" said The Tall One, and he began to pace up and down the room. After doing this a few times, he stopped and looked at Bo up close, and then he started pacing up and down the room again. This went on for a few minutes until, turning suddenly, The Tall One said to Bo, "Would you like to see Mimi Tian in private? I can arrange it."

"You mean you're going to release me and take me to see her just like that?" Bo was incredulous. "Oh, no, Boss, you're having me on. I don't think you would do that. I don't believe that's possible. I don't believe it. You are just testing me."

"No, no, I am not testing you. I can really arrange that. There is a condition attached, though. After all, I am doing you a very big favor."

Intrigued, Bo asked, "And what condition is that?"

"You will plead guilty to taking the ring from a Chinese American at the Thousand Island Lake."

"But I didn't do it, Sir. You know I didn't do it!" Bo recalled the words of Ah Fei in a flash.

"Alright, then, I will make you a better offer. You can not only see Mimi Tian. You can touch her and pat her. In fact, you can spend the night with her. You can sleep with her. But you have to confess to the crime. Is it a deal?"

Bo was taken aback and tried to think quickly. The offer was totally unexpected but struck him like a bolt of lightning. He was completely thrown. The idea conjured up in his young mind intimate images of in-the-flesh contact with his high school idol. His blood was racing fast. But his good sense prevailed and he said to The Tall One, "No, I won't do that. I didn't do it. I cannot confess to something I didn't do. You are making me a scapegoat and I won't do it."

The conversation stopped dead. Neither man moved. The Tall One stared hard at the young man in front of him. Bo tried to avoid his captor's gaze; his downcast eyes looked at the bowl that was now empty of noodles. He licked his lips in silence and savored the lingering taste of the soup in his mouth, half expecting to be struck on the head at any time. In an instant, The Tall One's hand phone rang. He took the phone out of his pocket, turned and faced Bo, saying as he did, "What was that? Your guy has caved in? He will sign the confession? Good!" After listening for another half minute or so, The Tall One switched off his phone and, looking smugly at Bo now, said, "You are in serious trouble, you stupid ass! Your mate has just confessed. He said you led him to commit the crimes, that you were the mastermind, and that he was just following you. He will get a light sentence and you will be carrying the can, you fool!"

Bo's facial muscles tightened but other than that he did not react. He was considering in his mind whether The Tall One was just making up the story. He could not believe Jie had betrayed him. They had been buddies since he left school and started touting in the streets, always sharing with each other the same hawking spaces and the same merchandise. He always knew Jie was worldly and did not care about other people, but never thought Jie would betray him. He was Jie's only friend.

At this point, The Tall One, sensing the need to pile on the pressure, said to Bo casually, "Your mate can now choose which of the two movie stars he wants to fuck."

A loud shriek from Bo pierced the walls of the room. The thought of what his tormentor had just said completely floored him. He was now shaking uncontrollably. He could not bear the thought of Jie poking into his beloved Liu Mei and squeezing every part of her soft heavenly body.

After suffering through these vile images which were flashing relentlessly through his head, Bo finally asked The Tall One, "If I do confess to the crime I did not commit, what is the maximum sentence?"

"I agree," gritting his teeth, Bo finally said to The Tall One. "But I have one request. I would like a wash and a change of clothing before I see her."

Bo was led into another room after his shower. He was given new clothes to wear. The room he now found himself in was more spacious and there was a rolled up bed at the corner. The light came in through a double window about ten feet from the ground. A double window was rare for a custodial cell.

There was a tray on the table with a pot of jasmine tea and a sweet sesame pudding. "That's for you," The Tall One pointed at the tray and said, "My staff will prepare the confession for you to sign." So saying, The Tall One left the room.

Bo gobbled down the sesame pudding quickly and started to drink his tea. The smell of the scented white tea leaves was to him particularly fragrant. The shower had relaxed Bo. The dry new clothes he was given fitted quite well and he liked the material of the beige color shirt and dark blue trousers. The soft cotton fabric felt good next to his young body.

Bo's mind now drifted back to the past. To his middle school, 401 High.

It was a sultry summer's day. The sun was at its most intense and the air smelled of wild flowers in full bloom. It should have been a very lazy, easy day. But his school had chosen this day to hold its annual Sports Meet at the stadium next to the hill that was covered in shrubs, short grass and very thin surface soil that was ready to give way in the unusually dry weather that year.

The whole school was there. And Liu Mei was there. Her tall and handsome boyfriend Fu Jing, he with the angular jaw and chiseled nose, was running in the 200-metre and 400-metre races. Because Fu was the tallest boy in the school and the head prefect, everybody called him King. And this was a happy day for King. He had won both the 200 and 400 meter events in record-breaking times and was the hero of many young boys' and girls' dream. Liu Mei had been cheering King at the top of her voice. She was radiant in the sunlight and jumping up and down with gay abandon, sweat coming through her pearly skin and her head of silky hair, which was tied into a pony tail at the back with a simple red ribbon. The curves of her young body were showing through even in her white school uniform. Every young student's eyes were on Mei and King, the Golden Couple of 401 High.

Then the last competition of the day – the Main Event – was announced. This was not any track-and-field contest but mountain-climbing followed by downhill racing and was only open to the winners of the day's other competitions. The starting point was at the far end of the stadium which backed onto the hill where the climb was to begin. This was where Liu Mei was now standing. King was favorite to win and knew it. Bo was too short and was at first pushed to the back. But he managed to edge his way forward through the crowd until he could see where his Mei was standing. She and her friends were at the centre of the front row.

The competing athletes, all in white and all of them male, had already gathered at the foot of the hill. They were told to position themselves for the sound of the starting pistol. The bang, when it came, was short and loud. As soon as they heard, the competitors shot forward and rushed up the hill, young and nimble bodies in the prime of their lives. King easily took the lead in the first hundred meters but was unable to shake off the others as the climb got higher and steeper, and the grass more slippery and treacherous. By the time King was half way up the hill, his hard trials at the two former track-and-field events were getting to him and he was slowing down. He could not turn fast enough at the top of the hill, lost his balance, slipped and fell. It was then that the two shorter, younger boys from behind got ahead of him. When the descent started, he was in number three position, in spite of all the cheering from the stadium that was rooting for the school's head prefect. "King Fu! King Fu! King Fu!" he heard them shout his name. "Come on, King! Come on, King!" Bo only heard Mei's voice calling, over and above the din of the crowd's chaotic shouting that was coming from all directions.

King didn't want to lose. He thought he could not lose. But he was now clearly behind. At the last descent, King was a good five or six feet from the two boys in front of him. He decided to do the impossible. Instead of just sweeping down on top of the grass and sliding his way along, he attempted to do a jump of twelve feet, hoping this would land him in front.

It was a stupid thing for him to have done. The pain of a breaking ankle transmitted right through his body and he let out several sharp cries. He had fallen heavily and couldn't get up again. The whole assembled crowd gave a loud roar of disbelief as the King crumpled in front of their eyes. Liu Mei darted forward and rushed to where King was, panting and crying on the sand and obviously in great pain.

She hugged and squeezed him in tears, the dirt and sweat now on both their faces, and blood coming out of his badly scratched knees and elbows. It was chaotic and it was heart-breaking – for the young couple who had been triumphant only half an hour ago. It was also heart-breaking for Bo. The ambulance team took King out of the stadium on a stretcher. Mei was crying out loud and was inconsolable. Her classmates led her away, as Bo watched from ten feet away, not knowing what to do.

Bo could not sleep that night. He slipped out of the workers' apartment after his mother had gone to bed and went walking along the banks of the lake. The cries of the cicadas were loud and insistent; they were pleading for the bodies of their mates in the hot summer night. The poor creatures' life span is short; they live all of fifty days before they die in the blast of the summer heat, some without passing on their DNAs. The macho male frogs that had lined up on the fringe of the lake were also at their most clamorous at this time of the year. Their ugly croaking was everywhere, orchestrating with the cicadas a cacophonous spring symphony late into the night. But nature can be cruel; it often arouses expectations but denies their fulfillment.

The sound of a cluster of frogs hopping into the lake was breaking up Bo's confused and scattered thoughts. He was just wandering around the lake now, lost and aimless, without any idea of where he was going. Bo was unprepared for such a turn of events at the Sports Meet and felt deeply disappointed for Mei. He so wanted King Fu to win the last trophy. Not for himself, but for her – his idol, his dreamboat, his teenage goddess.

Bo could not bear to see Mei cry. The tears that were streaming down her face went straight into his own broken heart and drenched it in brine. The pain was excruciating, much worse than anything he had experienced before. Lost in thought and without knowing it, he had waded into the lake and was waist high in the water. The cold water felt good. He needed something to cleanse his own suffering, so he went further and further out. It never occurred to him that he could not swim, until the mud and rocks under him suddenly gave way and he was totally submerged in water. He tried to turn and head back and moved his hands frantically. But it was no good. He had landed at the bottom of the lake. The rocks were slippery and the mud between them was trapping his feet. And he could not even keep his body straight.

A flash of his dead father's face moved across Bo's mind, admonishing him to look after his mother who had a serious heart condition. "You must be strong and brave, My Son. Your mother needs constant care. I can only count on you now." Recalling his father's dying words again, he suddenly woke up to the challenge of living and his instincts took charge. Bo held his breath and, one small step at a time, clawed his way back towards shore, exhausted and panting, with water in his mouth, nostrils, windpipe, and stomach, and mud all over his body. But he survived.

At school the next day, everybody was talking about the ankle-breaking incident at the last event of the Sports Meet. Bo had positioned himself at a corner of the school's basketball court to try and catch a glimpse of Liu Mei as she walked past. He had done this many times before. His beloved Mei would always be coming out of her classroom at recess time with two classmates on either side of her and walk across the court to the tuck shop opposite. On this day, however, Mei's two classmates came out with only each other, but without Mei. Disappointed at not being able to see her again and at not being able to find out how she was, Bo decided to cut class and left school early. On his way home and walking alone, Bo wandered out of habit into the flower garden next to a long and gentle slope by the side of a hill.

This place held special memories for him. Bo remembered walking into the azalea woods here one day some three months ago, looking for a quiet place to read the classic swashbuckling novel *The Water Margin*. The porous *Taihu* rocks with their see-through potholes made this an ideal site for playing imaginary bandits and swordsmen. It was late March and the dry winds from the north had finally given way to a welcome breath of warm and humid air from the ocean. The flowering season was late that year but had by now started in earnest, and the trees were heavy with pink blossoms. The chirping of the birds and the flapping of the butterflies made this Bo's favorite spot to lose himself in a fanciful reading of the exploits of Song dynasty outlaws. Being slight of build himself, he had a special fondness for the little yellow butterflies that are so light and deceptive they could rest on the tree leaves, close their wings and become part of the floral tapestry.

Bo picked a spot behind a big Chinese cypress and had just started his reading of Song dynasty intrigues when he heard a girl giggling, from somewhere deep inside the woods. Bo's curiosity was roused; he closed his book and, with body half-bending for fear of being discovered, tiptoed his way forward and followed the giggling sound into the overgrown shrubs. By this time, a male voice had taken over. When he heard it, Bo started slowing down. For he knew from morning assembly whose voice it was, and he could guess who the couple were. The skirt of a woman in school uniform was protruding from behind a rock and a man's trousers were pressed tight against the pleats.

Bo moved sideways to a place behind a big tree which afforded a better view and which gave him some hiding space.

He then arched his neck forward for as long as it would go. And as he did so, he saw, stretched out behind a big piece of *Taihu* rock, the interlocking bodies of Liu Mei and King Fu. Mei was now pushing King's hand away from her naked breasts and buttoning her blouse. He was smirking and she was blushing, pink as the azaleas around her. A crow flew past and gave out a cry. King turned and thought he saw a face disappear behind a tree. He quickly stood up and pulled Mei up with him, and they rushed away in the opposite direction to where Bo was hiding.

When the silence of the woods was restored and the place felt empty again, Bo came out from behind his tree and walked over to where the lovebirds were frolicking. He surveyed their love-nest in scrupulous detail to look for any trace of her belongings. He did not find any. Disappointed, he started his walk home. The novel of bandits and heroes no longer held any interest for him. For a very, very long time thereafter, that image of Mei, radiant in the white school uniform, with her rosy cheeks, her full and naked bosom, and the bounce of her body as she ran across the grass in quick retreat, were firmly implanted in Bo's head. His young eyes saw poetry in everything she did. She was the object of the young boy's burgeoning desire.

Bo went back to the azalea woods the next day and for three whole weeks thereafter, always at roughly the same time in late afternoon, always hoping to catch another glimpse of the Golden Couple and watch another scene of love-play. The area where they had installed themselves was marked by a big piece of *Taihu* rock and was well hidden behind the azaleas. He knew exactly where to look and wait. But he never saw what he wanted to see again.

School ended shortly after the Sports Meet. King Fu missed his final examination because of his injury and left school to find work in Hangzhou. Liu Mei, affected by all the trauma and worrying, did not do well in her exams, and never returned. There were rumors she had gone to Hangzhou to look for King. By mid July, everybody had left school for the summer. Bo and his classmates dispersed.

When school re-started in the autumn, the Golden Couple was not there anymore. Busy bodies would gossip from time to time about what happened to Mei and King after they went to the big city. Some said they were living together. Some said they had gone their separate ways. In Bo's young mind, there was only this one image of Mei among the blooming azaleas, a sweet, beautiful young girl in her radiant early splendor.

A few years later, when Bo was himself old enough to compete in the senior Sports Meet, he heard the Headmaster announce, just before the 400 meters event, that Fu Jing, a famous alumnus and former head prefect who still held the school record for the fastest 200 meters, had died in a cycling accident. He was only twenty-two.

There was no mention of Liu Mei. She was an average student and held no official position in the student body. Bo learned from other students that she had somehow found her way to Shanghai. But nothing more was known about her until Bo saw her again inside Assistant Commissioner Rong's mansion that evening.

B o was not the only one whose mind drifted back to the past that afternoon. David Han, alone in his hotel room and looking out at the garden in the spring drizzle, saw in flashes his sadly estranged relationship with his younger sister. Somehow the contours of that relationship appeared more clearly now that Carol was dead and he was stricken by his own pangs of regret. To friends and members of their extended family, David and Carol had a normal brother-sister relationship. Only he knew they had not been close. And it was more his fault than hers.

With family ties being regarded as so important in the Chinese culture, it is no surprise that Chinese guilt is often family induced. Unlike the feelings of guilt and shame in Christian and Jewish communities which spring largely from sex and religion, Chinese guilt and shame usually come from not having repaid one's debt to one's parents or siblings, or from having failed one's children. And David Han, the distinguished professor of humanities and author of two thick volumes on culture and behavior, knew this only too well.

There are not many engaging stories of brother-sister relationships in Chinese literature. But one that is required reading for Chinese intellectuals, and one which David Han knew by heart, was the famous Qing dynasty scholar Yuan Mei's obituary for his younger sister. This great literary work was a cry from the heart which laid bare the writer's inconsolable remorse when his sister died before he could make his way back to her death bed. This was what's haunting David Han now and pounding on his troubled soul. In the privacy of his room, as David seeped his tea slowly and hurt quietly, images of his sister and the very limited times they had together as children and as grown-ups were coming back to him. This stream of memories of things past was racing relentlessly through his mind.

David did not know Carol well, not only because of the ten-year age difference between them, but also because he had left home early. At eighteen, he was already a boarder at the University of Hong Kong and, soon after graduation, had gone to London for postgraduate studies when his sister was just getting into secondary school. When he returned to Hong Kong after getting his doctorate, followed by several years of teaching in England, David had become a stranger to his only sibling. England had changed not only the way he dressed and the way he talked, but also the way he thought. His sister, on the other hand, in demeanor and everyday habits, was typical of "the locals" in Cantonese-speaking Hong Kong. David did not read gossip magazines, which happened to be Carol's favorite source of information. He did not care about movie stars' scandalous lives or the conspicuous consumption of the idle rich, which somehow fascinated his younger sister and her friends. David had no interest in following popular trends and did not watch Chinese television at all, because he found the entertainment programs formulaic and the news coverage parochial. Apart from Cantonese food, he no longer liked most things Chinese. After coming back to Hong Kong, David was mixing with a different crowd that was essentially English-speaking, and he had stopped seeing most of his secondary school friends. There was more than a generational gap between brother and sister. By this time, there was a cultural gap as well.

One reason why brother and sister did not see each other more often was because Carol did not like her sister-in-law Dora, who came from a well-to-do, Westernized Hong Kong family and who did not show the kind of respect a Chinese daughter-in-law is expected to have for her husband's widowed mother. The only concession Dora made to Chinese tradition was to address David's mother as Mom. In all other respects, he might just as well have married an English girl, because his wife showed no deference towards his mother and made no attempt to please her. David did not see a need to change Dora's cool demeanor and occasional brusque manners. But Carol was quietly critical. She never told her elder brother she harbored such antipathy. Neither did she talk to him much about her own husband. But she was really not happy that David did not make any serious effort to get to know Andrew, who was a down-to-earth accountant with a lot of common sense but not a lot of intellectual curiosity. David found Andrew dull, matter-of-fact and unenlightened.

When brother and sister met for family dinners at their mother's flat, David would be embarrassed when old Mrs. Han heaped loads of food on his bowl, always giving him the choicest parts of the steamed chicken, while leaving the less fancied white meat for his sister. He knew that was the Chinese mother's way of showing love and affection. But he saw this as outright discrimination and secretly cringed when this was done to him, even though he was the beneficiary.

On one occasion, at a Chinese New Year's Eve dinner which David's wife Dora skipped because she was skiing with friends in Hokkaido, David decided to tell his mother she should stop giving him preferential treatment. "Mom, please don't do this. Please eat the drumstick yourself. I know you like it."

"I can cook this for myself any time I want. But you come home so rarely these days... I made this especially for you... you used to like drumsticks when you were little. I remember that."

"Yes, but what about Carol? You should leave her a piece too. Why give me both drumsticks?"

"Carol had her share when you were living in London. Carol doesn't mind not eating the drumsticks. Do you now, Carol?"

At which point Carol could only shake her head and say, "No, Mom, I don't mind."

David could press on but decided against it. He knew his mother would be upset if he did not take this demonstration of parental love graciously. He was not sure Carol really did not mind. He knew that traditional Chinese upbringing for a daughter would have conditioned her to accepting this kind of behavior as normal. Nonetheless, it offended David's Anglo-Saxon sensibilities and his innate sense of fair-play.

Very occasionally, Carol would let out an off-hand complaint about her husband Andrew, who had a fondness for horse-racing but little interest in travelling which Carol loved. David, however, would never go to her with any of his problems. He was the elder brother after all. He had to keep up the appearance that he was doing well in his career and in his marriage and was very much in control of his life. David never told Carol anything about the demons he harbored, that he was trapped in a quarrelsome relationship with his wife, that he suffered from this mortal fear that he had not fulfilled his early promise, and that he had failed to live up to their parents' expectations.

And when their mother died, brother and sister had a big row over the funeral arrangements. David was baptized and became a Catholic when he was in secondary school, but his mother and sister were Buddhists, and Carol knew their mother would want a Buddhist service with monks chanting and the burning of paper offerings dedicated to the dead. David always found Chinese funerals with their Buddhist rites, loud music and public grieving, distasteful and did not want any of this for their mother. But Carol insisted – strongly. She told David on no account must he disregard their mother's dying wish. It was the first and only time she stood up to her elder brother.

"If you don't want to pay for the monks, I will," Carol said to David, the expression on her distressed face and the tone of her voice both indicated she was digging her heels in.

"It's not the money, Carol. I just hate Chinese funerals which are like social events, with people coming and going and exchanging pleasantries, even name cards, in the midst of the monks' chanting and the paper burning. They have really no respect for the occasion or the dead. And the Chinese funeral music is something I just cannot stand. It is way too loud, almost bombastic, much too intrusive, even offensive, when all I want to do is grieve in private and get it over with."

"And that's all you care about, is it? Get it over with? We owe it to our mom to give her an elaborate funeral, after what she's done for us. Especially you, David, you were her favorite all these years. If you don't know it, I do."

As had happened in so many Chinese families before, brother and sister got into a prolonged argument. All the pent-up frustration and grievances over the years finally burst open, now that the matriarch who had kept sibling differences under wraps and who had held the family together was no longer there to mediate.

David abhorred Chinese funeral parlors for a reason. Unlike churches in England which host all kinds of family events like christenings, weddings and funerals, Chinese funeral parlors exist exclusively for funerals. And David never liked going there even when he was a child. On one such visit when he was just six years old, he had the unfortunate and horrifying experience of coming out of the lift in a Chinese funeral parlor and bumping his head against a corpse which was being wheeled out of cold storage into the make-up room. David had nightmares for months after that and had been dreading Chinese funerals ever since. But this time, at the insistence of his sister and with the greatest reluctance on his part, he had to stand in attention at the Hong Kong Funeral Parlor to greet and then return bows to the mourners who had come to pay their last respects. The Buddhist funeral was long and elaborate, and Carol was so overcome with grief that Andrew had to prop her up with his body. David himself was stoical; he never shed a tear. He had learned from the British and he had learned it well. He had developed the stiff upper lip as well as the stiff upper body.

In fact, David Han was the typical Chinese version of Ivan Turgenev's "marginal man" – an intellectual who knew what he wanted to do but was quite unable to actually do anything. He had read a lot of Russian literature and some echoes of the Russian soul have found their way into his being. In outward appearance, David Han was like an over-educated English gentleman, but inside his diffident exterior lived the archetypal Russian hero who thought a lot and knew a lot, who felt very strong emotions running through his body, who was often indignant about many things, especially the injustices of this world and the fatal deficiencies in the Chinese culture, but who was not really doing anything about any of it. He was ultimately just a thinker and not a doer.

The mind is a lonely drifter. When David thought about Carol now, the scene that stuck out and what really hurt was when he left her standing in the scorching sun in the cemetery at Pokfulam one grave-sweeping day two years ago.

After their mother died, brother and sister only saw each other at irregular intervals. Arrangements to meet were always haphazard and last minute. But not when it came to grave-sweeping, because this gathering had always been sacrosanct for the Han family. Chinese tradition mandates at least two such outings a year – the Spring Grave Sweeping and the Autumn Grave Sweeping. On this occasion, although he had the date and time marked in his diary, David had been working late on an academic paper the night before and could not get up in time to join his sister at the appointed hour. Even though it was early autumn, the day was particularly hot, more like an Indian summer, and graveyards in Hong Kong offer no overhead cover, not even a decent tree with enough shade to block out the relentless sun.

Their parents' grave was quite a long walk up the slope of the cemetery and several places to the left of the centre aisle. Because David was late, Carol had to wait for him, as by family tradition the elder son always made the first bow to the departed ancestors. And she waited more than half an hour in the sun, without even so much as a hat to protect her. She never expected him to be so late. The flowers she had bought were put into the stone vase at the graveside and water had been poured into it. The grave was already swept clean. She had made sure of that by clearing away the last scattered leaves herself. But there was no sign of David, and Carol could do nothing except wait for her elder brother to show up. She tried calling him on her hand-phone but there was no answer. If his phone was out of battery, Carol knew, this would not be for the first time. When David finally appeared on the scene in late morning, close to noon time, sweat was coming down her face and her blouse was soaked through, as was her handkerchief. He had somehow forgotten that Carol's husband had died and was cremated just a few months ago, and that, for the first time, there would be no one with her at grave-sweeping if he did not turn up.

Memories do not follow logical progression in time. Sequences of events surface in the brain as and when they please. David now painfully regretted not having seen his sister more, or helped her when she needed help and had summoned up enough courage to ask for it from her own brother. In Chinese family relationships, money always comes up somehow.

About four years before the grave-sweeping episode, Carol had called David one day and asked to see him at lunch at the end of the week. When they met, and after ordering food, Carol said to David, "Property prices are going through the roof this year. The 1997 issue appears to have been resolved and most people have turned positive about Hong Kong's future under Chinese sovereignty. Andrew and I do not own the apartment we are living in. But we think we must buy something now or we would miss the boat forever. So we have... er... we have identified a property, a good-size apartment in Happy Valley and we want to make an offer. But we are short by about a quarter of a million dollars for the down payment. Can you lend us the money, do you think?"

David knew he did not have so much ready cash in his own bank account, but he also knew he had the money in a joint investment account he shared with Dora. But this would have meant having to tell his wife, and he knew it would only end up in another fierce quarrel between them. In the Han household, this had been the inevitable outcome every time the finances of David's family came up for discussion, like when he had to pay his mother's hospital bills and his aunt's insurance premiums. Dora's rich parents had taught her that people who borrowed money were to be despised, and Dora always told David that. Their quarrels had become more frequent in the last couple of years, although David really did not like arguing with his wife. He could spend hours debating with his colleagues at faculty meetings and it would not have bothered him an iota. But arguing with Dora was something else, something he tried to avoid, because his wife could be downright insulting and didn't know when to stop.

Past quarrels with Dora were going through David's mind now, and he decided he did not want to talk to her about taking money out of their joint account. After a short but noticeable pause, David looked at Carol earnestly and said, "I'm sorry, but the answer has to be no, because I don't think this is a good idea. Property prices are very toppy now. You won't be getting value for money, and you might not be able to sustain the mortgage repayment if interest rate went up. I can lend you a hundred thousand, but I won't encourage you to buy the flat."

On hearing this response from her only brother, Carol's eyes drooped downwards. She was very quiet after that, didn't say whether she would take the smaller sum or not, but just finished her food quickly, excused herself and left.

David sent Carol a cheque the next day. But she never acknowledged it nor put the money into her bank account. And she did not buy the apartment. Not long after that, property prices in Hong Kong fell dramatically when the whole of Asia went into a tailspin following currency devaluations in Thailand, Malaysia and Indonesia, even Singapore. The Asian financial crisis snared every country in its ferocious sweep. David was glad Carol did not buy the property she had her eyes on. Maybe she was too. But both brother and sister knew that was not the point. He had turned her down on the only occasion she asked for help. Nobody except the two of them knew what transpired, so there was no shame involved, just his own feeling of guilt for having let his sister down. It was three years later that Carol's husband Andrew developed acute leukemia and died within two days of being admitted into hospital.

Carol never recovered from the shock of that loss; her husband was not even forty two when he died. She only saw David three times after that, twice at grave-sweeping and another time at Christmas. She did not know that Dora had started divorce proceedings, because David did not tell her. A year later, in March, when the azaleas were in bloom, she took that fateful trip to the Thousand Island Lake during her school's Easter break.

David Han did not really believe in burning incense for the dead. He never did. He had always regarded this as superstition throughout his adult life. But, notwithstanding that, he went to the Thousand Island Lake of his own volition – to burn incense for his sister in the nether world. It was ironic, he knew, but he just had to do it. Because he thought Carol would have wanted this if she were able to talk to him still. This was the last thing he could do for his sister. It was his act of contrition.

Thoughts of Carol and his own woeful neglect of her when she was alive were now becoming unbearable for David Han. Certain things in his past were just too painful to revisit in his grief. The past was not just a foreign country, the past was irredeemable. The living and the dead could no longer meet; they could not unravel what had been done or left undone. David knew that. But his guilt would not leave him and he decided to take a walk outside the hotel and around the lake, never mind the rain. He was hoping that when the eyes were busy taking in new and soothing images, especially the quietly calming scenes around the West Lake, the memory function of the brain might be able to take a rest.

And so he went downstairs and walked into the light drizzle this part of China has plenty of at this time of the year. It was springtime in Hangzhou, a city whose scenic beauty is long celebrated in Chinese poetry through the ages. David decided against going back and asking for a hotel umbrella; he simply turned up his coat collar and walked on. After he rounded the first corner on the left side of the road, he found, to his mild surprise, Anne Gavin standing by the lake and staring, motionless, into the water, with hotel umbrella in hand.

The air was heavy with humidity. The famous Hangzhou mists were drawing nature's own paintings across the lake, and these reached half way up the ageless mountains beyond. Some of the fleshy magnolias were still blooming with luscious delight. But the azaleas were past their prime. Many of their colorful petals now lay scattered on the dirt, having been beaten loose by the rain at night and stripped from the branches they had embraced the night before. A few stronger ones managed to hold on but now looked pitifully forlorn in their defiance.

As David made his way towards Anne and saw the weepy flowers up close, a line of poetry he had read as an undergraduate crossed his mind. He had imagined those tiny drops of water running down the petals of the magnolias were not just raindrops, he thought they might be tears. For Anne had been crying.

"April is the cruelest month…" David Han muttered the opening line of *The Waste Land* as he approached. He thought he was just talking to himself, but Anne heard.

"T. S. Eliot," said Anne as she turned and wiped away the tears from her face with her bare fingers, "I do love his poetry."

David nodded his head in acknowledgment and continued, "Breeding lilacs out of the dead land, mixing memory and desire." He stopped, lowered his eyes, looked at the wet dirt at his feet but without looking at Anne, and then he said, "How well these lines describe what we are going through… in this rain."

After a short pause, and seeing that Anne seemed to be pondering what he said, David went on with his poetic musing, this time from *The Four Quartets*. "Time past and time present are perhaps both present in time future, and time future contained in time past. That's what it really is, isn't it?… mixing memory and desire," David was talking to himself. "I can see it clearly now. Memory is time past, and desire is time future, the two of them connected by the conjunction 'and', which is time present – *the here and now* – the link between our past and our future. And so, here we are, in the middle of the journey, neither going forward nor moving back, but not really still either, and 'do not call it fixity', as Eliot says, just drifting, lost…"

"Between two shores," Anne turned her face up to look at David. She had woken up from her own unhappy thoughts and finished the sentence for him. "Lost between an end and a beginning. I have lost my husband and you have lost your sister, and we are not even sure how they died. There is no closure…" so saying, she lowered her head again. Tears were rolling down her face once more and she reached into her handbag for a handkerchief.

"We are trying to find out. That's why you and I are here. For us there is only the trying, I'm afraid," David said quietly.

"Yes, I suppose." Anne dried out her tears and began to stroke the petals of a white and purple magnolia that had been in her right hand all this while.

Seeing her doing this, David recalled a line of Chinese poetry which had been etched in his mind, and he started reciting this slowly, as if talking to himself, *"Lin hua xie le chun hong, tai cong cong ."* And seeing that Anne did not understand what he was saying, David quickly provided a translation. "I just said 'The flowers had bade farewell to Spring, and it was much too soon.' This is the first line of a Chinese poem. I am sorry for switching to Chinese."

"I don't read Chinese, which is a shame, I know, so I cannot share the sentiments of this poem you were referring to. I am told, though, by Victor, that many of the best Chinese lyrical poems are about friends parting or love lost, opportunities missed because a wrong turn was taken, bad choices in life which, having been made, become irredeemable, the very thing in Eliot's poetry. Isn't that so?"

"Yes, that is so." David affirmed. "For grief and loss, nothing plucks at the heart strings more poignantly than Chinese poetry."

"It must be fascinating," Anne said to David, "to be able to move so effortlessly between two cultures." As she said this, Anne started to walk back in the direction of the hotel, and David followed her. He also took her umbrella in hand and held it over her head.

"I was lucky. I studied the Chinese classics and Chinese poetry as a young man because my father forced me to. We came from a family of classical scholars before we became impoverished gentry. And then at eighteen, I rebelled and decided to do European History and English Lit, not Chinese Literature, at university – because I was engrossed in Thomas Hardy's novels. I completely shared his view that character is destiny and that God is indifferent to our sufferings. Well, my sister's death just confirmed that for me one more time."

"I read a lot of Hardy myself. Which of his books do you like best?" asked Anne.

"Oh, *The Mayor of Casterbridge*, by far! That was what convinced me that English literature can be every bit as deeply moving and profoundly touching as Chinese literature. I saw in Michael Henchard, the Mayor, the shadow of my own father who was hard-working, fair-minded, and deeply loving in his own way, but somehow could not see the grievous mistakes he was making and the harm he was causing to the people around him."

There was a long moment of silence after that as the two continued their walk. Both David and Anne were aware that he had just revealed himself to her. Anne felt emboldened by the personal nature of what David had just said and decided to ask him a personal question. And so she began, "Lyndon Johnson once said, 'A man is either living up to his father's expectations or making up for his father's mistakes'. Would that describe you too?"

"Yes, I think so…" replied David hesitatingly and, after a pause, finished his sentence, "except that I am trying to do both – to live up to my father's expectations and make up for my father's mistakes – but probably not very successfully." He turned slightly to look at Anne but without breaking stride. And he continued, "It was kind of you to suggest that I move effortlessly between two cultures, as if I had the best of both worlds. But the flip side of that is I often find myself falling between two stools. You know, not being good enough in either language, and not being accepted by either people. The British eye me with suspicion because I know how they think and argue – their speech-making tricks and their clever play on words – and I often catch them out. The Chinese regard me with distrust because I do not worship at the altar of Chinese civilization and Chinese culture but instead point out, when I see good reasons to, that the Chinese way is not the *only* way, and that sometimes the Chinese way is not even the *best* way. But I think I had already told you that."

"I hadn't realized being bicultural has its complications. I didn't know there was this dark side and that it had not been easy for you."

"It has its compensations. And most of that lies in literature – to be able to read the poet Li Po and *The Story of the Stone* in Chinese and to be able to read T S Eliot and Thomas Hardy in English. What really fired the imagination of my teenage mind was when I came across this description of Michael Henchard's wife in *The Mayor of Casterbridge*. Thomas Hardy described her as a woman who believed 'though one could be gay on occasions, moments of gaiety were interludes, and no part of the actual drama'. It is so well phrased. It described perfectly my own sorry predicament as a lost and emotionally insecure nineteen-year-old who had a great time at university and who didn't want those days to end, but who knew he would have to leave the Garden of Eden when he graduated."

"I think we all went through that at our last year in university. We really didn't want to leave, "Anne said.

"Ah, yes, didn't we all?" David nodded his head in nostalgic agreement and went on with what he really wanted to say. "But for this student of literature," he said, "what made such a discovery particularly satisfying was that it brought to mind a line of poetry which the Chinese poet Li Po penned. Li wrote, in one of his most famous poems, 'the lightness of being is like a dream in which moments of gaiety are ever so fleeting'. Reading these two lines together, you can see that somehow there was this communion of souls between two poets who lived four thousand miles apart and separated by eleven centuries. I found this enthralling!"

"I see what you mean. I do share your joy of discovery, and I am full of admiration."

Excited and speaking with his hands as much as his mouth now, David continued, "When I read Hardy, I find echoes of Chinese poetry; and sometimes when I read Chinese poetry, I feel the resonance of English literature. I once wrote about the joy of empathetic poetic imageries in a seminar I gave. I called it 'English chimes, Chinese echoes'. The double alliteration may sound affected, I know, but it does sum up what I wanted to say."

"I can see how exciting this must be for you. You are all animated. Your students must love attending your lectures."

"I'm not sure they do actually. They call me 'Earnest Han'. That's the name they gave me behind my back after I taught them *The Importance of Being Earnest*. In their book, being earnest is not a compliment, you know, not to today's generation of young people. I'm not really getting through to them. I feel like Father McKenzie in The Beatles' song *Eleanor Rigby*. I am just 'writing the words of a sermon that no one will hear'. That's right, that's me. 'Ah, look at all the lonely people.' And I am really one of them."

At the mention of lonely people, Anne's dark mood was taking over again, and she just said to David, "I think Eliot is right. April *is* the cruelest month. There's nothing for us to do here except wait and wait and wait."

David, who really wanted company and who was looking for a way to relieve his own dark mood, said to her, "If you don't mind walking in the drizzle, I can take you to do a little bit of sight-seeing, er, to take your mind off the boredom of waiting."

"Oh, what is there to see?"

"Well, there's a rather famous Buddhist temple, and there is a very famous tomb of a Song Dynasty general who was wrongfully accused of treason by a jealous Prime Minister, and sentenced to death by the Emperor."

"I have seen Chinese temples but never seen a traditional Chinese tomb. I wonder what that's like. Shall we go there?"

"Yes, of course. And instead of a Chinese temple, let me take you to the grand old mansion of China's richest businessman in the last dynasty."

"He lived here? In Hangzhou?"

"The richest businessman lived here. The richest man lived in Beijing. He was the Emperor."

The tomb of General Yue Fei of China's Song dynasty which ended with the Mongol invasion in AD 1279 was to Anne quite a disappointing historical site. It consisted of a large, roundish mound several feet high and covered in grass, with a rather narrow plaque by way of a tombstone. The inscription was straightforward, no more than ten Chinese characters from top to bottom. In the rain and with just a handful of visitors, the place felt deserted and forlorn. Anne and David had more than half the courtyard to themselves.

The few locals who entered the compound after Anne and David would step up to the tomb, bow, linger a while, then turn away and walk about ten paces out, to two figures in bronze who were kneeling side by side in the direction of General Yue's resting place. The two figures were those of a middle-aged man in mandarin garb and a middle-aged woman. They were positioned behind an iron fence of about three feet so as to keep them out of reach of passers-by. The local Chinese visitors, having paid their respects to General Yue, would walk over and spit at the two kneeling figures. And if they missed, some would spit again, until the saliva hit its intended targets.

"What is that?" Anne asked David, pointing her index finger at the two pitiful little figures kneeling on the dirt.

"That's the Prime Minister who had falsely accused General Yue Fei of treason before the Emperor and had him beheaded. The woman next to him was the Prime Minister's wife."

"I'm sorry, but you will have to give me the full story behind this," said Anne.

"Well, it's a story not unlike the story of Richard the Lionheart and his loyal knight Ivanhoe. I'm sure you're familiar with that." Anne nodded her head and David continued. "Except that in this Chinese version, it ended tragically for the loyal knight." David began the long story known to every Chinese schoolboy.

"The Eighth Emperor of the Song dynasty was on a personal crusade to crush the Manchurians who were plundering and marauding at the northeast frontier. Unfortunately, he was captured in battle and the Manchurians demanded a hefty ransom for his return. While negotiations were going on, the Prime Minister put the Emperor's son on the throne and brought in General Yue to secure the northern border. The Prime Minister never expected the General, who had been sidelined until then, would win one victory after another against the barbarians. But this was what General Yue did. In fact, he not only beat back the invaders, but was soon taking the war to the Manchurians and threatening their home base. To the Prime Minister and the substitute Emperor, however, General Yue was threatening much more than that. They were afraid he was going to bring back the Eighth Emperor and, with it, a full Restoration. Now fearful that he might be accused of conspiracy – for not paying the ransom and for putting the prince on the throne – the Prime Minister persuaded the Young Emperor to order General Yue to halt his advance on the enemy and return to court. The good general at first refused, sensing ultimate victory against the Manchurians might be at hand. But when the Emperor's orders got more and more frenzied, he relented and came back to the capital, whereupon he was promptly disarmed, thrown into jail and put on trial for treason – for disobeying imperial orders!"

"And was there no one in the Emperor's court to defend him? I mean the General was clearly the man of the hour," asked Anne.

"None," replied David, "did anybody defend Thomas More? No! And so, General Yue was sentenced to be beheaded." David paused for breath, and then, sensing that Anne was in the mood to listen, he continued. "On the day of General Yue's execution, when the executioner stripped him of his sweatshirt before the beheading, the assembled crowd gave out a huge, collective gasp that was so loud it became a roar which echoed around the square – the people saw on the General's bare back a large tattoo made up of four Chinese characters. And the characters read, "My life for my country". China's history books record that the tattooed characters were inscribed by the good general's own mother before she enlisted him in the army. That was the way she had brought up her son – to devote himself to the service of his country, which was what he had done. But that was not good enough for the Emperor who wanted personal loyalty and personal allegiance – to himself! They all did. And so it is to this day. Opposition to the Communist Party leader and his policies, even if this is in the bigger interest of the country, is regarded as subversive and must be summarily stamped out. General Yue was really not guilty of treason, but he was convicted of it nonetheless. And it was mostly the Prime Minister's doing. That's why he is kneeling there now – for posterity to spit at."

"Wow! That's a very powerful story, a very powerful cautionary tale," said Anne, "And what happened to the Emperor, er, I mean the prince who became Emperor. Should he not share the blame too? You know, for ordering the execution of the general?"

"In the Chinese culture, the top man rarely gets blamed. Someone else usually takes the blame for him. In this case, it was the Prime Minister and his wife," replied David.

"So in this Chinese version of the story…"

Anne had just started on her sentence when David interrupted her, "No, it is not a story; this really did happen. It is our history. Except now that Manchuria had become an integral part of China courtesy of the Qing Dynasty, the Manchurians are no longer referred to as barbarians. They had brought Manchuria onto China's territorial map and extended China's borders all the way to Vladivostok – this was really 'Cleopatra's dowry' in a manner of speaking – and as a result of that, Manchurians are now brethrens of the Han Chinese.

The account of General Yue's death, therefore, has had to be re-written in less rousing, less heroic terms."

"Alright then," said Anne, "so history had to be re-written, but the fact of the matter was that Ivanhoe was beheaded, Richard the Lionheart never returned, and King John stayed on the throne. Was that it? So what happened to the Magna Carta then? Was there a Magna Carta? "

"There was never any Magna Carta in our history, if you're referring to the idea of 'no taxation without representation' which the English nobles forced King John to accept and which is generally taken as the beginning of Britain's constitutional monarchy and representative government."

"No?"

"No." David was absolutely firm on this point. "It was not until the end of the nineteenth century, after almost five thousand years of absolute, dynastic rule, that a group of liberal-minded Chinese scholars started advocating the idea of a constitutional monarchy as the cure for the country's ills. This was called The Hundred Days Reform and it was really late in the day too. But the Empress Dowager of the Qing Dynasty would have none of it. Six of the leading instigators were rounded up and beheaded in public. And that was that. Constitutional monarchy and democracy have no roots in China. All that we've had, all that we've ever had for five thousand years are absolute monarchies, military dictatorships, and populist communism."

"That may change over time, no?" Anne was echoing the line her late husband Victor had been taking when he tried to convince her he should check out the New China this many years after its doors re-opened in 1979. "Why, in Eastern European countries," she continued, "once the communist parties were removed from power, free elections and democracies have taken over and some of these have even applied to join the European Union."

"Ah, but that's Europe," said David Han with a deep sigh and a shake of his head. He looked dejected. Despair was in his voice and also in his eyes. "In Europe you have a continent that had gone through the intellectual transformation brought on by the Renaissance, the Reformation and the Enlightenment. Among Europeans, you have the long-standing tradition of Christianity, liberalism, respect for the rule of law, respect for intellectual discourse and debate, so that after you removed the top soil of absolutist communist rule, what was underneath it was essentially wholesome, and the seeds of democracy could germinate in the spring rain, starting with Poland, Hungary, and Czechoslovakia. In China's case, if you remove the Communist Party of China, what lies underneath is five thousand years of feudalism and military infighting, ending with the winner taking all. Civilized, rule-based and orderly democracy, pitted against ignorant, brutal populism or no-holds-barred militarism, does not stand a chance. That's why I am not one who believes the demise of communism in China will lead to a Brave New World of democracy and free markets. In fact, quite the reverse," David was adamant now, and he continued, "the demise of communism in China will lead to a long period of civil war, violence and bloodshed, chaos on a grand scale – the Four Horsemen of the Apocalypse, no less. This is the pattern in Chinese history." David stopped here and took in a very deep breath after he had finished.

Anne looked at David but could not find the words or facts to rebut him. She also sensed that what she had just heard might be one of David's well-researched theses, one which he believed in passionately and argued with great intellectual rigor. And so Anne just kept very quiet, turned her head away slightly and continued walking by his side. David also needed a break to collect himself; he was quite exhausted by the vehemence of his own outburst.

The serenity of the West Lake had a strangely calming effect on people who bothered to loiter, breathe in the still air and take in the age-old scenery. This was getting through to Anne and David as they walked along its bank, wet and solitary though it might be. Soon they came upon a quaint little tea house in traditional Chinese wood architecture on the roadside. It had beautifully carved balustrades, frescoes on the ceiling and calligraphy on the wooden walls, and, notwithstanding the colors which were fading, a warm welcoming feel to it. The two walking companions decided to stop for a drink. And so they went in, sat down by the large picture window and ordered the fixed menu of jasmine tea and rice cake.

The drizzly rain had stopped before the tea arrived. As they sipped the fragrant tea, which was much too hot for Anne's taste but not David's, they could see, no more than thirty-five feet out towards the lake, two dogs fighting on the grass at the water's edge. Both were Chinese chows. It started with the small dog quietly enjoying a piece of bone with saliva dripping out of its mouth. The bigger dog appeared from behind and tried to tear the bone away from the little one. They fought ferociously over the piece of bone, with occasional grunts and a lot of animal noises. A group of young kids in their early teens started to gather, with long bamboo sticks in their hands. The small dog was losing the fight and started to back into the water, the bone finally coming out of its mouth and dropping on the ground. The big dog gave several howls of triumph, picked up the bone and made off with the spoil.

As the poor little dog came out of the water, down and defeated, the small boys, all five of them, started shouting abuses at the poor animal and beating it with their sticks. The dog went back into the water to try to escape punishment. But each time it tried to come ashore, the boys would beat it with their sticks, again and again.

Anne was horrified. She wanted David to intercede. Pointing at the boys, she said, "Quick, quick, you must stop them!" David rushed down the steps of the teahouse and started shouting as he did. He shooed the dog's attackers away with several waves of his hands and some very sharp words. After the boys dispersed, the poor little dog was finally able to come out of the water, panting and dejected, and quickly limped off. It looked like it had been hurt by the beating it received from the boys. David came back to his seat, looking serious and grim-faced, He asked for the bill. Before this arrived, Anne asked David why the small boys were doing such a barbarous thing to the hapless animal.

"I think I know why you are asking me this," David said to Anne, "I know you probably would not find American children doing this to little animals without the grown-ups telling them off and warning them never to do it again. I must be honest. There is a cruel, mean streak in some Chinese people. I don't know where it came from. I only know it is there. And it gains the upper hand from time to time to the detriment of our finer instincts, our peaceful nature, and our noble heritage. I am quite ashamed of it." David's head was bowed as he said this and Anne did not know what to do.

The waiter arrived with the bill and broke up the apologetic silence which followed David's last words. After paying the bill which, for just tea and refreshment, was really quite excessive, David looked up and said to Anne, "Let me ask you this, if you don't mind. In Britain, there is a tradition of rooting for the underdog. Would that be true of the United States too?"

"No, not to the same extent, I don't think…" Anne replied.

"Well, in China, people do the opposite. We only cheer on the victor but we spit on the vanquished. The defeated is called 'the dog in the water' and every dog in the water is fair game. You have just seen this cultural norm in action."

"I have, and I feel so sorry for the poor animal. Not only did it lose the piece of bone, it also had to put up with these senseless beatings." Anne said, looking for empathy from his traveling companion. They were getting ready to leave, but David stopped after getting up from his seat. He turned and was looking earnest.

"Unfortunately," he said and he pointed his index finger in the direction of the water, "this kind of behavior is not confined to animals. Beating a man when he is down is also a commonplace occurrence in the world of humans – there is even a Chinese proverb for this. On the one hand, nothing succeeds like success. On the other, the loser not only gets no sympathy, gets no cheer for putting up a good fight, but is even despised for losing. The victor could tease and taunt in his triumph, and the loser is often given short shrift by almost everyone."

"Do you not have the tradition of being 'magnanimous in victory and gracious in defeat'? We were taught to behave in this way from when we were children. A defeated candidate for elected office is expected to call the victor and concede graciously, and the winner is expected to be magnanimous in the way he treats his former challenger. I'm sure you know."

"Yes, I do know. But this is not the Chinese way. We are more likely to beat a guy when he is down. We worship at the feet of the victor on top, but we trash the underdog. The Chinese proverb says, 'A man in disgrace gets a hundred boots in his face'. Have you never heard this?"

"No, I have not. But that's a very cruel thing to do, surely?"

"It is more than cruel. It is at the heart of our inability to change. Let me explain…" David's mouth had become very dry and he took one last sip of the jasmine tea before finally leaving the table with Anne, "Rooting for the underdog gives British politics its self-correcting mechanism. With this kind of political instinct on the part of a discerning electorate, no single political party is able to dominate British politics for long. I remember a conversation I had with a famous British actor called Jeremy Irons when he was in Hong Kong to shoot a film called *The Chinese Box*. This was several years back, before 1997. Over dinner to which we were both invited, Jeremy Irons told me he was going to vote Labour in the next general election, having voted for the Conservatives three times before. When I asked him whether this was because the Tories were not doing a good job, he said not really, but he had to vote Labour this time to preserve a *working* two-party system – to keep the balance in public service appointments, he said, because these were crucially important – and that this was much more important to him than keeping the Conservatives in power…"

Anne was now walking alongside David and was still pondering the wisdom and significance of this interesting anecdote when David added the extra dimension. "In Chinese communities," he said, "this would not happen. In Chinese politics, people only want to back winners. In such situations, the incumbent, with all the powers of office at his disposal, especially the power of patronage, really could not lose. And it's always going to be winner takes all, winner walks tall and loser takes fall. I cannot see how that's going to change. I cannot see how we can change from beating up the underdog to rooting for the underdog. And, without it, it's going to be hard to sustain a two-party system. A one-sided culture, and a people who would rather ingratiate themselves with the people in power, than help the opposition make a comeback, will not give rise to true democracy. A functioning democracy needs a change of government from time to time."

The conversation was now getting too dense for Anne and she needed a distraction. So she asked David, "Did you really have dinner with Jeremy Irons?" Anne had been waiting for an opportunity to pop the question. She had been a fan of the actor since seeing him in the film *The French Lieutenant's Woman.*

"Yes, I did."

"I'm very envious. I would have loved to have met him. What was he like in real life, face to face?"

"He was very well-mannered and very forthcoming in conversation – very easy to talk to. And he listened; he didn't just speak at you as a lot of people tend to do; he was interested in what you had to say. And after dinner he also said good-bye to all the guests around the table, one after the other. He wasn't working his audience or anything like that. He was just being his natural self. He was comfortable in his own skin and I liked that. The women around the table all adored him. And I could see why."

Shortly after that exchange, the two walking companions arrived at the former residence of Hu Xueyan, the richest merchant in China in the mid 19th century until his political patron lost power and his business empire crumpled in its wake. David Han and Anne Gavin paid the entrance fee and walked into the grand reception hall. There were no guides to take them around and they were free to roam along the corridors and look at the many rooms on either side of the passage way.

This complex of interlocking buildings would have been a shining example of a hugely successful businessman's mansion in its day. But it was now deserted, dark and gloomy, even in mid afternoon, and was clearly suffering from lack of proper attention and care. There were rooms aplenty, spacious meeting rooms, receiving rooms, dining rooms, recreation rooms, changing rooms, bedrooms, guest rooms, maids' rooms, toiletry rooms, and one very curious one – a peeping room for Boss Hu to watch his business callers' interaction in secret and to eavesdrop on what they were saying to each other before he came out to greet them in person. This would have been useful in helping Hu Xueyan formulate his own negotiating strategy.

What might have been a grand and splendid mansion then was now damp, dimly lit and rotting away. Some of the wooden floorboards were uneven, and the air smelled of dirt. In the nineteenth century, the Chinese had been lagging far behind in both technology and creature comfort, compared to the fast industrializing West which was being propelled forward by new scientific discoveries and new technology. Inventions like the steam engine and the electric light bulb were fundamentally changing people's lives. The Manchurian dynasty called the Qing reached its zenith during the reign of Emperor Qianlong. He stayed on the throne for sixty years, until 1795, by which time he had become a stultifying presence. After that, it was all downhill for the Manchurian Empire.

Modern-day Chinese MBA students who studied Hu Xueyan's business model for success have found, not to their surprise, that it all boiled down to collusion between big business and government. Hu had an ally in the powerful General Zuo Zongtang. This was a symbiotic relationship which benefitted both parties. General Zuo gave the protection and political muscles Hu needed, and Hu gave Zuo a share of the business profits in return. This worked well for both partners until General Zuo lost favor with the Emperor and was stripped of his power. After that Boss Hu, who had over-leveraged in his business dealings, quickly lost his credit worthiness. His huge business empire came unstuck and collapsed under its own overweight. That same Chinese business model – of collusion between business and government – still holds sway in China today. Things have not changed very much in that regard after more than a hundred and fifty years.

David explained all that to Anne as they walked through the rooms in Boss Hu's mansion and wandered finally into the garden with its famous *Taihu* rocks, made up of porous limestone that looked smooth and delicate because it was full of holes polished by rainwater. Coming out into the soothing natural light again after the suffocating house tour, David asked Anne, "You know what I envied most when I was a student in Britain?"

"No, but please tell me," Anne half smiled and encouraged him not to break stride.

"British people's ancestral homes."

"Oh? Why?"

"Because we don't have these in China any more, not after so many years of war, dislocation and communism. Nobody owns an ancestral home in China. Nobody can point to a home where he grew up, where his father grew up and where his grandfather grew up. Everything's gone up in smoke and destruction. It's all so sad. But it's not just the wars and the fighting either."

"No?"

"No, that's not the full story. The other reason why there aren't ancestral homes in China is because this country never had the rule of law which would have protected the people's private property rights. The emperor had absolute power, and officials acting in the emperor's name could seize, impound and confiscate private property with trumped-up charges. When a small businessman got rich and got noticed, that's when these people would come calling and ask for a share of his profits. There was no legal recourse for the little guy who wanted to resist the bullying. The clever ones simply chose to collude, knowing it was useless to fight against people who wielded power, whether it was the government or the triads. Over the years, we have succumbed to a *triad culture*. This is when a people use force and violence to resolve conflicts, and apply physical threats to intimidate and exact compliance. You still see a lot of that in Chinatowns around the world, even today. Many shops have to pay the triads protection money if they don't want any trouble. In the Chinese language, socialism and gangster-ism share the same characters bar one. Gangster-ism is known as *black socialism.*"

"But, notwithstanding all that, China's businessmen have been able to achieve so much in one generation. How do you account for that?" Anne asked.

"I'd put it down to their innate practical sense, their head for figures, their capacity for hard work and their power of organization. China will soon have Fortune 500 companies of its own that will rival American ones in size and profitability. But with a vital difference. They would be owned by oligarchs, members of the revolutionary families and their networks or extensions. There may be a few outliers but they will be beholden to the Party just like everyone else."

"In that sense, the Chinese might not be very different from the Russians; it's mostly oligarch capitalism." Anne said.

"Ah," David Han continued, "but the Chinese are way ahead of the Russians in terms of their economic development. This is because there is something else which is not generally understood, and which might explain why China's attempt at modernization and economic reforms is surging way ahead of Russia's *perestroika*."

"And what is that?"

"It is the crucial roles the Hong Kong Chinese and overseas Chinese have played in aiding China's economic reforms. You see, the fire of private enterprise and entrepreneurship went out in China after 1949. It was subdued, then suppressed, and finally extinguished. Public ownership and collectivization ruled under Mao Zedong, until the Chairman died and Deng Xiaoping returned to power in 1978. Deng swung open China's doors again after thirty years of isolation and told the world China would now welcome foreign investors. As the world watched and waited, it was the Chinese businessmen in Hong Kong, and later the overseas Chinese, who answered the clarion call. They came back to China with capital, with equipment, management expertise, export orders and their knowledge of world markets. Some also provided scholarships for PRC students to study abroad because, at the time, the Chinese government had no foreign exchange for overseas tuition fees. But most important of all, like the Greek god Prometheus, the Hong Kong businessmen returned the spark of private enterprise to China's long extinct command economy."

"But people credit Deng Xiaoping for making the vital decision to open China's doors and go for economic reforms. Let me ask you this – what exactly were those reforms and why have they made such a huge difference?"

"Well, Deng should take the credit, no question, because he revised Marx. Karl Marx advocated 'From each according to his ability and to each according to his needs'. But Deng said this Marxist teaching merely produced in China a society where everything was backward and stagnant, where there was a lot of poverty and hunger but hardly any economic growth, because people who didn't work hard could still take as much as they needed from the collective pot. Before Deng's reforms in 1979, the standard chant amongst the peasants and workers in Southern China's factories and communes was salutary. They said, 'It's always 36 RMB, whether you work or let work be.' This was meant to be ironic. But to each according to his needs really did not work."

"So what exactly did Deng Xiaoping do?"

"Well, he gave the order that, from here on, it's not going to be 'to each according to his needs', but 'to each according to his contribution', and that meant anyone who produced more would get to keep more. That was the most important change since the founding of the PRC in 1949. That meant a peasant farmer who worked harder and produced more could keep more of his harvest. And it was the same with the workers – they would be paid for performance. The rise in productivity after that was what propelled China forward after 1979. In that year, China's per capita GDP was around US$300. Today, it is many times that and still growing."

"That's an amazing success story. Skyscrapers, first-class highways, modern airports – all of that in less than one generation. As I see it now on this trip, China is on its way to becoming a modern, First World country!"

"Unfortunately, it is just the veneer of modernity, Anne. Underneath it all, China is five thousand years old and still just as feudal. You are looking at quantitative change, not qualitative change. The standard of living has changed, but the culture has not. The Chinese perception of the world is still hierarchical; Chinese society is still tightly controlled; corruption and the abuse of power at every level of government are still rampant; the individual's rights and freedoms are still not being respected; and the judiciary is still not independent. I can name you a long list of what is wrong and why many Chinese people want to leave the country and get hold of a foreign passport."

"What qualitative changes are you looking for before you're convinced that China is now not just a leading economy but may be a leading light in the world?"

"I would go back to the French Revolution – the three things which encapsulated the basic changes the long-suffering French people were asking for in 1789, namely, liberty, equality and fraternity. Two of these concepts do not exist in the Chinese culture. Liberty and equality are alien to the Chinese people, and fraternity is in short supply.'

"I can agree with you about the lack of personal liberties. Many people have told me that the Chinese people are not free to criticize the Communist Party or government policies. But I am surprised you said there is no equality in China. Surely, after so many years of communism, China is now a more equal society than most other countries in this world?" Anne felt compelled to contradict David at this point.

"No, Anne. Throughout China's history, the Chinese as a people have never really embraced the concept of equality. It is ironic, but the Chinese view of the world is still hierarchical, even after all these years of supposed egalitarianism since the founding of the People's Republic of China in 1949. In the Confucian culture, you are either superior or you are inferior; Chinese people really don't treat other people, or even each other, as equals. Superior people are to be revered and inferior people can be kicked around. And that's the way many Chinese bosses treat their junior colleagues and the way many rich Chinese people treat poor ones."

"That's diabolical. It really is. And fraternity? What about fraternity? I see quite a lot of that in Chinese communities around the world," Anne sounded a note of protest.

"Actually, there is not a lot of fraternity either. Because of the intense population pressure and the fierce competition which results from that, it has always been a case of 'every man for himself'. In cultural studies, what we have found is that when an idea does not exist in a particular people's culture, there is no word for it in that people's language. The Chinese do not have a concept called *'noblesse oblige'* – the rich and fortunate among them do not see an obligation to help their poor and less fortunate brethrens. And the Chinese don't have the words for *'enlightened self-interest'*. We have a word for self-interest, for sure, but we don't have the term *'enlightened* self-interest'. The great majority of Chinese people do not subscribe to this idea that you are really helping yourself when you try to help others."

"How can you say that when Hong Kong, a Chinese city, donated the most money of any city, any country in the world, to the Live Aid campaign for Ethiopia some years ago. That's enlightened, surely? Victor was very proud of what Hong Kong people did when he read about it in the newspapers."

"Ah, but that's Hong Kong. Hong Kong people *are* enlightened. I was told this story by a primary school teacher in Hong Kong who really conducted this experiment. She gathered her class of thirty five pupils in a room and gave them a big balloon each, to write their own names on. The balloons were all the same color – pink. Then she led them out of the room and had an assistant change the positions of the balloons that were left behind. When the pupils came back into the room, they were told to find the balloon with their name on it. Pandemonium followed. There was a lot of searching, chasing and shouting and it took forever. The pupils were then led out again – to repeat the same experiment. Only this time, when they came back in, the pupils were told to pick up any balloon and return it to its rightful owner. And this time, it took less than two minutes for all the balloons to get back to their owners. And the moral of the story is: you are really helping yourself when you help other people. You can see from this that Hong Kong's young people are well taught. Hong Kong has the right values. Hong Kong people are enlightened, as I said. It is a modern city in the true sense of the word. I believe it is China's only modern city."

"I wish Victor were here to talk with you. He believed in a new China. He thought the country might have just turned the corner and was poised to take off."

"I would believe that if the Chinese people managed to fix a gaping hole in their political system."

"And what is that?"

"If they can find a peaceful and generally accepted way to manage their political succession – the transfer of power," replied David Han. "In the West, you do this through the ballot box. It is generally peaceful and orderly. You do not have *coups d'etat* and revolutions in the United States and Western Europe. And that is the ultimate strength of democracy. Not so in China. The country may look great now, but it cannot contain the individual ambitions and the self-seeking challenges of the power-mongers who can and will resort to anything to achieve their ultimate goal of taking over the Dragon Throne. And when they pounce, all hell will break loose and China goes back to the jungle again. I never get the sense that the country is really moving forward as a people and as a culture. As individuals, yes, it is possible; and as an economy, that too is possible; but as a people and as a culture? Well, let's just say I have not seen much of it yet, and I would love to be proven wrong, Anne. Nothing would please me more. Seriously."

"Do you not think China can break up like the former Soviet Union did? Or the former Yugoslavia?"

"No, not a peaceful break-up, I don't think that is possible. The break-up of China at the end of every dynasty was always violent. A prolonged civil war followed every major dynastic collapse in Chinese history, because there were no clear leaders after the emperor was overthrown. The incumbent would have made sure no one could command wide support, not even his own heir apparent. Chinese rulers are very insecure people. They see Brutus and Cassius all around them and often strike first before the other party makes his move."

"But Victor told me there had been many peasant uprisings and peasant revolutions in China's long history and it was these that shook up and eventually brought down Chinese dynasties."

"Yes, that was true. Some dynasties fell after peasant uprisings; but more had fallen as a result of military *coups d'état*. I call these two scenarios Brutus and Spartacus. In this day and age, with missiles and nuclear bombs and cyber warfare next, we can really forget about peasant uprisings upending the Communist dynasty. The threat to the current emperor's power lies within his own Party, within his own inner circle. And that is the conclusion China's leaders themselves had drawn after the collapse of the former Soviet Union. They blamed the dissension within the Soviet leadership itself for precipitating the final break-up."

"I am not completely convinced that a spontaneous, popular uprising could not up-end a government even in this day and age. I have seen this happen in East Germany, in Romania, and other countries around the world. When the crowds spill out into the streets and refuse to budge until their demands are met, there is precious little the government, any government, could do about it. They just have to give in."

"Maybe I did over-simplify," David conceded. "Sometimes, at the end of a dynastic period, after the foundation of state power had been undermined, eroded and shaken by corruption and maladministration, it was the combination of peasants' uprisings and generals' revolts that finally brought down a dynasty. Of course, the one could lead to the other; a popular uprising in the country could trigger off a power struggle at the court. Indeed, that is one way of looking at what happened on June 4th, 1989."

David and Anne had been walking back to their hotel all this while. David had a good sense of direction. He used the lake to navigate and he knew that as long as he kept the lake to his right, they would eventually find their hotel.

As the hotel came into sight, Anne suddenly asked David, "Why the Prime Minister's wife? Why did she have to take the blame too? Her husband framed General Yue, but what had she got to do with it?"

"Ah, she was really the Lady Macbeth of the story. She put tremendous pressure on him to press ahead with the sinister plot. These two culprits are immortalized in a piece of Chinese cuisine. In Hong Kong and Taiwan, you can buy these very tasty fried churros in the morning at roadside eateries. They always come in pairs and they are called "the fried prime minister and his wife". They are fried in burning oil because that's what they deserve. But, even if she was not involved in the plotting, she would have been condemned by posterity any way. It is called collective responsibility – guilty by association. "In case of treason, it was not unusual to kill several hundred people for one man's crime if they're part of his "nine relationships", each of which refers to one generation of his closest relatives. They and their families would all be executed along with him. This is normative control at its most brutal and most frightening. I would not want to be living in China's dynastic past. It was barbaric, though the Chinese called other peoples the barbarians."

Anne was lost in thought after she heard this. And then she found her voice and the question she wanted to ask. "Prometheus was bound, all tied up, his liver pecked at by an eagle, was he not? All for doing the good and noble deed of returning fire to mankind," she said to David. "So, do you think that is what's going to happen to Hong Kong too?"

"It is possible. It may even be likely. But Prometheus did not die. He suffered terribly. But Prometheus did not die." David Han pursed his lips, the look of defiance was on his face, but he did not say anything more after that.

"Saul, Saul, why doth thou persecute me?" On hearing this in his sleep, on his own Road to Damascus, David Han tumbled down from his horse and fell on the ground, dust swirling all over his body. The voice of Jesus took physical shape and appeared before him in the form of a fierce Chinese Dragon with outstretched talons whose every movement was accompanied by its hoary, fiery roars. Smoke and fire were coming out of the Dragon's mouth, ears and nostrils. After one particularly loud, thunderous outburst, the Dragon morphed into the bespectacled frame of Assistant Commissioner Li Neng who was now standing in front of David with an accusing finger.

"Dr Han, tell me, why are you so prejudiced against the Communist Party? Why are you so set against us? Could our country have come this far if we were all corrupt, self-serving, power-hungry, good-for-nothing country bumpkins? Dr Han, look around you. Look at the New China. Look at our roads, our trains, our airports and our skyscrapers. We have made giant strides. No country in the history of the world has grown as fast as we have, and achieved as much as we have done, in so short a time. We have in less than one generation moved out of the shadow of under development into the glory of an industrialized nation, and Chinese people around the world can now walk tall again, with their heads held high again. Could any of these have happened if we were all feudal Communist peasants who didn't know the first thing about governing this great country of ours? Or are you so blind you haven't even noticed, Dr Han?"

"I've noticed, Assistant Commissioner," and David Han raised his head to look at Li Neng straight in the face as he said this, "but all your achievements are economic. Have you done anything to loosen the nuts and bolts of state control to allow your people the freedom to enjoy the kind of life such riches as you described should bring? The kind of peace and stability they crave and deserve? A government that is not repressive, oppressive and corrupt? Why are they stashing money away overseas in such large quantities? Why do so many Chinese people want foreign passports? Why do they prefer to suffer foreign governments rather than their own? When can they live without fear and without always minding the long arm of the Communist Party meddling in their daily lives? It really pains me to see that Chinese people here in China enjoy so much less of what life has to offer than their brethrens in Europe, America and Australia. And I don't just mean material things, Assistant Commissioner. I am also talking about food for thought, and sustenance for the soul. It is not enough to have First World infrastructure, Assistant Commissioner, you need a First World mentality to go with it. Yes, your economic achievements are impressive. But your people are still living under the yoke of feudal, despotic rule. China is still a medieval country. And in that regard, nothing's changed!"

"You are an academic, aren't you, Dr Han?" Assistant Commissioner Li fired back, "To you and Liu Xiaobo and your ilk, it's all theoretical, isn't it? Open your eyes, Dr Han. Go out into our streets and take a look. How can anyone govern a country with more than one billion people, some of them barely literate, many of them low-end, low-level, low-grade, prone to unruly behavior and physical violence. How can any government do it without a tight and powerful security apparatus? We would not be here if we gave up our controls and monopoly on power. In any case, Dr Han, Chinese people put more store on higher income, better standard of living and modern amenities than they do on freedoms and rights. These things, which are so important to you, are the sort of things they cannot see, touch, put their teeth into and do not much care about. These can wait. Feeding a billion people and pulling them out of poverty must come first. Tight political control, coupled with inspired authoritarian leadership, is not only the Chinese way. This is the only way for poor countries to achieve prosperity and stability in record time."

"I do not mean to offend, Assistant Commissioner. But I just think you are on the wrong track and on the wrong side of history. You might think tight political control and the rule of fear will give you a docile population and political stability. They will not. The really stable governments I've seen in other parts of the world are the ones that govern with the manifest consent of their people. In spite of your awesome security apparatus, one day, perhaps when you least expect it, a coup d'état will materialize out of your own back garden, and the power struggle which follows will spill over into civil war. When that happens, the country will self-destruct, implode and disintegrate. And then, all these wonderful things you just mentioned – skyscrapers and fast trains and so on, all these trappings of modernity – will be blown to pieces. Assistant Commissioner, instead of concentrating your efforts on economic achievements, you should spend more time on forging good governance. You should respect your people's inherent rights as human beings, and not subject them to these one-sided, barbaric ways of yours in the name of socio-political stability and economic development. There can be no loyalty towards a government that is seen as an oppressor rather than a protector. And, unfortunately, this is a view that is fully justified by past experience and present orientation. Assistant Commissioner, the ascent of man is not just about improvements in material wealth. Western advances in science and technology which improve people's lives are built on the foundation of freedom, spearheaded by free-thinking individuals who are able to conduct free-ranging experiments and free-flowing intellectual discourses. Assistant Commissioner, if you want the Dragon's ascent, you must set the Chinese people's spirits free."

"That's where you're wrong, Dr Han. For all your learning, you don't seem to have any faith in the superiority of the Chinese way, the Chinese intellect, the Chinese head for figures and for the sciences. You might think the Americans are world leaders in science and technology now, but I can tell you, we are going to beat them at their own game, and we will do it without the freedoms you prize so much. Dr Han, there have been many attempts at modernization in China since the nineteenth century. They were called different names, but none has gone as far as this one has done. Oh, yes, you're going to see China overtake the United States. I know you don't believe me now, but you're going to see this happen within your lifetime. We do not believe there is any equation mark between freedom and scientific advances. We believe it's really all down to three things: material resources, innate human intelligence and hard work. We had two out of three in the past; we did not have the resources – both material and financial – that was what held us back. But we do now. The three requisites for scientific advancement are currently all aligned in China, and we're going to reach critical mass soon. After that, we're going to take off, and nobody, no country on earth, can stop us then."

"You are deluding yourself if you really believe that, Assistant Commissioner. China's success story is built on the foundation of Western science and technology, which the Chinese people have been able to borrow freely and apply usefully in their country. But your own contribution to basic scientific theories and scientific research has been minimal. China's entrepreneurs excel in the application of Western technology and Western know-how to the Chinese market. And, because of China's size, once something succeeds in this huge marketplace of yours, it tends to succeed spectacularly. It is really a function of scale and the economies of scale, advantages which no other country has with the exception of India and the United States. But neither your government nor your companies, state-owned or otherwise, can take credit for having achieved major breakthroughs in the advancement of basic scientific research."

"Dr Han, I know your kind. You are one of those people who want wholesale and full-scale Westernization. I don't think you understand that the next world war is going to be a race war. It's going to be us against them. You may think that because you are Westernized, you are now an internationalist and you can be one of them. Well, let me tell you this: there is no such thing as an internationalist in a race war. You are Chinese and can only be Chinese, because you look Chinese, and wherever you may be, they the Americans, the Europeans, the Hispanics, the Indians, the Arabs, the Jews, the Africans will regard you as Chinese – now don't argue Dr Han – and will treat you as Chinese. You should really study the accounts of what happened to the German Jews and the Japanese Americans during the Second World War. If you had done so, you would have known better. Don't be naïve, Dr Han."

"I am not naïve, Assistant Commissioner. It is you and your fellow cadres who are naïve, if you think you can win this next war against the might of America in the state that you are in. Do you not know that in that country many people carry guns? In the United States, even ordinary citizens have guns, not just one man one gun, but one man several guns, one man many guns! Nobody can conquer the United States, because the Americans will fight you on the beaches, in the hills, in the fields, in the streets, in the alleyways, and even in their homes. But conquering China, on the other hand, is not that difficult. Not only because you are inherently unstable, but also because in China nobody has a gun, except the People's Armed Police and soldiers in the PLA who have a monopoly on all arms and weapons. And so, once the Chinese military has lost its ability or its will to fight, the one billion Chinese civilians, in spite of their large numbers, will count for little, because they cannot put up any meaningful resistance. That was why the Japanese were able to massacre so many in Nanjing during the last war. Assistant Commissioner, the moral of the story is this, that while tight control might be great for the Chinese ruler and the country's ruling elite, keeping the Chinese people ignorant and cowed is not the road to great nationhood. It is merely the road to serfdom!"

"You really don't understand the realities of Chinese politics, do you now, Dr Han? You think giving people freedom is the answer to our country's problems, don't you? Do you really think you can trust the inherently unruly Chinese people to freely choose their own leader and govern themselves? Why, the moment we allow that to happen, the triads and warlords would be taking over. It is they who would be taking power in China, and not your kind. If we allow free elections in Tibet and Xinjiang, how could we keep the lid on the independence movements in these two provinces of ours? Please understand, Dr Han, it was always the law of the jungle in this country, and we are now the Lion King. What's more, it's a case of better the Communist Party than the triads and terrorists! Ask yourself this question: how can we be sure there is going to be a second election if we lose the first one? The history of African states has shown us quite the opposite. All too often, after the first election, there is no other. And the lesson of South American countries is not much better, because elections there don't mean a thing and didn't change a thing over the years. Don't just listen to Western propaganda, Dr Han, look at the facts. Let me tell you, science can develop independently of democracy, just as it can develop independently of freedom, and China can modernize without being Westernized! We want to keep our own identity, don't you understand? China will not blindly follow the example of the West!"

"Believe me, Assistant Commissioner, democracy is not the enemy of national identity. Communism might have been, in the way it had upended traditional Chinese culture, especially our hitherto strong family ties. You may or may not know this, Assistant Commissioner, but realpolitik was my research topic at graduate school. And so I am not so naive as to assume that, once democratic elections come to China, all our problems will be over. No! What I am really after is more fundamental than that. I want to see cultural change, and I want to see that change come about in a peaceful way. I don't actually believe a quick move-over from a single party socialist government to a multi-party democracy is sustainable without any change in the underlying culture. You should give me more credit than that, Assistant Commissioner. What I really believe in is that Chinese culture has to change before democracy has any chance. But that works in reverse too, because once a democratic form of government is in place, it will usher in the kind of cultural change that makes for a truly 'modern' society. An intelligent man like you must know that Chinese politics is determined and underpinned by Chinese culture. If the underlying structure remains untouched and unreformed, the change on the surface and in the façade is merely cosmetic."

"Ask yourself this question then, Dr Han. How do you change a culture that has lasted five thousand years and is embraced by well over one billion people across a landmass of some 9.6 million square kilometers? Where do you begin? How do you proceed? We both know that China's objective conditions will have to change first before the culture will. The economic reforms we have pushed through are easy by comparison, because the benefits to economic reforms are material, visible and immediate. But not so political reforms and cultural change for which cause and effect are blurred, and results take a long time to emerge. You are dreaming if you think China would ever embrace those Western democratic ideas of yours. Our country will follow its own trajectory and evolve in its own way in its own good time. We will eventually settle for a system of government which reflects our culture, our values, and our objective conditions. And I can tell you now, it will not be democracy."

"Assistant Commissioner, the mark of a great civilization and a truly intelligent people is whether they can manage changes of government without violence and bloodshed. This is the Holy Grail of politics, and in this most important test of political maturity, the Chinese have been found wanting. Yes, wanting! You must bring your people into the modern age in which government and society are ordered by the rule of law and civilized, humane behavior. Instead of focusing your mind on sustainable economic growth, you might spare some thought for sustainable government. You should know that absolutist, despotic government, backed by the threat and use of brute force, is not going to lead to political stability. You might want to take a close and enlightened look at what makes for a sustainable government elsewhere in the world. You might then realize how precarious your own situation is, because behind the tall skyscrapers and impressive looking shopping arcades, the Emperor really has no clothes!"

"Tell me, Dr Han, do you not feel even a tinge of pride, a tinge of delight when you see the economic achievements of China? Do you not feel proud of being Chinese now in a way you couldn't before? I mean, when you walk down London's Regent Street, or when you walk into Harrods, or dine at The Ritz, do you not notice the waiters and salesgirls treat you differently now – because they know you would be a big spender – as opposed to how they treated you before this Chinese revival and resurgence took place?"

"Yes, I do, Assistant Commissioner. Of course I do. I know most people respect material wealth. But, by itself, material wealth is not enough, and it is not going to last without the other support structures. Maybe you should ponder this question: has it never occurred to you that fast economic growth, which you prize so much, might be de-stabilizing? This is because your economic reforms, and the wealth creation that came with it, have already started to loosen the social fabric of Chinese society and have created tensions you now have to deal with. This is why many enlightened Chinese scholars believe economic transformation, if it is to last, must be accompanied by political reform. Or else someday you will just fall back to square one. The material wealth you have accumulated could all be sequestered on the altar of political infighting and civil war."

"You may think the Communist Party is bad, Dr Han. But you don't know what will come after us. There is a general and long-standing absence of trust in our country, and a tradition of violence. There are too many blood accounts to settle. We cannot let go, because we could not be sure we would come out of it alive if we did. I fear that after us it's going to be total chaos."

"All the more reason to find a way to improve the quality of your people's minds and their everyday behavior now! And one of the first and most important things you must do is to wean the Chinese people off the use of force to resolve conflicts and disagreements. The armed forces are there to defend the country against foreign invasion. It is not a private army of the ruling party. And it should not be used to crush dissenting voices just to keep the ruling party in power. You are an educated intellectual, Assistant Commissioner, how would you yourself like to be at the receiving end of such despotic rule?"

"Ah! But I am not, you see. And I am convinced ours is the only way to govern in China. This is the only form of government we have known since the dawn of the Chinese civilization. Your views are not only unorthodox; they are downright treasonous. I am going to charge you, Han. You are anti-Chinese!"

As he said these words, Assistant Commissioner Li turned his back on David Han and disappeared in a puff of smoke. David tried to wave him back with his right hand but discovered, to his horror, that somehow both his hands had been handcuffed to a baby's crib made of cast iron. The crib itself was embedded in concrete and not movable. The pillars of the crib to which his hands were chained were rock solid. He tried to pull the handcuffs; he moved them left and right and back again, until both his wrists hurt. But there was no movement and there was no escape. Only the sound of metals beating against each other – a loud, grating sound which pierced the depth of his soul. In desperation now, he hung his head down and cried. And what a despairing, heart-rending cry that was. Even his stiff upper lip could not stop the gushing tears.

At the sound of his own crying, David Han woke up.

Anne went out into the streets of Hangzhou to buy something to bring back to her mother-in-law. Old Mrs. Lin was a native of the city. But she left in a hurry with just two suitcases of valuables as Deng Xiaoping's Second Field Army advanced on nearby Nanking in the winter of 1948. And she had not been back since. At family dinners in the comfort of Mrs. Lin's apartment in Los Angeles, Anne had been told many times that Hangzhou was famous for its beautiful silk yarns and exquisite tea. But buying the colorful silk for her mother-in-law when they were both in mourning was hardly appropriate; so Anne decided to get tea for her instead.

She realized it might have meant something more if she could go to the area of the city in which her mother-in-law had grown up and get the tea for her there. But Anne did not know where that was. Victor might have known, his mother might have told him, but he was not there to advise her now. At the thought of this, Anne almost started crying again. Oh, how she missed Victor and his uncomplicated, good-natured company, especially his strong, muscular arms which made her feel safe even in

Downtown Los Angeles. Victor was a gentle giant of a man, well-built and protective, but his physical strength did not come with an overbearing personality. In Anne's eyes, his only flaw was that he was too focused on material success, more than was good for him. He never did understand that, in their marriage, Anne was really quite "contented with the morning that separates and with the evening that brings together, for casual talk before the fire". That was to her the epitome of marital bliss and all she wanted out of married life as she grew into middle age. But Victor did not believe she could get by with so little, because he always wanted more.

For Anne, visiting Hangzhou in the state she was in was not a pleasant experience. In fact, the city quite overwhelmed her, because she had not expected to find the haphazard mix of young and old, modern and ancient, wealth and squalor. These featured everywhere and not just in the architecture, although that was the most obvious. The high energy level and fast pace of life here would be impressive even for a New Yorker, let alone an unassuming, laid-back Californian. Anne kept thinking this was the city of Victor's mom and dad. It would have been Victor's city too, if he had not come to the United States, if his parents did not move to Taiwan, if Generalissimo Chiang Kai-shek had not lost the war against the Communists.

So many ifs, Anne thought, and the words of Ernest Hemingway in the opening paragraph of his short story *The Snows of Kilimanjaro* were coming back to her. Hemingway wrote that Kilimanjaro was the highest peak in Africa, at the summit of which laid the frozen carcass of a leopard, and nobody had been able to explain what the leopard was seeking at that altitude.

These words had special meaning for Anne now and she made a mental note to re-read her copy of the book when she returned home. As for Anne herself, she found the experience of her first encounter with China mixed, complex, and ephemeral. It was like watching floating images on the mirror of moving water along the West Lake, and she was not sure what to make of them all. On the one hand, the modern infrastructure on one side of the city was very impressive, at least from the outside. The new buildings made that part of Hangzhou look like a glistening First World city which put even Los Angeles in the shade. But, there were simply too many people jostling each other in the streets; the traffic was chaotic and the noise at the centre of the city deafening. All this was too much for Anne. But, that's China, she thought to herself, and these were Victor's people.

Everything was so cheap here compared to the United States. Anne bought the tea she wanted, the *dragon well*, for the equivalent of fifteen dollars. Coming out of the shop and walking back towards her hotel, she was stopped by a street vendor selling what looked like jade jewelry – pendants, brooches and necklaces, all for no more than ten dollars each. The merchandise looked quite attractive from a distance, but when she examined them up close, she realized she could not possibly wear them. The Chinese way of lumping all their merchandise together in no special order was a sure way to diminish individual value. There were just too much of everything, including the vendors themselves.

So Anne moved on. Another roadside hawker came forward. A fat, middle-aged woman with frizzy, disheveled hair was pushing in front of Anne some handcrafted necklaces made with dried red beans. These had been painted over and now appeared in three different colors – blue, green and Chinese vermillion. They were unusual and light to the touch and Anne really liked them because they were clearly handmade, not mass produced. So she asked the woman how much she was selling the necklaces for, and she was told they were two dollars apiece. Anne could not believe it when she thought about the amount of work that must have gone into making a necklace like that – the harvesting and drying of the beans, the painting and then the stitching. And all for just two dollars! She decided to take three there and then, one in each color. No polishing was necessary and no wrapping was offered; the woman simply handed Anne three beautifully crafted bean necklaces, for a total of six dollars.

Anne really wanted to buy more, especially a yellow one. If she could mix and match that with any of the blue, green and vermillion that she had already bought, they would make for an attractive multi-color roll of beads. The addition of a yellow necklace would make the other colors blend even more, she thought. And so, she asked the fat woman whether she had those same necklaces in any other color, but especially yellow.

"Yes," the woman nodded her head, "Sister has them, not here." and she raised and pointed her hand at some place which Anne could not see. So saying, the woman took the four corners of the piece of grey cloth that used to be white, tied them up in a bundle with her merchandise inside, and started walking, while signaling at the same time with a wave of her hand that Anne should follow.

Anne thought she had not really committed herself to a deal – all she did was ask – but decided to go with the woman anyway out of curiosity. Since the necklaces were so cheap, she thought it wouldn't really matter.

"How many you want?" the fat woman tucked her bundle higher up her shoulder as she asked the question.

"Oh, two or three, I don't know. I have to see them first."

"No, no, money first. Three for nine dollar."

"But I only paid six dollars for your three just now."

"My sister, better bean, better price."

At this point they had come to a road crossing and had to stop for the traffic to pass. It was then that the fat woman pushed an open palm in front of her and said, "Money now!"

Anne didn't like being forced into a sale, but considering it was only nine dollars and the woman had left her own roadside perch for her, Anne decided not to argue. So she opened her purse, took out a fiver and four one dollar bills and gave the money to the fat woman.

After another turn in the street, they came face to face with a young girl who was hawking the very same merchandise at the roadside. She was thin and short and did not look at all like the fat woman with disheveled hair that Anne had arrived with. But she did have the bean necklaces in yellow and brown and also in aubergine. They looked exactly like the ones Anne had just bought. Anne doubted they were better beans; and she doubted the thin girl was the fat woman's sister; they could not have been more different, in their looks and manners.

The fat woman said something to the thin girl in Chinese, took three of her bean necklaces, one in each color, and gave them to Anne. And Anne was putting the necklaces into her handbag when the thin girl smiled and offered her, from a pile she had just opened, the blue and green and vermillion necklaces as well, saying as she did, "One dollar, just one dollar each!"

Anne knew she had been ripped off, and it was not a good feeling. But then it was just a handful of dollars, and she couldn't buy these in California. So she confined herself to a curt huff and gave the fat woman one of her angry looks reserved for rude waitresses in New York restaurants. But she took the three necklaces from the thin girl all the same, and for just an extra three dollars.

Later, while thinking about the over payment she had been subjected into making, it occurred to Anne that the concept of fair price might not exist in the Chinese culture, and that the fat woman was just out to get the maximum she thought her customers would be willing to pay. And in order so to do, lying had become her way of life. There was no honor in the marketplace. Unfortunately, the marketplace was everywhere.

Each time Anne ventured into under-developed countries with ancient cultures, she found herself fascinated by their long and glorious traditions but at the same time repelled by the poverty, the squalor, the ignorance and, above all, the lying that goes on everyday – in the bazaars and on the streets. It was then that she counted herself lucky to be born an American and living in America. It was also then that she realized Americans who lied were much more reprehensible than these people who lived in the Third World, because Americans really did not need to. It was not for them a necessity; it was a matter of choice. And they had more choice than anybody else.

On her way back to the hotel on foot, Anne came across a fish farm. "Feeding time," an attendant at the door was shouting, "Look see, look see!" Two groups of European tourists were already making their way inside. Curious about what there was to see, Anne wandered in, along with a third crowd. They were led to three rather large ponds, each of them the size of half a basketball field, in which hordes of what looked like gold and yellow carps were waiting, their mouths wide open and eager to be fed. The routine must be well-known to the fishes themselves and it must have been well rehearsed, for as soon as the fish food was tossed into the ponds, the bigger fishes were shooting out of the water to get first bite, and the stronger ones were climbing on top of their smaller siblings and cousins. This was supposed to be a spectacle, and sure enough, many camera shutters were clicking. But all Anne took away with her was the thought that this might well be a microcosm of life in China. It was Darwinism in action.

There were just too many people and too much of everything, Anne thought. And if Darwin had been right, it was always going to be the survival of the fittest and most adaptable. The seasoned survivors that are still standing have no moral qualms about muscling out the weaker, smaller, less agile ones. To people who do not believe in God and the Last Judgment, what is there to restrain them? Survival *is* the end in itself. But it is survival of the most adaptable, not the most intelligent, the most deserving, or the most moral. Perhaps the obsequious, the hypocritical, the opportunistic and the violent would have a better chance in a Chinese millennium?

So thinking, Anne recalled that Victor always thought population control was necessary for China. She herself was against it, not so much the official One Child Policy itself, but the attendant forced abortion. Victor, on the other hand, believed limiting families to one child would be a very good thing for the country, and not just because there would be fewer mouths to feed and more food to go around. It was far more important than that, but few people realized just how important it was, according to Victor, and this was because smaller families might actually change the disciplinarian nature of Chinese children's upbringing, and this might make them less prone to following authority blindly when they grew up. If Chinese parents had only one child, Victor had explained to Anne, they would tend to be less authoritarian and more loving parents.

He was speaking from his own experience. Victor's father was a rare breed among Chinese parents in that old Mr. Lin believed in the power of, and the necessity for, reason, explanation and persuasion. The fact that he was a secondary school teacher had something to do with it. One time, when Victor was being naughty and did not want to return the bicycle he had borrowed from a neighbor's son, his father painstakingly explained to him why he must, and the consequences that would follow if he did not. Victor noticed that other kids were not so lucky. They either got whacked across the face for misbehaving or they got spanked with a cane. Many Chinese fathers just did not take the trouble to explain anything to their children; a strict, no-nonsense approach and corporal punishment for disobedience were the norm. This kind of upbringing produced individuals who respected authority and the use of force, but who were not convinced as to why they should. Without that understanding, they were prone to break the rules when they thought they could get away with it. Growing up in the close-knit émigré community that was Taiwan in the late 1960s and early 1970s, Victor also noticed that smaller families like his own tended to be happier families. When he was older, he put it down to the possibility that the father, as head of the family, was less authoritarian when all he had was a single offspring and knew he would have to depend on him in his old age.

From Victor, Anne's thoughts turned to David. Although David was at least a good three inches shorter than Victor, was ever so slightly built and very mild-mannered, he was no push-over. He was what Anne would call a strong liberal. It occurred to Anne that Victor and David were really non identical twins, except that Victor was positive about China and David was not. One was hopeful and the other was skeptical. One saw the bright side of things and the other saw the dark. This might be because one was an engineer by training and the other was a professor in the humanities. They were really the *yin* and the *yang* of the Chinese culture, the two sides of the same coin. In their different ways, both were patriots, although on first acquaintance David might give the exact opposite impression. To people less perceptive than Anne, David might appear to be anti China and anti Chinese. It took Anne who had married a Chinese husband to understand that both Victor and David were angry that China as a nation and the Chinese as a people were not more respected and not more respectable on the world stage. They saw much that was wrong with their native country and their own race but could not change either. They saw much to admire in Western civilization and Western culture but could not fully embrace them – because of the inherent, ingrained pull of their own. The clash of civilizations between China and the West is taking place within the two men themselves, within their own minds and within their own souls, as the two cultures vie for attention and ascendancy.

Anne noticed that quite often, when talking about China, the Chinese government, the Chinese people and the Chinese culture, both Victor and David would sometimes use the personal pronoun "we" and at other times the personal pronoun "they". The use of "we" and "they" might even occur in a single sentence. But Anne also noticed that it was not indiscriminate. "We" was used when they agreed, shared or identified with something Chinese. "They" was used when the men wanted to distance themselves. Consciously or unconsciously, both Victor and David were dissociating themselves from China's politics and political parties. Neither man would dissociate himself from the Chinese people. But David was more critical of many aspects of the Chinese culture, more so than Victor, who was himself more critical than many of his Chinese friends.

Walking back to her hotel along the lake, what David Han told Anne at the end of their dinner the other evening resurfaced and was coming back to her. David Han had said, with no particular expression on his face, "The Chinese story almost always ends in tragedy. The Japanese modernization which started with the Meiji Restoration of 1867 succeeded after one generation. But the Chinese modernization, which started with the Tung Chi Restoration of 1864 three years earlier, failed. In June 1989, the Pro Democracy Movement at Tiananmen Square ended in bloodshed and violence, deaths and tears. But five months later, in Europe, the Berlin Wall came down. It was ironic. The young people of China and the young people in Eastern Europe were really clamoring for much the same things. But one failed while the other succeeded. I cannot believe there is no rhyme or reason in the two different outcomes. I can only put it down to the differences in culture and tradition. But that is too general, too simple, for me."

In retrospect, it was at that moment that Anne got closest to being offered a glimpse of the tormented Chinese soul – of David, and through David, of Victor. The internal conflicts – of identity, of nationality, of race and culture – were there all the time and would not go away. But the Chinese ego was so sensitive and so guarded that these conflicts were hidden away in the deep recesses of the mind and of the heart. Behind the inscrutable and placid exterior of many Chinese gentlemen was an old and gentle soul that had roamed the plains of plenty and tasted their bountiful harvests for hundreds of years but had, in recent times, suffered the ignominy of rejection, deprivation and defeat. And it was hurting and burning inside. Anne was beginning to understand that now.

"Here, this is a standard translation of the Chinese death certificate authenticated by me, a consular official of the US State Department," Robert Denning said to Anne Gavin. "You can use this to file your insurance claim when you're back in LA. You probably won't need anything else. But if by any chance you do, please get in touch with me again."

"Thank you, but I am not done yet. I am not going back to LA until I have found out Victor's real cause of death." Anne looked straight into Robert's eyes as she said this.

"It says here that he was drowned at the Thousand Island Lake accident." Robert Denning pointed to the piece of paper he had put his signature to, just above the chop mark of the US Consulate.

"That may be what the Chinese authorities have put down. But I do not believe it. Victor was a very good swimmer; he could not have drowned unless if somehow his hands and feet were tied and he could not use them. I told you about this driver called Ah Sheng and I gave you the name of his company and his phone number. He was the driver who drove my husband to the Thousand Island Lake and he had told David Han – the Chinese gentleman who was at dinner with me last night – that he saw charred bodies being brought on shore. This suggests to me there was a fire or an explosion on board the boat. But nobody in the Public Security Bureau wants to talk about what caused it. I was hoping you could help me find out. Did you speak with Ah Sheng?"

"Not yet, we have not been able to track him down. Apparently he's off work sick and his company does not know when he will report back for duty. But, in any case, you need more proof than just one person's account if you are going to make that kind of allegation, you know. This is serious stuff. And this is China."

"I know; I wasn't born yesterday. But what can an American woman do in a foreign land except to ask for help at her own country's consulate?" Her female instinct told Anne a cry for help from a damsel in distress might be the best approach in dealing with Robert.

"We have asked for a copy of the investigating inspector's report, and the Chinese authorities have been very gracious about it; they sent this to me late this morning. I was told Assistant Commissioner Rong Hua had seen it and endorsed it. He did not raise any quibble."

"Assistant Commissioner Rong has been avoiding me," said Anne, her anger suddenly rising. "He was at the Thousand Island area, and then he was not. He was here and then he was not. Something very fishy is going on."

"Why would he want to do that?"

"I don't know. You are our man in Hangzhou. You are a seasoned diplomat. Suppose you tell me." Anne could not quite control herself when Rong's name came up in discussion.

"I do not speculate. I deal with facts and evidence. I *need* hard evidence before I can act, if I am to act, that is." Robert Denning was not going to commit himself to anything. The many years he had spent in the diplomatic service of his government had taught him the art of ambivalence above everything else.

"But if you don't go looking for them, the hard facts and evidence will not appear on your desk like a neatly typed-up report... like this one here!" A frustrated Anne Gavin was now waving her hands and pointing with her raised index finger at the report on Robert Denning's desk.

"You don't know how difficult it is to get anything out of the Chinese," rejoined Robert Denning.

"I know a senator on the Foreign Relations Committee." Anne was not going to say this but she now thought she had no choice.

"Oh? Do I know him?" Robert Denning raised an eyebrow but was otherwise unperturbed.

"You should. He is close to the Assistant Secretary of State for East Asia. His name is Gabriel Simon. He knows I am here."

"What? To see me?"

"Yes, I called him and I briefed him on what happened. He asked me to call him again after I have seen you today. He may want to speak with you himself. He has your number. I gave it to him."

"He is welcome to do that. I will tell him exactly what I have told you. Diplomats may be sent abroad to lie for their country; but we are not here to lie to our own people." Robert Denning knew this was not true even as he said it. But he also knew it sounded good and so he said it anyway.

"You will try harder to get to the truth, won't you? Please." Anne was pleading with him now. "This is not just a run-of-the-mill death-by-water kind of thing. I hope you appreciate that. I mean I saw my dead husband's ring being touted in the flea market by some hoodlum. If you get to the hoodlum and interrogate him, you might find out what really happened."

"We cannot just interrogate people here. We don't have the authority. This is not the United States of America. But, alright, I hear you. We have other sources we can tap into. We don't just rely on the Chinese officials to tell us things. Let me see what we can find out ourselves in the next few days. I'll call you if I hear anything different from this official report." Robert Denning was clearly taking a step back. He was now hedging and Anne could see that.

"How about dinner with me tomorrow night?" he asked, his white teeth showing in the slit of a half smile.

Anne was slightly taken aback by the dinner proposition. She was not in any mood for the dating game just now, and the suave Robert Denning was acting too much like her own philandering father for her to take an interest in the casual offer. And so she said to him, "If you manage to find out something new, I will see you at any time, otherwise I don't see…"

"I thought since you're alone here, you might like some company," Robert Denning did not give up easily.

"I have company. I have the Chinese gentleman from Hong Kong, remember?" She stopped talking in mid sentence and started putting the death certificate in her handbag, getting ready to leave. "You are not short of company yourself. I saw you with a Chinese girl the other night at dinner."

"Oh, well, that girl? She wanted a US visa and thought I could give her one."

Anne just shrugged her shoulders. She was unimpressed and showed it. Robert saw the expression on her face and quickly added, "Can I help it if they throw themselves at me all the time?" And, with a self-satisfied grin, he continued, "OK, so I go with the flow, but that's the only way to live, you know." He was not just being defensive; he was half suggesting that Anne did not know how to live.

The impertinence in his remark irked Anne and caused her to ask, with a slight disdain in her voice, "Have you read the novel *The Quiet American*?"

He noticed the change in her manners and came back to her in a flash, "Do you mean *The Quiet American* or *The Ugly American*?" He said this to impress, to show he was no philistine.

"*The Quiet American* by Graham Greene. If you have not, you should. You might learn something," she said. But, knowing she needed Robert Denning's help, Anne Gavin stopped at that and excused herself from his smug presence.

"You invoked the authority of an ex-Governor of Hong Kong and a Lord of the Realm to get me to see you. Was that really necessary?"

"Would you have seen me otherwise?" David Han shot back, quick as a flash.

Slightly deflated by the sharpness of the exchange from the word go, British Consul Quentin Maclean said to the well-dressed and upright Chinese gentleman in front of him, "I might as well tell you now it would not make an iota of difference to the outcome. We have our rules of engagement with the Chinese government and we follow them scrupulously."

"Even if the Chinese side does not?"

"That is a matter of judgment which we reserve for ourselves. It is not for outsiders and laymen to tell us what we should think or do."

"Even if that judgment is wide off the mark, I dare say. Some of us in Hong Kong think the British Government should never have raised the question of the 1997 lease at all, but should have simply carried on administering Hong Kong and waited for the Chinese side to come up with a proposal. Hong Kong might still be British if you had done that. Now what do you say to that?" David Han was being deliberately provocative. He sensed that the meeting had already gotten off on the wrong foot, and past experience in dealing with the British colonial officials in Hong Kong had taught him he must go for the moral high ground.

"That is a matter of opinion and we are not here to discuss that. In any case, *what might have been is an abstraction remaining a perpetual possibility only in a world of speculation.*" Quentin Maclean now quoted T. S. Eliot's poetry at David Han, not realizing that the Chinese gentleman seated in front of him knew *The Four Quartets* by heart.

"*What might have been and what has been point to one end, which is always present.*" David Han completed the line for him and continued, "And this brings me to exactly where we are now. You signed the Sino-British Joint Declaration and handed Hong Kong back to China. Some of us in Hong Kong always suspected the Chinese side signed the agreement in bad faith and hadn't any real intention of giving our city a high degree of autonomy for fifty years, nor of honoring the promise of One Country, Two Systems. Only now do we know the British side signed the Joint Declaration in bad faith too. You knew full well that Beijing might not abide by the agreement and that you had no way of enforcing it if this did happen, but nonetheless you sold it to the Hong Kong people as if they could really count on both. I call this hypocrisy."

"This certainly applies to the Chinese side if they never intended to honor One Country, Two Systems. But how were we to know that?"

"If you had read more Chinese history and understood better Chinese culture, you would know that if ever a Chinese person owns something, he would want to run it. Indeed that is the prerogative of ownership. It is against the grain of Chinese rulers to have sovereignty and not exercise it fully. Not for them the separation of ownership and management. Oh, yes, I have seen this separation in American and European companies. But I have not seen this in 5,000 years of Chinese history. Your queen reigns but does not rule, and that's a fine distinction. To you, there is also a clear distinction between sovereignty and administration; the two are not synonymous. But in the Chinese culture, they are completely inseparable! And so, One Country, Two Systems may work as between England and Scotland, but it cannot possibly work if the sovereign government is a Chinese government. The concept was just a convenient, expedient and catchy slogan to get Hong Kong people to accept the change of sovereignty. The virtue of tolerance for inherent differences is not a Chinese trait. Absolute control is."

"What other options did we have? What would you have done if you were in our shoes, Dr. Han?" Maclean fought back. He had asked those two questions before and successfully halted many hostile onslaughts when he lobbed them at antagonistic Hong Kong journalists and legislators.

"If I were to raise the question at all, I would have offered to give back Hong Kong Island, Kowloon Peninsula and the

New Territories – all three – to the Chinese Government. This would have gone down well with China's leaders and it would have put the ball in their court. Let them come up with a new arrangement which you can then help to modify. Who knows? They might even have offered you a new lease. An equitable one, mind you, not an unequal treaty, like leasing the use of a piece of land in Canary Wharf. Or more like Mayfair, since Hong Kong is expensive real estate."

"I don't see that it would have made much difference. Hong Kong still has a fifty year lifeline after the British departed."

"The difference is that Hong Kong might still be under British *administration* now instead of you having to give everything away under duress."

Quentin Maclean has no answer to that. But David Han was not finished with him yet, and he continued, "Strange, isn't it? You people pride yourselves on being able to see the endgame after the very first moves in a chess match. But this time you lot, the Foreign Office mandarins, got things completely wrong, didn't you? You did not trust Beijing's men in Hong Kong. You did not understand that they were really your allies, as they did not want to change the *status quo* any more than you did. They were not sure China could manage a sophisticated international financial centre like Hong Kong without the British."

"We always argued *the British presence* was vital to Hong Kong's stability and prosperity. If Beijing's representatives in

Hong Kong supported that argument, they should have told their own superiors."

"Ah! But you raised the question of the New Territories lease at the highest level, with Deng Xiaoping, and you did this without preparing the ground for it – without first briefing Beijing's men in Hong Kong. You sprang a surprise on them and also on Deng. You didn't understand that after the paramount leader rejected your proposal of a rolling lease, the underlings could no longer say or do anything in your favor. You always knew the British presence argument was facetious. Just look at what happened at the Suez Canal after you pulled out. The Egyptians could and did manage without you."

"We had to try that one first. That was our opening gambit. But our fallback position was always to try and keep British institutions going even after the change of sovereignty, if there was to be one. We were hoping that, in Hong Kong's case, with the signing of the Joint Declaration and the guarantees crafted therein, British institutions could survive without the British presence after 1997. Things like the separation of powers, the rule of law, the use of English and a politically neutral civil service etc. And let me ask you – what is wrong with that as far as daily life in Hong Kong goes?"

"Nothing, if things were really working out as you envisaged, but they are not. In Hong Kong now, British institutions are dying on their feet. They are being eroded – undermined invidiously or dismantled openly – by people who either don't know any better, or who are simply currying favors with Beijing and doing its bidding without questioning. Because *you* did not deal adequately with the problems arising from 1997, now *we* have to deal with them, in addition to new problems that are coming up even before 2047."

"If that is your view and if all you're interested in is the venting of your own anger at the British government, then I see no point in us having this meeting at all. Goodbye, Dr. Han. I am sorry I cannot bring myself to say it was nice meeting you."

"I am holding you to your obligation as a consular official, Mr. Maclean. You cannot *not* protect British subjects in a foreign land. My sister had a British passport, she died at the Thousand Island Lake, and no convincing reason has been given by the Chinese authorities as to the cause of death. It is your duty to find out and inform her next of kin, namely, me." The words were coming out of David Han's mouth like in a rehearsed presentation, and he had not finished with Maclean yet. "I am not convinced that you have done your best to find out what really happened and I shall so inform the Foreign Secretary through my sources as well as write to *The Guardian.*"

Quentin Maclean now realized that David Han was not someone he could just brush off and dismiss easily; and so he decided to change tack. He began slowly, "The difficulty for us is that your sister, when she came into China, traveled on a Mainland Travel Permit issued by the Chinese Government and not a British passport. That being the case, she would be regarded, under Chinese law, as a self-declared Chinese national on a home visit. The Chinese authorities have already told us she was not a British national under Chinese law and that, therefore, her cause of death is no business of ours. Now the difference in the compensation the insurance company is willing to pay out is this – 40,000 yuan for a Chinese national and two and a half times that for a foreigner. We can make representation, but…"

"That is not what I am interested in. It is not the money; I am not concerned about the money," David Han told the British Consul. "I want to know what killed her or who killed her."

"The Chinese Public Security Bureau has given us a copy of its own report to Commissioner Ma, as a matter of courtesy, they stressed, not by right, and the report says the boat your sister was travelling in capsized and she drowned, along with all the people on board."

"I do not believe that is the full story. Maybe not even the true story, Mr Maclean. Some of the bodies which were brought on shore were charred and might have been burned to death. They did not die of drowning. I have an eye witness, a driver called Ah Sheng, and these are his contact details." David Han handed over a piece of paper and continued, " I suggest you send someone to interview Ah Sheng and, when you have done, contact the Public Security Bureau and get them to investigate further – until they find out the full details. Somebody is trying to hide something alright. My heart will not rest until I know what really happened to my sister."

Quentin Maclean looked at the piece of paper David Han had just given him and was pondering what to say next when

Han volunteered another piece of information. "An American woman who has lost her husband is doing the same thing as what I am doing here – she has gone to the US Consulate to report what we both found out at the Thousand Island Lake yesterday. And she is asking her consulate to do what I am asking you to do now. You are going to be in good company, Mr. Maclean. And, by the way, the US Assistant Secretary for East Asia Pacific is a friend of hers."

"Who is she seeing at the US Consulate? Do you know?"

"Robert Denning."

"My men didn't mean to kill anybody, Pa. You have to believe me. They were just after the money. It was a robbery gone wrong, that's all." Di Di, Assistant Commissioner Rong's son, was on his knees and pleading with his father who was not even looking at him. Young Rong dared not tell his father his men had not been paid for three months because he had lost a bundle at the gambling table in Macau. The Assistant Commissioner's two henchmen, The Tall One and The Short One, were standing behind Rong Junior who wore a loose Giorgio Armani jacket on top of very tight-fitting dark trousers and colorful trainers. Waiting in the next room was Boss Pang, the movie mogul from Hong Kong – he who liked to stand out in the shine of light-colored suits.

Assistant Commissioner Rong was stony-faced, his spiky hair on edge. When he was furious with his subordinates, he would swear and bark insults at them non-stop and at the top of his voice. But when he was angry with his son, his anger was much more subdued and internalized. He would clench his fists; he would breathe heavily; and his body would shake; but he would not verbally vent his anger. Di Di was the Assistant Commissioner's only son and the apple of his dead wife's eyes. Their first son died of meningitis at the age of two. The little boy was already feverish in the morning, but Rong had to leave home on urgent Party business, and his hapless wife was left alone to deal with the very sick child. She did not know what to do and blamed herself for not taking her son to the hospital that night. She was exhausted by the crying, the worrying and the chores she had to do on her own and thought she could go to the hospital in the morning. But that turned out to be a fatal mistake. Her son died in the night. She didn't even know, because when the crying stopped, she was so tired she had already fallen asleep.

Mrs. Rong never forgave her husband for leaving home when she needed him there, even though she knew Party business came before everything else. The relationship between husband and wife was very strained after that. But Di Di's arrival brought a change of sorts. Her second son brought back the smile on Mrs. Rong's face and she was enjoying being a mother again. Husband and wife decided to call the second son Di Di because they still wanted to be reminded of their eldest son Da Di. The good times started to roll after Rong Senior joined the Public Security Bureau in Hangzhou and rose steadily through the ranks by dint of hard work and an uncanny ability to anticipate and please his bosses. With every promotion, his official pay packet swelled and his unofficial emoluments got even bigger. By offering protection to various rackets and syndicates that operated on the fringe of society, Rong managed to amass for himself a considerable fortune.

But tragedy struck a second time when Rong's wife of fifteen years died suddenly in a spring epidemic. Di Di was then barely nine years old. Not long after, Rong married again, against the vehement objection of his son. His second wife was well connected in the local Party hierarchy and helped him move up the ladder on a fast track. She also bore him a daughter soon after marriage, and mother and young child manoeuvred to make Di Di feel unwelcome around the house. Rong had to deal with the growing antipathy and decided to set the son up in an elderly aunt's household in Jin-an County while he lived with his new family in Hangzhou. The remorseful father made sure his son did not lack any of the good things in life. But the son saw this as banishment. He never forgave the father and deliberately made a mess of his studies to spite the old man.

Di Di got into all sorts of trouble in his teenage years – disorderly behavior, street fights, drunk driving on his motorbike, illegal bookmaking, gambling debts, soft drug offences – the lot. Each time, the Chief Inspector, as Rong had then become, would send Dragon the Tall One and Tiger the Short One to his rescue. With such strong muscles behind him, Di Di soon became known as *the* Princeling of Jin-an County. Everybody there knew he was above the law, because the law was being administered by his father.

After Rong Senior was made Assistant Commissioner and while on a private visit to Hong Kong, someone called Boss Pang came to see him and introduced him to the world of celluloid glamour called film-making. Assistant Commissioner Rong became an investor and then a sleeping partner in Boss Pang's film company which made mainly action movies. The ever courteous, smooth-talking Pang would bring movie starlets from Hong Kong for his carnal pleasure, and Rong became a sleeping partner in the true sense of the word.

"Why did you have to kill these people?" The Assistant Commissioner finally burst out, shouting at Di Di at the top of his voice, which shook and shocked everyone in the room, most of all his son. Rong could not control his wrath any longer, and Di Di was so stunned by the sudden outburst, the kind his father reserved for servants and subordinates, that all he could do was cower his head and body even further; he could not say anything in response. He had never seen his father this angry before.

After he was able to pull himself together, the much shaken and very nervous Di Di began, "We did not mean to, Pa. We only wanted their money and valuables and they were quite willing to part with those. But one Indonesian Chinese woman had a big emerald ring on her finger and it would not come off. So Young Hong took out a knife and was going to cut off her finger to take the ring from her. It was at this point that the big Chinese American lunged and pounced on Hong and a fight broke out. Other male passengers joined in and the women screamed and ran all over the place. In the chaos which followed several people were stabbed, and some women fell into the water." Di Di had been speaking very quickly and had to pause for breath. He then took one peep at his father's angry face and continued, "The

Chinese American was very big and very strong. We just couldn't hold him down. So Hong's younger brother took out his gun and tried to shoot the guy. Some bullets hit the LNG tanks and triggered an explosion which blew up the boiler room. The fire swept quickly. More explosions followed. People caught fire. The boat disintegrated and sank."

"So there were several explosions? And it was the explosions that sank the boat, yes? Why didn't you tell me this before, you dumb stupid idiot!"

"I thought... I thought with the help of these two," Di Di pointed his fingers at Dragon and Tiger, "We could just report a boat capsize accident and sweep everything under the carpet."

"You thought? You thought? If there's any sense in your thinking, you wouldn't still be in this monkey business by now!" He was now barking at Rong Junior. "Do you think it's going to be that easy? When so many people were killed? I now have the Commissioner breathing down my neck. And he has the Vice Mayor to deal with. Did you know Vice Mayor Sun has called me because the US Consul and the British Consul have both called him? This is now too big, far too big, even for me! You've got me in boiling water this time, do you know that, Di? Boiling!"

"Boss, Sir," at this point Dragon the Tall One intervened and said, "It is the upstart Li Neng that really worries me. His men are interviewing our collector Ah Fei now, and Fei might not hold out for long. If he spills the beans, then Di Di will be in serious trouble." When the Assistant Commissioner did not say anything, Dragon continued, "You might be too, Sir. Although Li is just *Acting* Assistant Commissioner, he is really Vice Mayor Sun's man in our Bureau, and the Vice Mayor is responsible for Party discipline and anti-corruption investigations. We know Li sends secret reports to the Vice Mayor; even our Commissioner cannot touch him, because the Vice Mayor has a direct line to the Party Secretary in Beijing. Before the Vice Mayor called you, Li would have briefed him. We must try to find a solution quickly and not waste time shouting at Junior Master here. We must protect the Syndicate and do a blanket water-tight cover-up. That should be our number one priority now."

"That's right, Boss," Tiger the Short One, joined in, "We have an idea which might work and we want to run this by you and get your nod before we make our move."

"Alright, so tell me! If there's a way out of this, why didn't you tell me! So tell me, tell me. Let's hear it." The Assistant Commissioner shouted again. He was getting very agitated because he could not yet see a way out of the mess his son had created. He knew Acting Assistant Commissioner Li could not be trusted, because Li was relatively new to the Bureau and was not part of the Syndicate. He had no lien on Li.

"Junior Master Di Di's gang must go into hiding immediately," said Tiger. "Junior Master himself will need an alibi. He needs to prove he was not even in the area on the day of the accident. We will tell whoever asks that he was with Boss Pang in Shanghai. You need to talk to Pang about this – we have arranged for him to be in the next room. He's waiting for you there now. After this is all set up, we will go through the motions and conduct another investigation to satisfy the American Consulate and the British Consulate."

"And what are you going to tell them after the investigation?" asked Assistant Commissioner Rong.

"We will tell them there was a robbery and the robbers set fire to the boat." Dragon butted in. "We cannot deny this anymore. There are eye witnesses who saw the charred bodies and the burned wooden planks being brought ashore. One of them is a driver called Ah Sheng. We ransacked his flat but could not find him. He is a fugitive now. We need to shut him up before the Consulates or Li Neng's men get to him." Dragon butted in.

"And so, Sir, this is what we will do. To divert the pointing finger away from our Jin-an Syndicate, we announce we have arrested seven people and we charge them with the crime," said Tiger.

"And who are these seven people?" the Assistant Commissioner asked.

"We already had six in custody for various serious crimes in the past few weeks, now we are adding one more as of yesterday. The first six had been arrested for arson, murder and conspiracy, and had been charged for those. We are just adding one more crime on their list – the robbery and killings at the Thousand Island Lake. But we need to charge one more person, Sir, because he had been *seen* by the American woman touting her dead husband's ring. This is that troublesome American woman who insisted on seeing you at Jin-an County. So we are including this youngster who is willing to plead guilty to the crime."

"But the crime of robbery and manslaughter carries with it the death penalty. Why would he want to do that?"

"He doesn't know that. We are going to trick him into signing a confession. He thinks he is confessing to a different crime – for taking a ring from a dead body and for selling stolen goods. We will bring him before our Judge Xu, the one who had worked in this Bureau before he crossed over to the bench two years ago, we produce the signed confession and we prosecute him for killing the Chinese American. After all, you must kill a man first before you could take the ring from his dead body."

"But young people are not stupid these days. They know how to read and write. How do you even get him to confess to the lesser crime?"

"We offer him a trade-off to sign on the line."

"What kind of trade-off?"

"He gets to sleep with a movie star in Boss Pang's film company."

"And he will give up his life for that? No, I don't believe it. Think again. Try something else. This won't work."

"It has a good chance of working, Boss. The girl was the boy's high school dream-girl, but he never got to sleep with her. He would agree to anything to bed her now, since she's become a famous movie star."

"Oh? And who is that?"

"Mimi Tian. You've met her. She was the girl who played the Hong Kong policewoman that got raped in the film Boss Pang made – you know, that movie we showed in your house a few nights ago? And we brought her there for your pleasure too, remember?"

"Oh, her!" Assistant Commissioner Rong's mind quickly conjured up flashbacks of his own sexual encounter with the young actress, she with the ivory skin and dreamy, smiling eyes. He paused, but not for long. And then he asked, "But what about the other young guy you arrested? What's his role in all this?"

"He has no role. We won't charge him, but we will keep him in custody until after the American woman has left the country. We will only release him after he gives us an iron-clad triad's undertaking never to tell. He will agree to that for sure because we are letting him off lightly. As for his mate who will be standing trial for robbery and manslaughter, we will tell him he won't get the death penalty if he pleads diminished responsibility under the influence of drugs. We've done this before. We won't make any mistake with Judge Xu. He likes sexual favors and we have him in our pocket."

"You have not set my mind at ease. It is high risk."

"We don't have anything better, Sir. This young man is the one who broke into your house several nights ago and he would have seen you entertaining Boss Pang, and Pang is Di Di's only credible alibi. We really cannot afford to have this young guy running loose. The American woman can identify him. They had a tussle in front of many people at the Lake's pier side. She said he was wearing her husband's ring on his finger. There is no way we can shake her off if we do not pin the crime on this guy."

"Time is running out Sir," Dragon joined in. "You still have to speak to Boss Pang and put this proposition to him. He is in the next room."

"Pang, my dear man, it's good of you to have waited this long for me. I've had to deal with a complicated case just now. Didn't they give you something to drink?"

"Boss Rong, you are too kind. I don't take liquor so early in the day. I am just here at your service, and the Commissioner's too, of course. Where would I be without the two of you? I just heard from my staff the latest film we launched a week ago is doing fabulously well in Hong Kong and Southeast Asia. We have grossed over a hundred and fifty million so far and your share is likely to top twenty five after expenses. The Commissioner will get slightly less, but he doesn't need to know." Boss Pang gave the Assistant Commissioner a knowing wink and they both laughed loudly.

"You have a very good head for business, Pang, I'll give you that." Boss Rong complimented his guest and Pang's ghostly face lit up. "Who would have thought of making movies as a way of getting money out of China?" the Assistant Commissioner chuckled as he said this.

"I should not claim credit for the idea, Boss Rong. I learned this from the movie moguls in Hollywood. In the 1950s, these guys' fathers were taking in a lot of Italian liras from showing their American films in Italy. But Italy had exchange control after the Second World War and there was no way to get the box office money out. So someone in Hollywood came up with this brilliant idea – shoot a big budget movie in Italy, pay the crew and all production expenses in Italian liras out of the company's Italian bank account, get the finished footage in the can and take it back to Hollywood for editing and worldwide distribution. The global box office receipts would all be in hard currencies after that! Simple, but it worked beautifully. And that's what we are doing now. Even if the films don't make the investments we put into it, whatever we take from the box offices in Hong Kong and other parts of the world is good, clean money. And hopefully lots of it, ha, ha, ha!"

"Like I said, Pang, quite ingenious! And by the way, I want to plough back my twenty five millions into our company and increase my equity stake since it is doing so well, and since you have been honest with me from the day we first went into this business together."

"Boss Rong," Pang had summoned up his anguished look as he said this to his business partner. Through knitted brows, he said, "There is just one complication."

"And what's that?" The Assistant Commissioner was surprised to hear Pang say that.

"The money you would have made from Mimi Tian's latest film? Well, it's not really there anymore," said Boss Pang.

"What do you mean not there? You just told me the film made a lot of money and my share was about twenty five millions."

"I know, but your son, Master Di Di, he was in Hong Kong and he, er, well, he took the money."

"What?" The Assistant Commissioner gave a sharp cry.

"Yes, Di Di took the money to pay for his gambling debts in Macau where he lost big, really big, playing craps against an American syndicate of professional gamblers."

"So the twenty five million is gone? It's not in my account with you anymore?"

"I'm afraid he lost more than that, Boss Rong, much more! You should ask him yourself – face to face."

"I can't do that now. I have just dispatched him to Shanghai. You must tell me."

"One hears rumors…"

"Pang, let's have everything out in the open. How much did these rumors say my son lost?"

"Over a hundred million," says Pang.

"What? But that's impossible. Where did Di Di get the other millions from?"

"I lent him another thirty because he's your son. You know your name is as good as gold in my organization."

"That leaves another forty five… is that the extent of Di Di's losses, Pang? I need to know the final figure. I must know if I am to deal with it."

"I believe the final figure is more than that, Boss Rong, but I don't have a precise number."

"This means he owes other people too, not just you. So that's why he has been so reckless lately," the Assistant Commissioner said with a sigh and slumped in his chair, his eyes downcast and unfocused, his mind anxious and confused.

"Don't be angry, Boss Rong. I know you would want me to tell you everything; I know. So, here it is. I understand Di Di had lost millions in the Hong Kong stock market. He didn't buy the actual shares. He bought, instead, the stocks' derivative products. These derivatives are gambling instruments. If you make the right bet, you win a lot of money because they are leveraged many times over. But if you make the wrong bet, all is lost. There is no value in them after a certain date, unlike actual shares. Well, Di Di bought heavily into the derivatives of two companies of which he was director. He told me they were sure wins, because he had inside information that the share prices of these two companies would rise as a result of a soon to be announced merger."

"And did the share prices rise?"

"Yes, to begin with. But then the trading volumes got so big and the price rises were so strong that they caught the eyes of the market regulators in Hong Kong who ordered the suspension of all trading in the shares of these two companies pending an investigation into possible criminal activities. The suspension was continuous and indefinite, Boss Rong, meaning there was no end in sight. When that happened, the share prices of the stocks slid in the grey market and the derivatives got clobbered. That's where Di Di lost the most money. The banks, the lenders and financiers of his derivative purchases, all wanted their money back."

"But what's wrong with buying on insider information, Pang? What business is that of regulators? A lot of people do that here."

"In Hong Kong, it is against the law because this is not fair to the other shareholders and investors who do not have that insider knowledge."

"But whoever told you the world's fair? This is just hypocrisy, Pang. You and I know there is one rule for the poor bastards in the street out there and another for the likes of us. We are the governors and they are the governed, because we are the clever ones, and because we have power and they don't. All human societies are like that. There can be no real equality anywhere, as you must know."

"The British built the financial markets in Hong Kong. They made Hong Kong the international financial centre that it is today. They have their rules. They say they believe in fair play and that markets can only thrive if there is credibility, and *that* depends on a level playing field and transparency. And so, in order to be fair, minority shareholders must be protected, conflicts of interests must be steered clear of, and buying on insider information before this is public knowledge is a crime in Hong Kong."

"And I say bollocks to all that!" said Assistant Commissioner Rong. "We are going to build an international financial centre in Shanghai, one which is bigger and even more vibrant than Hong Kong's, without any of that bullshit. We can have a financial centre with Chinese characteristics where insiders rule. When Shanghai becomes that, we won't need Hong Kong. If we throw enough crumbs to international investors, they will come and play ball."

The sophisticated but wily Boss Pang was too savvy to contradict his patron. He really only wanted the practicalities of debt and debtor acknowledged and sorted out. While he was not completely sold on the idea of British fair play, having seen not a lot of it in Hong Kong's colonial time, he was intelligent enough to understand a stock market controlled by insiders was not going to attract many international investors, especially not institutional investors, and if this was going to be the case, Shanghai might be a domestic financial centre but could never replace Hong Kong.

"Don't worry too much about Di Di's debts, Boss Rong." Pang tried to put a positive spin on things. "We can make the money back with our next film if Mimi continues to have the eyes of the audience." So saying, Pang added, "But the next film is going to cost us more, though, much more. For one thing, Mimi Tian is a big box office draw now, and it will be worth our while to invest more money on a blockbuster movie with greater production value. That way we will get an even higher return.

To do this, we will need an 'A List' director and co-stars, better quality sets, more exotic film locations and so on. In short, we will need to put more money into it. I've already worked out the numbers. If you are going to be in on this, it's thirty million apiece. But it will be worth it. This one could be an international hit." Boss Pang did not stop to give Rong Hua time to think. He quickly pressed ahead and asked, "Do you want me to get the money from your Macau accountants, or are you going to go through your Hong Kong bankers?"

The Assistant Commissioner was not one to beat about the bush either. With just one roll of his deep-set eyes, he said to his savvy business partner, "My Macau guys will deal with this. Just wait for their call. You will hear from me personally if there are any changes." And then, without pausing, he went on to say, "That's settled. Now I need you to do two favors for me, Pang."

"But of course, anything you want." Boss Pang, having got what he wanted – the thirty million would cover Di Di's debt – was quick to acknowledge his willingness to return a favor and his obligation to a major investor.

"First, I want you to tell everybody my son Di Di was playing cards with you in Shanghai the Saturday before last."

"That's easy. As it happened, I was in Shanghai that weekend and I can easily say Di Di was with me in my hotel suite. My staff will also testify to that. They would say anything I tell them to. Triads' honor, you know. They have sworn to that. No problem there. And the second favor?"

"The second favor is – I need to have Mimi Tian for a couple of days. I have something important for her."

"You want her a second time? Would this be for business or pleasure, Assistant Commissioner?" a smiling Boss Pang asked knowingly and obsequiously in equal measure, but knew he had spoken out of turn the moment he said those words.

"You don't need to know. Just bring her to my hotel and have her ask for Inspector Dragon. She should know Inspector Dragon by now; he holds a few rooms at our hotel for just this kind of business."

"And what instructions do I give to Mimi?"

"Tell her she will be entertaining a VIP in private, and that she must not say anything to anyone afterwards."

"Yes, of course. That goes without saying. She knows the rules. She is under contract to me. I can make or break her career." Boss Pang said this matter-of-factly, without any emotion in his voice. "But if I may change the subject, Boss Rong," he knew this would be an opportune moment to ask for something in return. "I have a favor to ask of you myself."

"Of course, Pang. Just say it."

"I would like you to give me an introduction to Sunny Kong. I'm sure you know him. He is the top businessman in Hangzhou."

"That's easy. I do know him. Is there anyone important that I don't know in these parts? I'll give a dinner to introduce you, and when an Assistant Commissioner of Public Security gives a dinner, no one, but *no one*, would turn it down. Sunny Kong or whoever just cannot *not* come. As a matter of fact, I am a shareholder in his company."

"You bought his company's shares? You must expect good results then, no?" Boss Pang would like exactly this kind of financial information for his own investment dealings.

"No, he just gave the shares to me. He does that every year to ward off any potential trouble. That's the way we do business here. You have to be an insider and you have to get on the inside track if you want anything done. The Americans either don't understand this or, if they do, they still cannot match it because they have laws against this sort of thing in their own country."

"In Hong Kong, we use the race course or the casinos to do such things. There is an organization called the Independent Commission Against Corruption and we have to be careful. But it's a lot easier now after 1997. The locals are running the government and we have access; they listen to us. Before, we had to work through intermediaries, because the Brits were in charge and we didn't speak their language. Now, we can go to the Chinese heads of departments direct. There is no need to go through intermediaries anymore."

"So the change-over is a boon to your business?"

"You bet!" Boss Pang and Boss Rong both chuckled at the thought.

When Mimi Tian walked into Suite 804, Bo was already there waiting. It was late afternoon and the thickening mist outside the hotel was casting a shroud over the greenery; soon it would engulf the whole compound. Bo did not notice that when he first entered the room half an hour ago, for the net curtains in front of the windows were drawn. Tiger the Short One told him not to touch anything and left him there all by himself. Since then, he had been sitting on a comfortable sofa, with his elbows resting on the down-filled cushion, and was skipping through the many channels on offer on the hotel's cable television network. He showed no interest in the Russian ballet *Swan Lake* in which a young Diana Vishneva was making her debut at Berlin's Staatsoper in the double roles of Odette-Odile. He settled instead on an NBA game featuring The Houston Rockets. His hero Yao Ming, China's most famous sportsman, was being rested due to a thigh injury but Bo decided to watch Yao's team anyway.

Anyone who should come into the hotel suite now would notice that Bo's white shirt and simple blue trousers really did not match the opulent red and gold décor of this ultra luxurious hotel suite. The young man was now totally engrossed in the American basketball game and was raising his arms to cheer on The Houston Rockets when, without knocking, Dragon the Tall One suddenly opened the door from the outside and ushered a beautiful girl into the room. Once inside, the Tall One gave a cursory nod to Bo who had turned to greet them. With an authoritative sweep of his muscular arm, Dragon now guided his charge forward in the young man's direction, saying as he did, "Here you are, Bo. I have brought you Hong Kong's hottest movie star, Mimi Tian."

Mimi managed a smile as she heard this. Bo stood up from his sofa. The two young people looked at each other, Bo intensely, Mimi only fleetingly, and with disinterest, although she kept the smile on her pretty, well powdered face. The smile was just reflex action on her part. Boss Pang had told her this was an important client meeting. She knew what was expected of her and she knew what to do.

"I will leave you to it. Mimi, a car will be waiting for you outside the hotel at ten tomorrow morning. As for you, Bo, move over and sign here." Dragon produced a pen and a piece of paper which had Bo's admission of guilt typed out. He put it on the desk, pushed the pen forward and signaled to Bo to sign.

Bo crossed the room and sat down at the desk. He really wanted to read what was written on that piece of paper and so he picked it up and brought it close to his eyes. But Dragon raised his voice and said to him, "You don't have time. Just sign."

Dragon's tone and demeanor towards Bo suggested to Mimi that the young man might not be that important after all. As Mimi watched, Bo signed. Dragon took the sheet of paper from him, walked to the door in rapid strides and let himself out. It was all over within a minute. And the lock clicked shut from the outside.

An awkward moment came to pass after Dragon left. Bo's eyes were fixed on Mimi's face. It was pearly white but with a pink flush to her cheeks just the way he remembered her that day in the azalea garden. That mole which gave teasing character to her face was still there, close to her upper lip. But the hairstyle she was now donning was very different from that of her student days. She had straight hair then which she sometimes tied into a pony tail at the back of her head. But her hair was now perm and wavy and no longer black; it was a shade lighter than auburn. Her nose looked slightly different. It might have been lifted at the arch; he was not sure. As he watched, Bo said nothing and did not move from his seat at the desk. Mimi started to sit down on a sofa a few paces away from Bo. She also said nothing. But her eyes wandered around the room and settled momentarily on the rich, expensive furnishings. Bo went over to another sofa and sat down. She was not looking at him but could feel he was staring at her.

Mimi had noticed the young man's clothes the moment she walked in – she could see that they had nothing to recommend them. And then she noticed his age. She had never entertained anybody this young before. To her mind, he did not look like a VIP at all, more like just any youth in China's many city streets.

She had seen a lot of those, in Hangzhou, in Shanghai and in Hong Kong, and they did not interest her in the slightest.

Feeling bored with the inaction of the young man, Mimi rose from her sofa, walked over to the window, opened a slit in the curtains and looked out onto the lake in the fast gathering dusk. Some swallows, the day's food searching done, were making their weary way home and already chatting happily to their mates. But Mimi was not impressed by natural beauty of any kind. Having grown up in the countryside with few modern conveniences, she was naturally drawn to cleanliness, creature comfort and gracious living, the kind represented by warm toilet seats, thick wall-to-wall carpets and central heating. Except she didn't particularly like hotel rooms; they always reminded her of work.

Mimi had used this hotel before on earlier calls, although not to this particular suite. And she knew the hotel kitchen could do a bowl of spicy Hangzhou noodles. Feeling an urge for some food now, and knowing she had a whole evening of toil ahead of her, Mimi looked around for the hotel phone to call room service. And when she had found it and started walking across the room to make the call, she noticed Bo's eyes following her. As she picked up the phone and pressed the button, Mimi turned somewhat theatrically and said to Bo, "I am ordering some noodles. Would you like a bowl?"

Bo was startled and jumped out of his seat – because she was speaking to him, she was actually addressing him now! He could barely answer the question but somehow managed to nod his head and say the words, "Yes, yes, I would."

"Any kind in particular?" Mimi was finding his almost comic reaction quite amusing.

"Er, whatever you're ordering. I'll eat anything. I'm actually very hungry," replied Bo.

"Alright then, I will ask for three bowls of spicy Hangzhou beef noodles, a plate of fresh water prawns fried with tea leaves and some pork dumplings. Do you want anything else?"

"No, that's good enough for me." Bo was not sure who would pay and how but trusted Mimi to know what she was doing.

"Well, I'm going to order some tea to go with the food. Do you like dragon well tea? You must do. You have a local accent."

"Yes, I am from these parts." He said and watched as she made the order and put down the phone. "And so are you," he continued, "You are from these parts too. I can tell."

"Can you?" She moved towards him. "I thought I had lost my native accent. I think you are just bluffing."

"It's not your accent, Liu Mei. It is who you are."

At the mention of her real name, Mimi Tian was startled, completely taken aback and went scarlet all over.

"Who told you my name? How come you know my name? Did Boss Pang tell you that?"

"No, Liu Mei, I don't know who your Boss Pang is, but I went to the same school as you – 401 High."

Complete silence followed the unexpected revelation. Mimi moved forward towards Bo and was looking at him closely for the first time since she came into the room. She did not know what to make of this young man; she could only ask him, "Which year? What is your year of graduation?"

"I never graduated. Neither did you, if I'm right."

Mimi was even more intrigued. As she sat there waiting for the next question to come to her head, Bo continued, "You and King were the Golden Couple of 401 High."

"You know about me and King too?"

He nodded three times in response, slowly.

"Were you following me? Stalking me? Was that it?" Her voice was frenzied; and her breath was short.

Bo shook his head.

"How did you know Assistant Commissioner Rong? Are you related to him?"

"No," Bo said emphatically, "I am most certainly not related to Old Rong, but he owes me a favor." After a short pause, he continued, "That's why he has sent you here. We have a deal, Old Rong and I. He is keeping his part of the bargain, and I will keep mine. I just signed. You saw me sign, didn't you?"

Many things crossed Mimi's mind all at once. She knew she was under contract to Boss Pang and must do his bidding or he would just put her in cold storage — he wouldn't promote her fledgling film career. She was a professional as far as selling herself went, and she had done this kind of assignment many times before. But she would not want any of her teachers and classmates at 401 High to know about it. Her whole native village would know then and that would be downright degrading. She wanted to keep up the façade of being a glamorous movie actress based in Hong Kong, living the fast life of the rich and famous, followed and admired by fans everywhere she went, with photographers and paparazzi trailing – the very embodiment of many Chinese girls' dream.

She wanted to ask Bo about the deal and the favor Assistant Commissioner Rong owed him, but hesitated. She had heard stories about people ending up in the lake or left hanging by their necks in the woods because they knew too much. She had been warned to steer clear of the dealings of the Assistant Commissioner, and also those of her own Boss Pang. But her curiosity had been aroused; this really concerned her as well and she wanted to know. She thought if she just confined her probing to this young man in front of her called Bo, it might be alright.

So she walked across the room to switch off the television. In the sudden silence that had just descended, the ambiance of the room changed and she could now think more clearly. And then she began, hesitatingly at first, "Bo, that's what they call you, isn't it? But what is your full name?" She paused and waited for his answer.

"Chen Bo. I am called Chen Bo,' he said, suddenly very pleased with himself, pleased because she now knew him for who he was. Noticing the pleasant change that had come upon him, which was written all over his face, Mimi continued, "And have you gone back to 401 High since leaving school, Chen Bo?"

"No, I have not. Don't know anybody there anymore. Headmaster Feng has retired and most of the teachers who taught me have left. So, what's the point?"

"And your schoolmates, those in your own class, do you still see them?"

"No, I don't see them. In my line of business…" Bo was about to tell Mimi what he did but decided against it. Selling stolen and counterfeit goods was not something he was proud of. "Let's just say, my school chums and I, our paths have not crossed since I left school. Fate has dealt us different cards, and we're doing different things now."

Mimi was very relieved to hear this. It was an important piece of information to her. Now slightly off her guard and gaining in confidence, she asked Bo, "What do you remember most about 401 High then?"

"You," he paused and looked straight at her, as she smiled a broad smile and showed her gleaming white teeth. "The last time I saw you – on the day of the Sports Meet when King fell and broke his ankle and lost the mountain climbing race."

"You remember that?" Mimi Tian's smile disappeared. It was not her most cherished memory about 401 High. "That race broke King and it broke me. He never recovered from that, do you know? I mean he did physically, but he changed after that incident and became a different person. We never used to quarrel before, but…"

The doorbell rang and the door swung open. A liveried waiter pushed his serving trolley inside and food was delivered on a silver-plated platter. The two young people, both hungry and ready for a break in the conversation, consumed the noodles in slurps, followed by the prawns and dumplings. All the food was downed with great speed and gusto.

Now pouring the fragrant dragon well tea into two delicate porcelain cups, Mimi began again. "Did you know King died when he was barely 22?"

"Yes, I did know. His death was announced by Headmaster Feng at morning assembly. It was during my last term at school."

"Did you know he was racing with a truck? On his bike?"

"What? Racing with a truck on his bike? Why did he do that for?"

"He was angry at the truck driver for having overtaken him at a crossroads when the lights were red. So he gave chase and was hit by a car that was speeding down the cross-section from the left side of him. I'm afraid King had become easily irritable and very bad-tempered when he found the outside world didn't treat him like the superstar that he was at 401 High."

Bo nodded his head to show that he had understood, but King really did not interest him any more. After a short silence, he just had to ask the question he had been longing to ask for a very long time. "And you? Where did you go after you left school? I heard a rumor that you were living with King against your parents' wishes and that they had disowned you."

"I did follow him to Hangzhou, but my parents did not disown me. I was too ashamed to tell my Ma I was living with King, and just never went back. I learned afterwards that she had died of a stroke in the same month that King died, but I didn't know at the time. My father – actually he was my stepfather, not my real father – well, he never even bothered to find me and tell me. He left me to fend for myself alone. I never got on with him anyway and I don't know where he is. He's probably dead by now and I don't really care. He wanted a son and told my mother to give me away so that she could get pregnant again. Only I was so adorable even as a baby girl… Ma said I had lovely rosy cheeks and big rolling eyes and she just couldn't bear to give me to someone else. So she defied my stepfather and kept me. Maybe because of that he never really liked me and the feeling was mutual."

"Unlike you, I loved my Pa," Bo volunteered the information to Mimi. "He was an intellectual, a learned man born into the wrong century. He loved to read; that was his world. Although he made the right choice in supporting the Party, he was never trusted because he had a mind of his own and loved beautiful things. They made him a barber; that was the job he was assigned after the revolution. They told him he could make people look neat by cutting out their dirty hair. But he was really not very proletariat – he wanted to wash his hair every day. He taught me 'beauty starts at the top' – that was his favorite saying. He had dreams and he lived in them. He really didn't care for the real world around him. He told me once, when we were out fishing on the lake, that he enjoyed being close to nature, surrounded by little animals and flowers; for him that was the way to live. The real world he inhabited was too stark and unlovely; he wouldn't know where to put his 'un-communist' emotions, he said. My mom always complained that he was impractical and useless around the house, but I believe she loved him in spite of that. She nagged him all the time and he didn't fight back. But he couldn't change who he was. When Pa died at the age of forty-three, my mom was shattered, she was never the same again. I always thought my mom was the strong one, the pillar of the family. But it turned out Pa was the mainstay of her life. His mere presence was what had sustained her. And she did not live long after he went."

"It's all in the stars, isn't it? We really can't change our lives, can we? A soothsayer had said to my mother when I was born that I would have a very hard but eventful life. The hour of my birth and my eight characters had foretold that, he said. And so it has proved. I was all alone in the world after King and Ma both died and I went to find work in Shanghai…"

"Where you found fame and fortune," Bo finished the sentence for Mimi.

"No, no, not so fast, not until I met Boss Pang and joined his film company a couple of years later. He saw something in me, took me under his wings, arranged for me to go to Hong Kong, gave me a new name, a makeover, and put me in his movies."

"It must be fun making movies and being worshipped like a goddess on a pedestal." Bo said in childlike admiration. He finally got to voice his adoring wonderment in front of his teenage idol.

"Making movies is no fun at all. It is actually bloody hard work when you're on the set. The directors treat us like shit. But attending gala premieres and cutting ribbons at fashion launches, yes those are things that I do enjoy. You cannot have the one without the other, though," the worldly wise Mimi said matter-of-factly. "But, hey, why am I telling you all this?" So saying, she shot up from her sofa and went over to the mini-bar to open a bottle of red wine.

"Do you want some?" Mimi said to Bo. She had picked up the habit of drinking wine from Boss Pang, but did not really know good wines from bad or when to drink them. The bottle she had just opened had a foreign looking label but was actually produced in China's Shandong Province on the coast. It was a far cry from the expensive Burgundies that lined Boss Pang's wine cellar in Hong Kong.

"I'll try some, yes…" replied Bo.

"Now, tell me something about yourself." Mimi started to coax Bo after hurriedly gulping down her wine like drinking water. Bo's face was soon scarlet and they had moved closer to each other as the drinking progressed.

"There is not much to tell. Both my parents are no longer living. They died of heart diseases. My father died first and my mother followed him to the grave five years later. My grades at 401 High were just average. When my mother died, I was really quite lost. She had cooked for me and looked after me all these years and kept me on my best behavior. After she died, I didn't need to go home for my meals and started associating with bad elements on the streets. I skipped classes and didn't do my schoolwork. I thought I could catch up closer to exam time, but I couldn't of course. I was too far gone. And so I didn't make the cut. I did not graduate and the school would not enter me for university entrance, nor did I expect it to. When the money my mother left me ran out, I had to resort to selling things on the sidewalks and at the pier by the lake. There was just no other way."

"Any yet, you are important enough to be doing deals with Assistant Commissioner Rong."

"Did I say that? No, I did not say that. I only said he owed me a favor."

"It must have been a very *big* favor then." She knew. She did not come cheap any more. Those early days in Shanghai and Hong Kong were far behind her now. She heard Boss Pang had been talking to several Hollywood film producers about casting her in an international blockbuster.

As she said the word 'big' with insinuating emphasis and looked at him up and down with pouting lips, Mimi Tian became the alluring temptress she could be, not only in her movie roles but also in real life. The rising alcohol level in his blood, the perfume which floated across with every toss of her perm hair, and the inviting look that promised sensuous pleasures he could only dream of before – all this was making Bo's head swirl and he could no longer tell Mimi Tian from Liu Mei, or Liu Mei from Mimi Tian. In his fast swelling head, they were one and the same girl now, although they were really many years apart, and many worlds apart.

Bo lunged forward and fell on top of Mimi's soft perfumed body with gay abandon.

She had never experienced anything like this since King died. Over the years, Mimi had slept with different men, in different cities, in different positions. Most of them were much older than she, many had big fat stomachs which could not be held back once their belts were loosened; quite a few were bald and oily, from their heads to their faces; some had bad teeth and bad breath; nearly all had bad skin she could not bear to touch. Yes, she had slept with them all and did their animalistic biddings. But to her it was just a job, a role she had to perform, like doing a scene in a movie. Her soul was never there. She was always very relieved when it was over and she could quickly disappear into the bathroom to wash herself clean again. Viagra might be God's gift to older men, but it was no gift at all to a girl in her profession. It only meant longer working hours.

But this time it was different. Whether it was the connection to 401 High, the reminiscences about their old school, the fact that the young man she had just slept with knew her and adored her as one half of the Golden Couple – something about the experience just now had taken Mimi to a rarefied part of her consciousness where she had not been for a very long time.

The young man, tired from his own physical exertion and the worries of the past two days, was sound asleep now. Mimi looked at his smooth young skin which was quietly glowing in the light, his head of rich healthy hair, his strong muscular abdomen and she just could not help wanting to touch him again, gently, as she would have done her young King.

At the thought of her ill-fated first love, and the tortuous route her own life had taken, tears welled up in Mimi's eyes and she started to weep and sob. Her sobbing woke Bo. He took her in his arms and wiped the tears from her face with his fingers, again and again. "What is the matter, my lovely?" he asked, whereupon she burst out crying, with a loud shriek which startled him. Her crying was non-stop and went on for a long time. The poor girl was inconsolable and the young man did not know what to do.

When at last the crying turned into sobbing again and finally died down, Mimi Tian fell into a deep stupor. It was her turn now and she had gone, in her dream, to another world, the world of her youth, the world which belonged to her glorious teenage years when she was happiest and felt safest, ensconced and secure in her young lover's tender embrace.

Bo really wanted to study Mimi's face. But with her lying over him and inside his left arm, all he could see was the lower part of her body, from the hips down. She had long and slender feet, and her buttocks were firm and well proportioned, and he thought she smelled divine with every breath she exhaled in her sleep.

Bo had finally done it now, and a self-satisfied grin came to his face. He wanted to do it again. But not before he had taken another long and greedy look at her naked, sensuous body in its quietly alluring repose. He pushed her over. Mimi gave a sigh and Bo slipped his arm out from underneath her. Having detached himself thus, he could now look at her whole body, inch by lovely inch.

Bo bent over and kissed Mimi on the lips. She stirred in her sleep and kissed him back and the two were locked in a tight, passionate embrace. Bo could hardly hear Mephistopheles' gathering footsteps when his heart, his mind, his body and his soul were all racing away into the darkness.

"Wake up! Wake up!" Dragon was shouting at Bo and shaking him up from his slumber. Bo could feel the rough and muscular palm of the hand that had taken hold of his right shoulder and it was hurting. The slightly bent frame of Dragon was next to the bed and blocking out the sunlight. "Get out of bed now, you scum! Your time's up, hell!" Dragon was physically dragging him out of bed as he barked out his order.

Bo wanted to linger and savor for a few more moments. He wanted to take a long last look. But Dragon would not let him.

Liu Mei had gone, disappeared, and left not a trace, except for a whiff of perfume on the pillow. In the prisoner's car on the way back to custody, Bo was left wondering whether last night had meant anything to her. It meant everything to him. But she would never know.

"Rise!" The Court Guard shouted out the order as the Chief Magistrate and his two deputies in black robes took their seats on the podium behind their tall desks. Judge Xu read out the case that was on trial, "Robbery, arson and manslaughter of forty two people on board Boat 9413 at the Thousand Island Lake on March 30th this year." He stopped, put down his court file, acknowledged the two deputies on either side of him and continued, "Bring in the accused."

The people at the back of the courtroom that had gathered for the hearing started to look in the direction of the court's inner entrance. The accused, all dressed in dark brown prisoner's outfits, were brought into the room in single file by the prison guards. Anne Gavin and David Han could count up to seven. There were seven accused. One row behind Anne and immediately to the right of her sat Robert Denning who was there for the U.S. Consulate. Another row back and sitting next to the left aisle was Quentin Maclean, British Consul in Hangzhou.

Anne tried to look for the young man who had taken her husband's ring but could not recognize any of the faces as they trooped past with heads bowed and at nine or ten paces from her. They all looked dejected and drawn; all were unshaven and expressionless; all of them quite young, at most in their thirties. Only one seemed to have combed his hair. In a matter of seconds, the accused were all lined up with their faces towards Judge Xu and Anne could only see their backs.

As the names of the accused were read out, The People's Court proceeded to take their pleas. It transpired that six of the accused had already been tried and found guilty a week before for multiple serious crimes. They now pleaded "guilty as charged" to the additional charges of robbery, arson and manslaughter but sought leniency. The last of the accused, to everyone's surprise, professed his innocence when the charges against him were read out. A small commotion descended in the courtroom as people moved their bodies to one side and whispered into one another's ears. Now Anne recognized the young man in the dock – he was the one who had taken possession of her husband's graduation ring. And he was the only one to have said he was not guilty as charged.

Judge Xu threw down his pen; he looked really upset, the prosecutor even more so. Judges in China only needed six months' training if they were seconded from the Security Bureau. They were used to trying easy to handle cases which only required them to convict. But this one had complications the sitting judge was not prepared for. The prosecutor quickly stepped up to the bench and conferred with him; the lawyer for the accused also joined in. Robert Denning leant forward and whispered to Anne, "This is highly unusual. The young man on the right pleaded not guilty! Normally the accused would have confessed before he is brought to trial, and at China's law courts the defense attorney is only there to plead for a lighter sentence, not to argue over the guilt or innocence of the accused." Anne nodded her head to show she had understood.

Judge Xu had a very serious look on his face now. He declared the court adjourned until the following day and sent the seven accused back into custody. As the august judge rose to leave, Dragon and Tiger appeared from behind the far corner of the courtroom and dashed towards the judge's chambers. Robert Denning left his seat and came around to talk to Anne Gavin.

"I'd like you to know, Anne, that we have done our bit. We put so much pressure on Commissioner Ma through the Vice Foreign Minister that he ordered a fresh investigation into the incident, after which the Commissioner told us that it was not just a simple case of boat capsizing and people drowning, but a case of robbery, arson and manslaughter. That was the gang that did it, these seven guys you saw at the dock just now. That's why they are having this trial. I left you a letter in your hotel to explain all that and tell you about this trial. You must have got it since you are here this morning, even earlier than I, I've noticed."

"Yes, Robert, I have read your letter and shared the information with David, thank you." As Anne said this, David looked across and acknowledged Robert with a nod of his head. "That's why we're here." Anne continued. "But so what happens now? One of them pleaded not guilty to robbery, arson and manslaughter. Six of them did, but not the last one; and I know he was the one who took my husband's ring. I can point him out in an identity parade."

"That may not be necessary, Anne. We will know tomorrow. I'm afraid we cannot interfere with their judicial process. But we can hope that justice will be done."

"If these were indeed the people involved," David Han who was standing behind Anne butted in.

"Do you know something that I don't?" Robert Denning was annoyed at being contradicted after all that he had done and showed it in his voice.

"Only that justice as you called it is not always done in China," replied David, "The semblance of justice? Perhaps. Our Scottish friend over there would know." He motioned to Quentin Maclean who was just putting his notepad and paper back into his briefcase and getting ready to leave. "I assume you two know each other since you're both stationed here." David raised his voice deliberately to engage the British Consul.

With the briefcase in his hand, Maclean stepped forward and said, "Yes, we do. But the United States and the United Kingdom are two countries divided by a common language. We do not always see eye to eye. Oh, sorry, I am Quentin Maclean." He introduced himself to Anne.

"Anne Gavin, and I am Irish American. Interestingly enough, although we all speak English, the only one with an English ancestry among us is Robert Denning here." Anne was really trying to calm David down with a touch of humor. And then she continued, "But British and American diplomats do confer from time to time on matters of mutual interest, do you not? And maybe also share intelligence? Is there enough common ground in our particular case for the two of you to work together on this, for instance?"

"I am not at liberty to divulge what we do," Robert Denning gave a cool response. He did not trust David Han and was in no mood to volunteer any information or offer any help.

"We should wait another day and see what happens," said Quentin Maclean to Anne Gavin. "I think we may be getting somewhere. The fact that the young man pleaded 'not guilty' means the prosecution will have to prove its case in court tomorrow. It's not just a simple matter of going through the motions anymore." Maclean tried to be a little more reassuring and less stand-offish. Now turning to Robert Denning, he said, "I don't know about you, Robert, but I'm getting back to my office. Does anybody want a lift?"

"I'll come with you," said Robert and the two of them started hurrying away before Anne and David had a chance to respond. When the two diplomats thought they were out of hearing of Anne and David, Robert Denning said to Quentin Maclean, "So, what have you heard? About this case, I mean."

"Our sources told me it's basically a highway robbery gone wrong," Quentin replied, "The three charges of robbery, arson and manslaughter tell us almost as much now. But the gang involved has protectors in high places and cannot be touched. So they just got these guys we saw today to take the blame; these seven guys are the scapegoats. The chap from Hong Kong whose sister died might have sensed that. I think maybe he knows. The Public Security Bureau has done this before. The only surprise this time is that one of the young men is not playing ball."

Quentin Maclean opened the doors of his car and signaled to Robert Denning to go in. Once inside the car, Maclean asked, "And you, Robert? What have your people found out?"

"We went to Commissioner Ma," Robert began.

"I wouldn't trust the old fox if I were you. He has a mountain of cash stacked away in Hong Kong and Switzerland, and he is a business partner of the movie mogul Boss Pang." Quentin continued, "You must wonder where he got all his money from. As you know, the official salary of a Commissioner is just 5,600 *yuan* a month. And that's not much, is it? But his daughter is at Stanford and his mistress is driving around in the latest BMW Six series."

Quentin Maclean started the noisy engine of his cantankerous car and drove off, saying as he did, "You must get your ambassador to go directly to the Vice Foreign Minister. Now, there's a good egg for you. The Vice Minister is always straightforward in his dealings with us. He would not tell us something which he knows is a lie. So far as we know, he is not corrupt either."

"We did exactly that after we got absolutely nowhere with Ma who just gave us the usual spiel about Chinese justice being different from American justice. Why do you think they have put together this public trial at such short notice if it weren't for the Vice Foreign Minister's intercession? Tell me, Quentin, do you think Ma is the gang's protector? I know he's on the take, but is he their protector in this particular case?"

"I really don't know. But I smell a rat. It's very ironic, but the quasi reformers in this country are corrupted by money and their feudal Marxists are corrupted by power!"

"Strange, isn't it? That this country which has five thousand years of written history behind it, which was the first to have invented printing and spread valuable knowledge around, and also the first to have introduced a civil service exam to select the best and the brightest for a meritocratic bureaucracy, has never been able to rid itself of serious corruption. At the heart of the Chinese soul is a bundle of American greenbacks, I always say!" Robert Denning was staring at the modern and impressive looking buildings either side of the road as he said this to Quentin Maclean.

"I had this discussion with a Chinese diplomat in London once," Quentin replied. "Like all educated and patriotic Chinese gentlemen that I have come across in my career, he was a defender and an apologist for his country. When the subject of official corruption came up, he said he had seen this in all the countries he had served in – France, Japan, the United States and even the United Kingdom, and that, therefore, this is a universal phenomenon which afflicts 'bad people' in positions of power, not just the Chinese."

"And what did you say to him when he said that?"

"I told him there's a difference between Chinese corruption and corruption anywhere else in the world, because Chinese corruption is *dynastic, nepotic*, and *astronomical* in scale. I said I had chosen those three adjectives carefully and I wanted him to remember them clearly."

"Bravo you!"

"Wait a minute; I haven't finished," a delighted and self-satisfied Quentin Maclean continued, glad to have a captive audience in his car. "I then told my Chinese diplomat that if you've had this for five thousand years, it would have become part of your nature. Listen to this, Ambassador Meng, I said, corruption in China is *dynastic*, because the powerful syndicates get passed from father to son. They are self-perpetrating, because there is no change of government within the duration of a dynasty, so that's D. And then, corruption in China is *nepotic*. Whole families are in it together, not just the head of the household, because in China, 'The Son Also Rises', the wife and daughter too, and that's N. Finally, I said, the sums involved are *astronomical*. We are often talking about hundreds of millions of dollars in graft. Corruption in the West pales by comparison; our MPs at Westminster only take freebies to Paris, for Christ's sake, and that's A. Now, put these three characteristics together and what have you got as acronym? It's DNA! Corruption is in the Chinese DNA!"

"Oh my God, Quentin! You Brits are such clever bastards!" said Robert Denning in sincere admiration.

"Yes, that's right, Chinese corruption is dynastic, nepotic and astronomic! Or should I say astronomical? Those are its distinguishing features. The three adjectives even rhyme. May be I should patent this, Robert. What do you think?" Quentin Maclean smirked and chuckled at his own cleverness and brought the car to a temporary halt in front of a set of traffic lights that had gone red.

"Well, the obvious antidote against entrenched corruption is a change of government from time to time. That will break up the *dynastic* bit for sure. Then vigilant opposition parties and a free press will do the rest."

"You are right of course, Robert. But China has none of the above. Instead, Chinese governments have, since time immemorial, put their faith in heavy punishment to deter corruption and other crimes. This had proved not to work in Britain. In the mid nineteenth century, our then Home Secretary Robert Peel was the first to recognize this. He believed crime was not deterred by the severity of the punishment but the certainty of conviction. You could threaten criminals with heavy penalties how you liked, but if the chances of their being caught were slim, they would still play the probability game. The Chinese are especially good at that. They are natural gamblers. Robert Peel started London's Metropolitan Police to make sure that crime would not pay. That was the birth of the world's first police force as the custodians of law and order, I'm proud to say."

"Ah ha! But if the custodians of law and order are themselves corrupt, what can you do then?" asked Robert Denning.

"That, my friend, is precisely what I think we have here. There are really no effective checks and balances in the Chinese system of government, I'm afraid. They put their faith in so called sages. They don't seem to understand that sages can get corrupted just like everybody else if the system gives them easy opportunities to do so. And they have a system that is ideally made for corruption!"

As the two diplomats watched the Chinese crowd mill past at close quarters, Robert Denning said to Quentin, "Just look at them – self-seeking people all, held together by the rule of fear, the use of force. Essentially a medieval, feudal, hierarchical society, ordered by the teachings of Confucius, but superimposed with supposedly egalitarian Marxist values which really do not sit well with their natural, selfish instincts. Nonetheless, in less than one generation, this country has grown to become the second most powerful nation on earth and is now throwing its weight about on the international stage, even threatening to challenge the United States in some areas. Astonishing, isn't it? Really impressive! But do you know what I think is wrong with this country, Quentin?"

"No, but you are going to tell me, aren't you, Robert?"

"What is really wrong with this country called China is that their intelligent people are not very brave, and their brave people are not very intelligent," said Robert Denning. "Their intelligent people are willing to play subservient roles and leave the decision-making to gungho army commanders and bullies with guns. The generals in the People's Liberation Army that I've met are really not the most intelligent Chinese around. They are busy feathering their own nests for one thing, and building up strong syndicates to protect and perpetuate their own business empires. The corruption is not just dynastic, nepotic and astronomic as you said, but also *syndicated*. Some of their own history books blame their defeat at the hands of the Japanese navy in 1894 on the Empress Dowager of the last dynasty. They say she had taken the money intended for the Chinese navy to build this glorious Summer Palace for her own enjoyment. Well, it is now over a hundred years hence and China has gone from a dynasty to a republic to now a communist state, but the corruption in the armed forces hasn't changed at all. That should tell us something about this land and its people. They don't change much, do they? They will never make the transition to a modern nation with the rule of law, an elected government, a market economy, and a free people. What a shame!"

"Yes, I know what you mean," rejoined Quentin. "This is the world's most populous nation. These guys account for almost a fifth of mankind. But as a country and a people, it is less than the sum of its parts. You see this in the games they are able to win in world sports. They may excel in individual competitions. But in group events, their performance is less than stellar. They are not a force in basketball or football, or even in volleyball now. In soccer, for instance, they have never won the World Cup. It's not just that they don't work well together, it's also because of corruption. If you can win matches just by bribing people, why do you need excellence? Why do you need to train hard on ball control, dribbling, scoring, tactics and strategy?"

"The sad thing is," and Robert Denning said this with a sigh, "This people have not known anything but despotic governments for five thousand years. For them, government is about rulers and rulees and, while rulers should look after their rulees in the way parents look after their children, they do not have to listen to the rulees or respect their rights. In fact, rulees have no rights, period. And when the rulers act against you, there is really no redress, no recourse, nothing you can do. You just have to swallow it. There is no concept of Rousseau's 'social contract' between the ruler and his subjects. The surprise is that this otherwise intelligent people have put up with it for so long."

"Well, I can think of two explanations for this state of affairs — two explanations for why Chinese governments are so dictatorial. The first is that because the people are unruly and not law-abiding, the only way to govern them is to use the threat of force and violence. The second is that because the people are naturally timid, they invite bullying and despotic rule. You can pick which one to believe. Speaking for myself, I tend to go for the second explanation based on my own boarding school experience. At my school, the timid ones got picked on all the time and were bullied left, right and centre. One just has to stand up for oneself and fight, or get organized; one has to push back and not *kowtow* so readily. But instead of doing that, weak people would just take things lying down and pray for a hero and protector to come forward and save them, a Messiah, like the Israelites did in Biblical times."

"I dare say you are right, Quentin," said Robert, "But this Messiah syndrome is not just one for the Jews. It is deeply rooted in many cultures. I've noticed the overseas Chinese penchant for *kungfu* movies and the undying popularity of the legendary Bruce Lee. I've always felt that this is a people looking for protection and security because they are inherently weak themselves and because they do not want to band together with anybody else. They will go to Canada, America and Australia to look for this security – just simple law and order, protection of private property and the rule of law. With those elements in place, they can live their lives in peace, go about their businesses and rise to as far as their natural abilities will take them, which is very high indeed."

"But," Quentin came in at this point, "what they do not appreciate is that they will subvert a system that is in good working order if they do not *contribute* their share of effort to uphold it. This inherent selfishness, this lack of public spirit, is their undoing. After a hundred and fifty five years of British rule in Hong Kong, you would have thought that some British values would have rubbed off and that British institutions which have provided this city with its stability and prosperity would survive. But this is not what has happened, I can tell you that. Many of the city's top businessmen and some of its best British-trained civil servants, people who have benefitted the most from British rule, are now singing a different tune – a Chinese tune. Instead of defending the institutions which have served the city well, they are busy currying favors with the new power wielders and doing their questionable biddings for them. Bending with the wind, not pushing back, leaning to one side, all these Chinese norms are reasserting themselves. Hong Kong is fast becoming just another Chinese city now, if the truth be told."

"It's ironic, isn't it, Quentin? The United States is ever changing and China is never changing – intrinsically I mean. I don't mean their skyscrapers and fast trains."

"Having just learned to use the Internet after resisting it for some time, I'll agree with you. Yeah! America has never stopped changing and has never stopped evolving; and it's always among the first to lead the changes too. But, notwithstanding what you've just said, Robert, the PLA is a formidable fighting force and can win any battle its soldiers can walk to. It is also developing a brand new cyber warfare capability from what we know."

"Well, they can't walk to San Francisco. And, from what I know, their navy or air force has not won a single important battle at sea or in the air. They look good on paper, but in actual combat? We'll just have to see. In one respect, however, you're right. They are putting a huge amount of resources into developing their cyber warfare capability, and they may yet surprise us there. Nobody's ever fought a cyber war before, not on our side and not on their side."

"I think we are agreed that, to win a war, you need people who are both intelligent and brave. You need, shall we say, the guile and audacity of Horatio Nelson at the Battle of Trafalgar? And his willingness for self sacrifice! Speaking for ourselves, upper-class Brits have never shied away from self-sacrifice and from serving in the armed forces. King and country are powerful rallying calls throughout our history. It was said that the Battle of Waterloo was won on the playing fields of Eton, then by far and away *the* school of choice for our aristocracy. Our best and brightest are also some of our bravest. Many recipients of the Victoria Cross which is awarded for bravery are Etonians. The Chinese elite might be over educated, I don't know, but they do put self preservation above everything else, it seems to me. There is this Chinese saying, 'Your best iron does not nails make, nor your best son an army post take!' Do you know that one, Robert? Not for them serving in our Queen's Guards, that's for sure. Mind you, in the First World War, the Germans did make fun of the quality of our British officer corps too. They used to tell our men through their propaganda blasts that they were 'lions led by donkeys'. So, maybe we Brits shouldn't be too proud of ourselves either."

"You know what, Quentin?" said Robert Denning, "Self deprecation is a peculiarly British trait, and an endearing one. It is also one that is in short supply in the Chinese culture. They take themselves much too seriously, especially the leaders." And then he continued, "I worry about *our* professional army actually. They are a killing machine driven relentlessly forward by our country's military-industrial complex. Eisenhower warned about this in his last major speech at the end of his presidency. That symbiotic relationship will get us *and* the world into serious trouble one day."

"But you have an elected government, just like we do. It's hard for me to imagine the British armed forces not taking orders from the elected civilian government. The tradition of a civilian-led government is very well entrenched in our country. First the separation of church and state, *then* a civilian government sitting on top of the military – it was these two developments that have transformed politics in Western Europe. In Third World countries, on the other hand, the military have always played an inordinate role. They are not much good at the battlefield, but they wield too much power at home – over their own people!"

"I can only agree with you. Your country is better placed than mine. You don't have a military-industrial complex the way that we do. One day, these guys will be strong enough to put they own man in the White House. And then America will *change* for the worse. As you said, America is ever changing and China is never changing."

The next day, at ten o'clock in the morning, the courtroom was already packed full of people, much more full than it was the day before, because word had spread that one of the accused pleaded not guilty and a legal tussle was expected between the prosecution and the single attorney for the defense.

At five minutes past ten, the Court Clerk appeared and declared the hearing would be conducted in camera and asked the assembled crowd to leave. David Han was the first to protest in his native putonghua, but it was to no avail. He was ushered out along with Anne Gavin, Robert Denning, Quentin Maclean and the rest of the courtroom gathering.

Some people in the crowd walked away cursing, but the four of them chose to stay outside the courtroom to wait for the outcome. By eleven o'clock, the hearing was over. All seven accused had been found guilty of robbery, arson and manslaughter and had been sentenced to face the firing squad. The judge did not accept their pleas for mitigation. The confession Bo signed was enough to convict him. Judge Xu did not believe he had signed that piece of paper under duress.

"I want my husband's ring back; they must still have that," said Anne to David. "And they must have my husband's suitcase. I also want to collect Victor's ashes."

"The Public Security Bureau should have all of that. Here, I'll go with you. I want to take Carol's ashes with me too." David replied.

During the taxi ride from the courtroom to the Public Security Bureau, Anne said to David, "At least we now know what really happened. I'll be able to tell my parents-in-law that Victor didn't drown. They did not believe he drowned anyway, but now I can confirm it."

"Yes, but this does not make our pain any less... well, speaking for myself..."

"I know what you mean, David. But at least now we have caught the culprits, the perpetrators of these dastardly acts."

"Mm... I wonder."

"You don't sound convinced," said Anne.

"Well, let's just say I have a few questions for Assistant Commissioner Li if we get to see him. I wouldn't ask Rong because I don't trust him. I don't think he would ever tell us what really happened and who the real culprits were."

"But you trust Assistant Commissioner Li? Why?"

"Oh, just instinct. Let me put it no stronger than that. Being Chinese, I think I can tell what is a good egg and what is a bad egg among my own people better than you can. If I am being presumptuous, I apologize. But it's like this business of looking at women across the cultural divide all over again. I don't think I can be easily fooled. I might be able to catch them lying from the tone of their voice, the twitch of an eyebrow, or the shifty look in their eyes as they try to stare away."

"In that case, I will let you do the talking after I have asked my first question."

"Good afternoon, Assistant Commissioner. I believe the Bureau has my husband's ring. I would like to collect that, together with his ashes and his belongings. I will be leaving for Los Angeles after these have been returned to me, and after I obtain the official death certificate and a copy of the judge's verdict. Could you help me deal with all this please?"

"Yes, our bureau can arrange that, certainly," said Assistant Commissioner Li who was trying to help wrap up the case amicably for his American interlocutor. He knew that, behind the scene, his own scheme is also now close to its denouement. "In fact, you can collect your husband's suitcase and anything else that belonged to him at any time this afternoon. The Bureau has inspected them all and can release them to you. It is really Assistant Commissioner Rong you should be seeing, not me. But you asked for me at reception…"

"We don't trust Assistant Commissioner Rong," Anne said this point blank, and with noticeable disdain in her voice. She was not holding back.

"He knows much more than I about this case. It is his case. I'm sure you know that. And, with the judgment having been delivered by the court, the case is now closed, I hope to your satisfaction." The Assistant Commissioner was trying his best to look benignly at Anne now.

"Not really, Assistant Commissioner." David Han butted in, "Many questions remain."

"Oh? Such as…?" Li Neng acted surprised.

"Why was the trial held in camera? Why was the first version of events materially different from the second version? Why witnesses were not called? And why there was only one defense lawyer for all seven accused?"

"Dr. Han, you have to understand. This is China. This is not Hong Kong. We have a different legal system here. We do not practice the common law. There is no presumption of innocence. There is no jury. The prosecution does not have to prove its case beyond reasonable doubt. On the contrary, it is the accused that has to prove his innocence. None of the accused was able to do that. And so, the judge convicted them all." Unlike Assistant Commissioner Rong, Li did not rise through the ranks but joined the Public Security Bureau from the Law School of Fudan University in Shanghai. He understood very well the distinction between the legal systems in a common-law jurisdiction like Hong Kong and the Communist legal system in China.

The Assistant Commissioner made a pause at this point before continuing. "Actually, Mrs. Lin, we have you to thank. You gave us a witness and a lead. You told us we should interview a driver called Ah Sheng and we did. And you told us we should track down a young man who was selling stolen goods by the lake and ask him where he got his goods from, and we did. Their testimonies led us to find out what really happened, and Assistant Commissioner Rong has had to change his whole report – from one of boat capsizing to robbery, arson and manslaughter. Hence, the convictions. Now you can leave China in peace."

"Not yet, Assistant Commissioner," David Han was not one to let go easily. "Last night at dinner, Robert Denning, the American Consul, told us that many of these gangs that rob and loot and prey on people around the lake are under the protection of powerful local cadres. Might not this be one of those?"

"Foreigners will say such things, but where is the evidence? We haven't had much time to work on the case, as you know. I can assure you we want to get to the bottom of this if there is any truth in the allegation. You can leave the matter with me. I give you my word that if new evidence turns up, I will pursue the matter to its logical conclusion."

"Why are you helping us to the extent that you are?" Anne Gavin smiled as she said this. She thought a slightly different tack might help get more information out of the Assistant Commissioner.

"Because I am a law enforcement officer," Li responded, in a voice that was at once serious and dignified and which he thought left no room for argument or doubt. "I stand for law and order. I am proud to say I joined the Public Security Bureau to keep the peace and to see to it that justice is done and criminals are punished."

But David pressed on, "And you think justice has been done? Do you really?"

Assistant Commissioner Li was cornered. He knew something David and Anne did not. On the secret orders of the Vice Mayor, he and his team had been quietly investigating Assistant Commissioner Rong and the way he had conducted this whole Thousand Island Lake case.

Li decided not to answer their question. "Have a safe journey home," he said to David and Anne.

Acting Assistant Commissioner Li knew that if he was to get anywhere with this investigation of a colleague of higher rank, he must go above Assistant Commissioner Rong. That meant he had to go to Commissioner Ma with hard, incontrovertible evidence of corruption and miscarriage of justice on the part of Rong, and not just Rong, but also other people in his department, probably the entire syndicate. Li knew he had to get the Commissioner on his side. If he failed to do this, his own position would be in jeopardy, because this was a very serious allegation; the reputation of the whole Bureau was at stake.

Acting Assistant Commissioner Li's instinct for survival told him he had to handle this with the utmost care and circumspection. But the problem was that he could not be sure of his own superior, he could not be sure of Commissioner Ma. From what he had seen and heard in the last twelve months since his transfer here from Yangzhou, Li was sure Old Rong could not have gotten away with so much for so long if he did not have a powerful backer in a high place, and perhaps more than just one. Rong would have made sure that many palms were oiled so he could slip through with ease.

Li's own subordinate, Senior Inspector Deng, was quite sure Ah Fei, the Fat One, was the wholesaler and distributor for Rong's syndicate, and that Rong's two subordinates, Dragon and Tiger, were the extortionists who collected the bribes and monthly dues and acted as protectors, trouble-shooters and cover-up agents for these gangs. Deng also told the Acting Assistant Commissioner his suspicion that the Thousand Island Case was the work of Rong's son who ran the notorious Jin-an Syndicate in the Thousand Island area. Young Rong was a menace, a bully and the local big shot who ran night clubs, casinos, brothels and counterfeit rings. Those exploits of his were well known but they were not crimes for which he could be easily nabbed and put behind bars if no one would come forward as witness. The Acting Assistant Commissioner did not dismiss his subordinate's strong suspicion that Rong's son Di Di was the real culprit in this particular case. But what was still a mystery to him was why Junior and his gang would stoop to highway robbery and killing. He could only assume they must be desperate for money. Maybe it was the fact that Assistant Commissioner Rong was near retirement age that made Rong Junior so anxious to reap the last harvest?

"Boss, Sir..." an elated and animated Iron Finger Deng rushed into Acting Commissioner Li's office after knocking on the door twice. He was so excited he forgot to close the door behind him until Li Neng told him to do so. Having collected himself and his thoughts, he began to present his report to his commanding officer.

"I have interviewed Ah Sheng, the driver, Sir. And he confirmed he took the Chinese American to the Thousand Island Lake in his car last Sunday afternoon. The American was going for a boat ride and told him to wait in his car, and to take him back to his hotel in Hangzhou afterwards. Ah Sheng waited but never saw his hirer again. What he saw later that evening were quite a few charred bodies being hurriedly taken ashore. He counted more than twenty. Local public security people were there to direct the whole operation, he said. He was sure of that. He noticed the locals feared them."

"Go on," said Li, as he scribbled something down on his notepad.

"I also interviewed the young man called Bo who, the American woman said, was wearing the ring of her husband, the dead Chinese American. This young guy, now convicted of robbery, arson and manslaughter, was adamant he bought it from his mate and business partner, another young man called Jie, for 500 *yuan*. This other guy insisted, in turn, that he had bought the whole pile of jewelry and watches from Ah Fei, the fatty you saw in our custody, the one we netted. He is the distributor for stolen goods and counterfeit merchandise in the area."

Assistant Commissioner Li had drawn a sketch of the four characters on the piece of paper in front of him, with arrows and words to indicate who did what to whom. Iron Finger Deng understood his superior's routine and stopped to let him finish the drawing of big and balding Ah Fei. He then continued.

"When I interviewed Ah Fei, at first he wouldn't say anything. But then, after several rounds of sleep-and-food deprivation, and after I offered him the prospect of plea bargaining and twenty-four hour round-the-clock protection sanctioned by you and supervised by me, he began to hesitate a little but still wouldn't talk."

"And…"

"Then I told him Old Rong is retiring in November and his own minder Tiger has lung cancer and will soon be in hospital for surgery. I also told him you are the rising star in the Bureau and will be taking things over. Once he heard that, his whole attitude changed. He knew he had to work with us. It was then that he decided to take the lifebuoy and spilled the beans."

"Well done, Deng! What exactly did he say?"

"He said the haul of jewelry and watches had come from Di Di's gang. Di Di is Old Rong's son."

"Ah, ha! Bravo, Deng, bravo! Do you have that confession in writing?" Assistant Commissioner Li was almost jubilant now.

"Yes, I do, Sir. And here it is." Deng took out the standard confessional form from his breast pocket and handed this over to his boss.

As Li read Ah Fei's confession, an excited Iron Finger Deng asked, "This time, we have them nailed, haven't we, Sir?"

"Not so fast, Deng. This may be enough to get Rong's son. But we still need to draw up a fool proof plan to catch Old Rong himself. And after that, Old Ma. My suspicion is that these two are in league; they are in this business together. But we need more proof." So saying, Li rose from his chair and walked to the window of his office. He was just staring down at the courtyard out of habit when he saw Rong's car speeding out of the compound. It was then that he realized he did not have any moment to lose and must summon help. "I think I'd better go to the Vice Mayor and consult with him straightaway," he turned quickly and said to Deng, "and I want you to come with me. We need to report this to the Commission on Party Discipline and Inspection. We want to work with them and get a search warrant to go through Rong and Ma's offices, residences, and bank accounts – I am sure they have many warrens. We need to work out a strategy with the Vice Mayor to net both men. Go get my driver."

"I suppose it's time to say goodbye," David said to Anne the next morning after they had both sat down at the breakfast table and ordered. "What time's your flight?"

"Six twenty-five in the afternoon – from Pudong International Airport in Shanghai. I need to take the train to Shanghai first and then transfer to the airport. I should leave the hotel by about 11:30 this morning." Anne gave David a straightforward answer as she looked at him and noticed that he was in the same dark grey business suit with matching black tie that he wore on the day they first met. David Han was ready to resume his academic routine again.

"And you? When are you going back to Hong Kong?"

"My flight is from Hangzhou to Hong Kong; I don't need to go through Shanghai. But my flight leaves here at 3:50 in the afternoon. So I should be leaving the hotel at around 12:00, about half an hour after you."

"The company is sending this same driver Ah Sheng to pick me up at 11:30. If you like, he can drop me off at the Hangzhou train station and then take you to your airport. Would that work for you?"

"That's very kind of you, Anne. Shall we exchange email, phone number and other contact details now? In case we need to get in touch with each other again?" asked David. "If Assistant Commissioner Li comes up with anything important and lets me know, for instance, I will contact you."

"Of course, David. I'll get my card and give this to you when we meet up at the hotel lobby at, shall we say, 11:20?"

"Well, here's mine." said David Han as he gave Anne his name card.

"Look me up please if you should visit or pass through Hong Kong. I should have given you this when we first met, but we met in unhappy circumstances…" David was trying to find the words to express the unusual bond that had developed between them.

"I would like to do that, David, very much.' Anne said, very quickly, before David finished his sentence. "I've never been to Hong Kong and really want to see it someday. I should also thank you for the support you've given me this past week. I don't know whether I could have come this far if you were not there with me." Anne said as she looked at David in sincere appreciation.

David was slightly embarrassed; he managed a half smile and, with his earnest look, said to Anne, "Let's just say we both needed support and we were there for each other."

After a pause and as they exchanged a glance without saying anything, Anne's scrambled egg arrived and put a stop to whatever might have followed.

David's rice congee with chicken looked a mouthful and was also steaming hot. He did not want to slurp while he ate and was stirring his bowl of congee to help it cool. He did this with his usual intense concentration. Anne saw what he was doing and thought it best not to distract him.

After the eating was done and Chinese tea and coffee had been served, Anne decided to ask David a question which had been in her mind for a long time. "So, what's going to become of Hong Kong?" Anne asked when she had David's eyes.

"Just another Chinese city like Guangzhou, I think. China's leaders have never had any experience in running an international financial centre. Many of them don't know what that is. They think it would be as easy as running Shanghai. They will want to control Hong Kong and dismantle all vestiges of Hong Kong's colonial past, not knowing that British institutions like the common-law tradition, the use of English and the free flow of information are the essential requisites of international financial centers around the world."

"You don't think they will have the wisdom to leave Hong Kong alone?"

"Let's just say I do not know of any Chinese businessman who would own something and not run it. This would be against his whole nature. Singapore had a very tough time immediately after independence in the 1960's but on the advice of a Dutch industrial economist, Prime Minister Lee Kuan Yew had the wisdom to reverse his own natural instinct which was to dismantle the British legacy. Following the recommendation of this Dutch advisor, who told the Prime Minister to 'Let Raffles stand where he stands today', Lee decided to keep the British institutions. The Singapore economy which had plunged after independence soon stopped contracting; it stabilized and took off after that. But we do not have a Lee Kuan Yew in Hong Kong and we have an overlord called China. Hong Kong's demise is inevitable. It is a Greek tragedy with Chinese characteristics."

"Are you going to do anything about it? If so, what are you going to do? Or are you going to stay and just watch it come down as it were?"

"Greek tragedies are tragedies foretold, but there is nothing anyone can do to avert them. So I suppose I will just be there to 'watch it come down' – as you said"

"But, given your views and beliefs, why are you still there at all? Why have you not left Hong Kong?"

"Inertia… job… I love my job… familiarity? At my age, it's very difficult to leave… home."

There was a moment of silence between the two which Anne really wanted to break. And so she asked David again.

"And China? What's to become of China? It seems to be riding an economic boom right now."

"In China, stability and prosperity are interludes and no part of the actual drama, Anne. I am paraphrasing Thomas Hardy, of course. This is where my reading of Chinese politics and English literature comes together. What you are looking at, what the people of China are living through, is an interlude. What lies ahead, what will come hereafter, is the actual drama."

"And what is that?"

"For China, the actual drama is political strife and never-ending power struggles. It has always been like this and it will always be like this… for as long as the use of force to resolve conflicts is the *modus operandi* of the Chinese people. There is no sustainable stability for this country of over one billion and, that being the case, I'm afraid no sustainable growth either. They are building castles on sand. The inevitable tide of civil war will come one day and take everything away."

Anne wanted to continue with this line of enquiry but noticed that David was looking at his watch. "Do you come to the United States much?" Anne finally asked.

"Only to attend academic conferences," replied David.

"Come and visit me in California. You might like the Golden State."

"I might? You think?"

The moment passed and the conversation drifted to the hotel bill and check-out matters. When they met up again at the hotel lobby at 11:20, Ah Sheng was already there to greet them and take them to the waiting limo.

As Ah Sheng took his car down the main thoroughfare in Hangzhou, another black limousine was turning into the same road from his left side and almost rammed into the front of his vehicle. Ah Sheng braked quickly and his passengers were thrown violently forward and then backward even with their seatbelts tightly fastened. But Ah Sheng made light of the rude driving they had just witnessed and sheepishly let the other car get ahead of him. When the two limos pulled level at the next set of traffic lights, Anne strained her neck to have a look at the people in the other car. She could see two passengers in the long limo. They were the two glamorous girls she saw at the hotel restaurant the other evening. One of them was talking on the hand phone – again – and the other was just staring listlessly at her own finger nails.

"Why didn't you honk to show you're angry? This other driver was clearly in the wrong," David said to Ah Sheng.

"If you had to work here, Sir, you would know which girls are off limit and which cars are beyond reproach. All the long Mercedes and BMWs belong to people in high places and you just do not trifle with them. Because if you do, you would only get yourself into trouble; you always end up the loser. The biggest, most expensive cars have the worst traffic record in our city, because they have got used to not following the rules. The men who drive them are the chauffeurs of powerful bosses; and the girls who drive them are the mistresses of the rich and untouchable."

"Is it still like this after all these years of communism and reform?" David shook his head as he asked. It was a rhetorical question and he knew it.

"You bet," said Ah Sheng and held back a vituperative remark.

"Do you recognize these two girls in the car next to us?" Anne motioned to David with her eyes.

"Yes, I do. I had a look at them too. We've seen them before – at our hotel restaurant. But why do you ask?"

"Because they don't look the same to me in broad daylight. The sheen has come off. Is it the make up? Or is it something else? I wonder."

As Ah Sheng waited for the lights to change, another big black vehicle was speeding down the same road but in the opposite direction. It was a Public Security Bureau lorry and it was taking convicted prisoners to the execution yard at the other side of the city, just outside the city border.

Shortly after the black lorry passed, two other government cars were following closely on its wheels, this time with sirens blaring and with a motorcade of riders in front, alongside and closely behind. The whole entourage smacked of power and authority. In one car, Assistant Commissioner Li was accompanying the Vice Mayor to interview Commissioner Ma. And in the other one, Senior Inspector Deng was taking the Secretary of the Commission on Party Discipline to interview Assistant Commissioner Rong.

The lights were just turning.